# THE HOUSE ON LIBERTY STREET
## HOME OF SECOND CHANCES

BY

FRANCES RIVETTI

E Book ISBN: 978-0-9904921-5-3
Print Paperback ISBN: 978-0-9904921-4-6
Hardback ISBN: 978-0-9904921-6-0

Other books by Frances Rivetti/Fog Valley Press:

Fog Valley Crush — Love at First Bite — At Home in the California Farmstead Frontier

Fog Valley Winter — Pioneer Heritage, Backroad Rambles and Vintage Recipes — A Farmstead Fireside Companion

Big Green Country — A Novel

Illustration: Copyright @2022 Gail Foulkes gailfoulkes.com

FOG VALLEY PRESS

For Giuseppina

*"An old house that had lived its life long ago and so was very quiet and wise and a little mysterious. Also, a little austere, but very kind."*

L.M. Montgomery

# PROLOGUE

Nobody took any much notice of Adamaria's place. The house on Liberty Street simply did not call any special attention to itself, a shabby exterior having no unique features to differentiate it from the time-worn neighboring Victorians it rubbed shoulders with, mid-sized, two-story homes of a similar age and style, several of which had been turned into apartments in the 1950's and 60's.

And even if she had the funds to fix it up, to restore its detail and shine of the latter decades of the 1800s, the formidable power and restrictions of the city's strict preservation code posed daunting obstacles.

The average passerby saw its sagging structure as another residential relic of the city's bygone era; its upkeep a taskmaster beyond most aspiring vintage homeowners' reasonable means.

Nevertheless, it was a home that was loved unconditionally by the small family who dwelled within its walls. It meant far more than a familiar box of wood and plaster. It was as important to them as they were to each other; its windows like a pair of wise, old eyes overseeing an increasingly unpredictable, troubled world.

It breathed, it sighed, it creaked. It groaned and seasoned and aged along with each new generation of Adamaria Uccello's lineage, its floorboards bending in allegiance to their footsteps and its many-layered rooms absorbing the essence of all who'd shared its space.

In the summer it was deliciously cool. In the winter months, the entire house frequently shivered, the nuances in its framing and woodwork susceptible to the elements. In high wind and rain, its wooden structure swayed — dignified, yet doddery. During the bone-chilling damp of a December night, however, its tidy, orderly interior was freshly polished, fire-lit and doted on as a shrine to the past, an extension of self.

What a passer-by on Liberty Street might easily overlook was that the old house with its shabby, faded and partly peeling exterior was in

1

fact a time capsule. It had more-or-less stayed the same through over a century-and-a-half. It had withstood two major Bay Area earthquakes, the Great Depression, wars that had stolen beloved sons and a regretful period when homes of its era had been flattened in favor of the modern.

The house was unaccustomed to the company of guests — invited or otherwise. It had never been an especially social home. Adamaria and her people were homebodies for the most part who preferred to keep the sanctuary of their abode to themselves. Except for other species that snuck in consistently to take advantage of its shelter, racoons especially, that occupied the secret spaces that lay between the humans, the earth and the sky.

The house, if it were to express such a preference, was accustomed to the passing herds of black tailed deer, the males with their antlers that munched on the neighbor's rose bushes after dusk, the vegetation of its own front yard having been largely devoured by these four-legged browsers over the years.

Noxious-scented skunks tended to make themselves more of a nuisance, as did an increasingly large colony of tunneling Norwegian rats that ran wild through the wall space and attic in the hours between dusk and dawn.

A big-horned owl topped this compact hierarchy of inhabitants, coming and going as he pleased, frequently perched on the tip of the slightly lopsided weathervane, the perfect spot for patrolling the sidewalk after dusk and the parcels of Victorian picket-fenced neighboring yards that led up to the church.

The house existed for two separate world orders, that of Adamaria and its people and that of the creatures of the wild who sprang into action under the cover of night.

> *"There was a roaring in the wind all night,*
> *The rain came heavily and fell in floods."*

William Wordsworth

# Chapter One

# Run, Rudolph, Run

It was the afternoon of Christmas Eve. Faded trowel marks on the dense lath and plaster of the walls in the upstairs hallway were cool to the touch. Though thick layers of old-world horsehair and plaster dampened the transfer of noise, the tarnished brass ceiling lamps in the parlor below squeaked and wobbled in tune with the children's unsupervised playtime above.

"I'm a fire-bweathin' dwagon," said the smallest of the two little girls as she swayed side-to-side and whipped around within the confines of the narrow corridor. A small chunk of plaster dropped from a crack in the wall. She stopped, still, captivated by a visible cloud of warm vapor in front of the crumbling framework.

"Don't be a dummy. You're not a dragon. You're a reindeer," her sister replied, kicking the plaster to the side. "And you gotta start sounding your r's. You're not a baby no more."

For Izzie and Rosa, their energetic game of make-believe served as a fun and practical method to keep the blood flowing until the heating kicked in. Theirs was a private drama club with an exclusive membership of two. It was their special time together, away from the grownups and their whispered secrets, a chance to be kids, to goof around without an audience to subdue their exuberant play.

Still, thin air nipped greedily at their fingers and toes in the gloomy afternoon light.

"Brrr . . . it sure is freezin' here in the North Pole," Izzie announced, interrupting the production script that ran in her head. She raised her right hand and held it over her mouth. The warmth of her breath on her palm was a reminder of how cold the house could be. The fast-pumping of her heart had heated her core but her small, cold hand demonstrated the chill of the afternoon.

"As long as we keep on movin', we'll be fine," she said, dropping her hand and shrugging her shoulders.

Rosa puckered her bowlike lips and puffed a short series of toasty breaths into the two tiny, circular voids that formed in the space between her small, blue-veined, thumb and forefingers.

The sisters knew from experience to bide their time by jumping around until later, when the noisy, forced heating system of their grandmother's high-ceilinged house would clank into action.

It was getting on in the afternoon, they could see, judging by the lengthy shadows that cast across the hallway at the top of the stairs. The hardy children were looking forward to accompanying their mother on a last-minute, pre-dusk holiday shopping expedition the few short blocks into town. Afterwards, there was the promise of coming home to supper, a cozy fire in the parlor and the lights of the Christmas tree. Wind rattled the shutters as they picked up the pace in the murkiness of their makeshift playground, prancing around at intervals as they raced up and down the narrow space.

A rich scent of stovetop onion, garlic, celery and carrots sauteed in olive oil had snaked its way at a sluggish pace over the course of the long early hours of the winter's day, finally making its way upwards, despite an absence of heat, into the confines of the second floor. A diffusion of odor particles had infused its crumbling insulation with the warming notes of Adamaria's bubbling, stovetop Ragu. This comforting aroma registered in Izzie's mouth before it hit her nose, coating the tiny taste buds inside her tongue, her throat, the roof of her mouth.

The girls had discovered, much to their delight that their brand new, bargain-bucket cherry red, microfiber holiday tights made for the most effective slip-and-sliding along the smooth, unpainted, tongue and groove boards that stretched beneath their small, stockinged feet.

Left by the grownups to their own devices for an afternoon of screen-free quiet time, the excitable children had set about gleefully gathering dust balls as they cycled through countless laps of emotional circuits in their one-act, holiday play.

Fantastic games of creative hide-and-go-seek had kept them similarly entertained throughout many a long, wet afternoon in the rainy-season. But this afternoon's imaginary play was different, special. Neither of them knew exactly why the solemn air of Christmas Eve made for the most thrilling play day of the year. Their jitters in overdrive fueled the sisters' adrenaline-filled action, making it all the more exciting by the minute.

Izzie, aged seven, was self-appointed show director. She'd generously assigned herself the lead role of Santa's helper. Her younger, smaller and more naturally anxious sibling stood upright before her, hopping from foot to foot, since skidding around on all fours had proven cumbersome by then.

Rosa, age five, was decked out in the guise of a reindeer, her curly-head topped by a fuzzy, dark brown hat, her small body draped in a short, tan, musty-smelling woolen coat of their grandmother's that they'd unearthed from the back of the coat closet along with the hat. "We've over half the planet to cover before the night's up, so step on it, Dasher," Izzie urged, tugging a little too vigorously for Rosa's liking, attached as she was to the other end of a pair of makeshift reins, the empty sleeves of the coat. She raised her eyes in a show of dramatic exasperation.

The intricate, silvery lacework of a fat and contented spider dangled tantalizingly in the low light of the ceiling lamp above her head. There was a tin pail positioned nearby, a familiar obstacle during the rainy season.

"Where to now?" Rosa the reindeer inquired, lowering her eyes and hopping on the spot as she turned her attention back to her leader, thus leaving the spider to its own devices. She was gap-toothed and earnest and wishing to please as she was wont to do. Rosa swiveled her slim neck to take further instruction from her bossy big sister, who was dressed from head to toe in assorted, flowing, flimsy layers of red and green nylon.

Izzie clutched a heavy pillowcase stuffed with a selection of one-eyed and sagging soft toys. The two of them resumed their slide-skating back and forth from one side of the hallway to the other, giggling and shrieking from a stubbed big toe on a gap in the floorboard and again on the thick, wooden trim at the foot of the wall.

"Head west until we hit the Pacific. Next up, ranch kids out at the coast."

"Oh, yummy, fwesh gween gwass," Rosa improvised, lowering her head in a munching motion before launching off spontaneously in the direction of their mother's bedroom where she subsequently skidded to a halt at the door.

She curled the outstretched fingers of her right hand into her palm and dropped it to her side. How tempting it was to nudge the door open, to tip-toe in and explore in the shadows for hidden treasure. And yet, if she were to follow such an impulse, she knew from past experience that the second she took hold of the doorknob, an immediate tell-tale sound would signal its guilty alarm throughout the otherwise silent house.

A loud chime broke a brief silence, the doorbell scrambling her thoughts. Rosa was afraid of strangers, just as she was terrified of thunder and lightning — and the prospect of any combination of which was thoroughly off-putting in her contemplation of breaking a rule.

She stood perfectly still as she and her sister strained their ears in an attempt to decipher the muffled conversation below. It was hard to hear above the wind as it wrapped itself around the trees at the front of the house. A gust whistled its way through the open door, reverberating up the staircase. Such an interruption struck the children as odd seeing as they barely ever had visitors. The grown-ups appeared to prefer it that way, keeping their own company. Play dates happened at other people's houses. And the girls were astute enough to have figured out that an unexpected visitor might be a cause for concern.

"What's goin' on, Iz?" Rosa asked of her older sister, her sweet little face at once serious. "Who is it?" She moved closer to Izzie's side. Their Nonna, Adamaria, they heard speaking in muffled, yet decipherably firm tones.

"How do I know, nosy? And anyway, you'd best not be pokin' around in Mommy's room," Izzie warned, as she changed the subject. Her clear blue eyes darted back and forth from the staircase to the shuttered door of their mother's room. She hadn't said a word previously, but in the run up to Christmas, she'd spent considerable time weighing up whether or not she should settle things, to discover once and for all if the whole dubious grownups' story of the Santa deal was real or not. But she'd been wise enough not to spoil the illusion for her younger sister if it turned out to be nothing more than a fairytale after all.

Although she had an inkling that gifts destined for the pair of them were indeed tucked away in a hidden spot behind their mother's door, the whole idea of how they'd wind up in a pillowcase at the end of each bed remained somewhat of an unsolved puzzle to Izzie. She likened the feeling to a long, sharp fragment of wood, a nasty slither that had buried itself deep beneath her skin. She worried it might hurt more to force it out, the truth, to examine it for what it was rather than to leave things be for another year. It was tough being seven.

It would be better, Izzie figured, at least for now, if she held on tight to the knot at the end of the big, red Santa bubble. Besides, she feared there were plenty more bewildering mysteries of life that might threaten to spoil the magic of Christmas if she were to start with her questions.

Besides, she had rituals that she held on to. Rituals that kept her from bearing the weight of too many of her own worries. One of these was tasking herself with looking after her sister. If she could keep on doing that, then everything would be alright.

For the two of them, the house provided a treasure trove of secret and not-so-secret spaces in which to hide and play. Izzie appreciated its protective shield — a place to forget about the outside world and one in which she managed for the most part to stifle the more confusing thoughts and concerns that sometimes attempted to take hold in her head.

She shook it off, a growing need to want to know more about the complicated world that the grownups lived in. And with Rosa following her prompt, unquestioning as ever, the two of them raced one last energetic lap of the upstairs hallway before they tumbled together in an exaggerated fashion, a tangle of limbs, squealing, laughing and leaping back up.

Izzie had expected their mother to reprimand the two of them at any moment for all the racket they'd made. It was the time of day when they were expected to be on their best behavior, respecting their elders with a period of peace and quiet. Before any such scolding ensued, she set about shedding the red and green — multiple layers, dance gear and nightclothes mostly, that she'd retrieved from her dresser drawer in order to assemble her make-believe guise.

"But have you seen him?" asked Rosa, suddenly wide-eyed, as she peered downstairs into the darkening shadows of the lower hallway. Whomever it was at the door had retreated.

"Who?"

"Santa."

"Not the real one, no. I would've told you if I had. Besides, he's way too smart. He'd never risk it."

"But what if we stay awake? The whole night long."

"We mustn't."

"But it's kinda spooky, don't ya think? I mean, how he gets down the chimney an' all?"

"Hey," Izzie put her arm around Rosa, easing her little sister's anxiety with her protective gesture. They huddled side-by-side on the top step of the narrow staircase.

"He has a special key, see. He uses it to put the fire out. Somehow it opens up the chimney so that he's able to squeeze in."

Rosa's face expressed a mix of further confusion and alarm. It was the look she signaled when she was close to tears. A similar thing had happened when their grandmother had taken the two of them downtown to the Turning Basin on the river, to see Santa, the Saturday after Thanksgiving.

Rosa had flat out refused to shake his outstretched hand after he'd disembarked from his decorated boat. She'd simply stood her ground, scowling and stared at him, suspiciously. This particular embodiment of Santa sailed into town along the Petaluma River at the start of every holiday season. It had become a family tradition, for they had been amongst the crowds for this annual spectacle ever since Izzie was in a stroller. And Izzie looked forward to the downtown merchant's annual holiday open house, for she was old enough to have grown accustomed to its marking the start of the festive season. Rosa on the other hand was not nearly as confident as her sister when it came to a face-to-face with a grown up, let alone Santa. Izzie remembered how Adamaria had responded to Rosa's evident concern, her fear of 'stranger danger', by sweeping them along for warm apple cider and sugar snowflake cookies. Izzie smiled when she pictured the blue and white sprinkles that had stuck to Rosa's cheek.

"Santa's cool — he's a kind of shapeshifter, I guess," she added reassuringly, she hoped. "I guess he has superpowers an' all."

"Oh," the younger of the two replied, a frown crumpling the soft, pink skin of her brow, this new, even more complex information not helping.

"Anyway, I'm gonna be right here beside you, lookin' out for you, as I always do," Izzie promised.

"Okay, I guess," Rosa said, gripping her sister's slightly bigger hand in hers. "If you say so. But maybe Santa gets scared too. I mean, what if it's not the wight house? What if there's no kids?" A current of cool air clung to the surface of the floorboards — an indoor version of the low-lying Northern California coastal fog that rolled in and blanketed the hills on either side of the city during the late afternoon hours.

"Dang, I dunno, he has his list though, remember? Now, let's head down and see if Mommy's finished the dishes," Izzie suggested, cheerily, scratching her head as she moved on to address the afternoon's more immediately pressing matters.

Holiday lights of neighboring homes on Liberty Street reflected through the window at the front of the upper hallway lighting their path as the children tip-toed half way down the stout staircase, step by step. The wooden structure sighed beneath the soft sound of their stockinged feet.

In the middle of the staircase, at the same step where they always stopped, Izzie grabbed her sister's hand in hers and together, with one last squeal, they jumped.

# CHAPTER TWO

# RAINFALL
# AND A DECKING OF THE HALLS

Rain had set in around midday, a slight drizzle at first, its silent pitter-patter dampening the sidewalk in front of the house. The change in atmospheric pressure registered with the onset of a dull, tell-tale ache that settled itself into Adamaria's arthritic joints. Still, she'd shrugged it off as a mere shower — a sprinkling that would, she prayed, be sure to pass over by evening. With two overly-excitable youngsters in the house, what they needed most was a good night's sleep.

The last storm had hit hard earlier in the week. Its deluge had kept her and her daughter Gracie up for two nights running. Together they'd stuffed strips of absorbent fabric cut from a stack of threadbare towels into the rain-softened window frames of the ramshackle Victorian. This was in addition to having maneuvered around an entire battalion of battered and rusted pails in an effort to prevent the more unreachable leaks from doing any more serious damage to her prized wooden floors.

Adamaria refused to resort to the employment of bigger, more unsightly plastic buckets, the green colored behemoths that her neighbors on Liberty Street purchased by the dozen from the big box lumber store during the rainy season. Neither would she deem to subscribe to the country-chic, reproduction "Petaluma" ranch pails that were snapped up mostly for show by amateur interior designers during the annual warm-weather antique fair that crowded the bustling, downtown streets behind her house. Tin pails and old paint cans had been good enough for her folks and it was the exact same misshaped brigade that were still working well enough for her. These dinged and time-worn vessels had played their trusty part in preserving the place since its early days and if they'd out-lived the generations that came before her, they'd continue do the job just fine while she was alive.

Why spend money replacing what's not broke? she asked herself, a common mantra of a self-confessed curmudgeon. Any slight temptation she fought to reconcile tradition with modernity followed this same old pattern.

Some work had been done on the roof's main trouble spots during the summer months, upgrades to gutters and downspouts but still, the ever-persistent rainwater continued to find a way to seep, squirt, drip and, heaven forbid, occasionally stream its way in. The price of a new roof was out of the question. The wet winter months promised a test of resolve as to how long the old roof shingles could possibly hold with only a patchwork of sporadic repairs.

Adamaria was grateful for a kindly neighbor who helped her out with whatever she could manage, money-wise, when it came to fixing up the worst of the roof. Ned was a seasoned old specimen of a local treasure in her mind, lizard-like, his skin wrinkled and folded from a working life spent entirely outdoors. He had long-since retired from the roofing trade but he would make time when it called for it and mess up his hands good and proper in hot tar for fellow old-timers such as herself.

The children, she would wager a bet, were sure to be up and about by the break of dawn. It was with this early hour in mind that Adamaria set about preempting the leaky roof by repositioning a bunch of freshly emptied pails into the usual trouble-spots.

By three p.m. she was no longer able to fool herself that what had by then escalated to a steady downpour would be over before nightfall. Her ears tuned in to the wind as it whipped through bare tree branches lining the triangular plaza by the church. Dense spirals of gunmetal grey gusts swirled skyward from the saturated concrete walkways, encapsulating the park and its central fountain in a haze of heavy mist.

Adamaria turned to scan the washed-out scene, the street barely visible beyond the sheen of slim, silver nails that pinged against the window panes. Her eye settled on a washed-out stick figure that appeared to be walking towards her house. Whoever it was seemed almost to emerge from the center frame of a life-size watercolor painting. Though she'd always been drawn to moody, impressionistic cityscapes, the kind that hung in the windows of the galleries downtown, a deep scowl formed on Adamaria's brow as she peered through the glass for a closer look. She had no time at all for the sudden appearance of any unannounced caller, especially on Christmas Eve.

Just paint him outta here, she advised herself, scrunching her eyes shut, willing whoever it was to simply absorb into the opaque cityscape so that she wouldn't have to show him how gruff she could be. She pictured a flourished sweep of brushstrokes and a thick glob of imagined gouache on the ball of her thumb as she blurred the lines of what was real and what was imagined, at least in the controlled universe of her own mind.

In order for her to make time to wield a brush and even half way proficiently act-out her unspoken, uncharacteristic desire to take up painting one day, something in her routine was going to have to give. Anyone so bound to the relentless upkeep of home would surely bury such a notion? It was one of a substantial litany of regrets when it came to allowing herself some leisure time. The word hobby did not exist in Adamaria's vocabulary.

And yet, that afternoon, contemplation crept on in, regardless, that of the playful blending of an especially pleasing pallet of greys and greens and shades of dark blues. She couldn't help herself as she went so far as to add in a splash of imaginary color here and there for passing headlights and such — a flourish of a softer, muted yellow for the street lamps.

How odd it is to look clear through the air around us, most of the time, Adamaria mused. She doubted she'd ever allow herself the freedom required to even attempt to capture time on canvas. Still, it was the white noise of nature that she found most fascinating in the rare moments she allowed herself the time to stop and think about it.

It's as if the air itself is altogether invisible, she considered, though she knew this not to be the case at all. With one swish of a heavy, damask curtain, a screen of dust mites hovered before her eyes, reeling her immediately back to the minutiae of reality. However meticulous she was in her house-keeping, it was impossible to prevent the build-up of these pesky little particles. Meanwhile, plump drops of precipitation strummed against the porch roof and, as the rain bounced off its gutter, a steady increase in its velocity made it impossible to deny that they were in for a wild night weather-wise.

Adamaria lingered by the window. Her stance locked, her shoulders a rigid line above an arched back as she peered out. Privacy was paramount within her home, more so than ever these days. A shiver crept along the length of her spine, upwards to rest at the base of her skull.

Oh well, she consoled herself, whoever the fella was, whatever his business on such an afternoon, he must've gotten the wrong address. She would do best to put it out of mind, to reconsider the long list of holiday chores yet to complete.

Though the bleak December rain contained a slightly sinister beauty, Adamaria had to admit she found the afternoon's inclement weather oddly soothing, all the same. After all, she was perfectly secure inside the confines of the house. Her daughter and grandchildren were out of harm's way beneath its roof — Gracie in the kitchen, taking care of the lunch dishes and the girls, as she was rudely reminded by their boisterous afternoon play, above her, hopefully keeping out of mischief.

The old house was her fortress, their castle. And she the gatekeeper. An imposing one at that. Adamaria was damned if any outsider, random or otherwise should dare to interrupt and spoil the peaceful, private mood of the holiday while she was on guard.

A dove-colored veil of low laying cloud shrouded the already dwindling daylight. Visibility tapered as she stood sentry-like, feet planted firmly within her vantage point at one of two, long, narrow sash windows positioned in the front parlor overlooking the porch. Neighboring two and three-story Stick Style and Queen Anne homes, most with their own assortment of missing shingles and chipped paint, a couple more recently restored with coats of smart new exterior color, cast long, dark, watery shadows across the plaza — ghostly echoes of the city's architectural heyday.

Adamaria rubbed a circle in the condensation and squinted for a better look, this time a study of the mysterious, watery shapes that were punctured by the patterns of intricate cut-outs of decorative, wooden curl — gingerbread trim and design, wings, bays and a turret or two each reflected in the ink-like puddles. It was never lost on her that these staunch, old structures had withstood the first earthquake in 1906 and a second in 1989.

She winced as a sudden, sly gust whipped up a bunch of mixed yard debris, leaves and small fragments of lichen-covered tree branches and smacked them into the center of the windowpane. The room was breathing damp air from the fireplace flue. A pre-dusk fire she'd set in the cast-iron grate picked up a slight odor of creosote that wafted down from deposits on the insides of the terracotta flue. Adamaria had set a dish of apple cider vinegar beside the dancing flames. She swore it worked wonders in reversing any unpleasant air flow.

What a day she'd had.

All that preppin' and cookin', plus the settin' of the table in the dinin' room, she commended herself with smug satisfaction as she glanced around the parlor, assessing the many holiday rituals completed and those yet to accomplish. It was a list that she and only she insisted on. It wasn't like they were expecting guests. It was just the four of them for Christmas, after all, for she was widowed these past two years and Gracie an only child and now single mother.

I have my standards regardless, she figured, in justification of her formal ways.

Adamaria stifled a yawn. Caring for the house was proving a near constant physical strain on her aging body. Though her mind was agile as ever, she huffed and puffed in the slow unfolding of her short, squat, broad-beamed frame after she moved across the room and lowered herself to her knees to check on the progress of the fireplace blaze.

"Good riddance 2019," she declared, as she stared into the flames, trancelike for a second or two. Though she was pleased to see the back of the last ten years and its troubles as a whole, she couldn't help but consider the imminent launch into the unknown of an entirely new decade as nothing less than formidable. She had still so much to do with regards to securing her family's future. The house required an heir and Gracie was it. How would the girl ever manage when it came her time?

A new calendar, filled with its clear, empty squares of promise and uncertainty, month-by-month, sat face up in its clear, plastic wrapper on the side table by her armchair. Her eyes swept the cover, a photograph of a red barn, before which stood a small herd of healthy looking black and white Holstein dairy cows on a field of impossibly green grass. The calendar came courtesy of the local feed store where she occasionally bought small cans of cat food for the neighborhood strays. She was not a cat person, but the cats were good for keeping down the vermin and the children loved them. It was a compromise she made so as not to be sweet-talked into having a house cat of their own.

She walked over and stooped to pick up the calendar and turn it over in her hands. As she unwrapped its cellophane layer, she held it closer to her eyes and studied its declaration of the fast-approaching year, 2020 — printed in large, bold, white numerals.

To think, a new decade was just a week away. It appeared before her as fantastic, unimaginably futuristic. Adamaria was a child of the 1940s. She scratched her head. How she wished her Aldo had been there beside her to see this strange new decade into being.

What a thing! She pondered. Though never mind what the future holds, she consoled herself, it had to be better than the more recent past.

Gracie was forever on at her about being so set in her ways to be at risk of being stagnant. She should be more willing to be open to new things. But what other option did she have than to stand her ground, hold it all together the way she knew how, for the four of them? Young folk these days had no patience with constancy in her opinion.

Adamaria pushed aside a strong urge to double check the street as she set the calendar back on the side table and instead, returned her attention to the glowing flames that danced within the ornate fireplace and mantel, original fixtures from the 1860s.

The fireplace was flanked by an imposing and intricately carved, solid redwood surround, its mantel supporting a wide, classic mirror feature, much clouded with age. She'd been planning to replace the glass someday, but this was just one of a long list of non-essential updates her dear old house deserved.

What was it Gracie had recently been intent on pointing out? Oh yes, the cost to the ancient redwood coastal forests of the fireplace surround, as well as the rest of the interior framing, paneling, doors, trim and built-in cabinets of their home as a whole.

"Mass commercial logging, it's outrageous by today's standards, Ma. With what we now know about green building," her daughter had declared during a recent, largely one-way discussion with her mother on Adamaria's pride in the structural merits of the House on Liberty Street. Gracie, as a member of a generation that Adamaria privately considered somewhat tireless and hairsplitting in its vocal, eco-conscious ideals, had been insistent on hammering her sentiment home.

Adamaria had been upset by the suggestion that she was at fault for what had happened to the forests all those years ago. She didn't appreciate being to forced think too hard with regards to the millions of lengths of solid virgin redwood that Gracie bemoaned, the vast mounds of precious first-growth sacrificed during the logging of the Gold Rush years. It made her uncomfortable. What could she do about it now? The damage was done long before she was born. Gracie had said the rise of the western states came close to devastating the vast tracks of ancient coastal forests to the north. This was not something Adamaria in her blissful ignorance had ever even considered until her daughter moved home with the airing of her new-fangled lectures and principles.

It wasn't that Gracie didn't appreciate their old home's integrity, its craftsmanship and beauty, Adamaria was sure of that, but the younger woman, what with her passion for the planet and all, well, she had to admit she had been most articulate and insistent in her criticism of what she'd called the Gilded Age of Rapid Growth.

At least Adamaria had preserved the precious materials that had gone into her home's early construction. She'd been a good steward, hadn't she? It struck her, in the quiet of the afternoon as some small miracle that not one single, misguided soul had taken the notion in the name of progress to rip any of these fine, craftsman made fixtures, including her precious fireplace clear out of the house she'd called home since she herself was a girl.

Plenty of early Victorian gems in the neighborhood had been gutted, split into apartments, or devastatingly worse — torn down by the time her folk had taken ownership of the house that her mother's parents had scrimped and saved for. It was a constant regret of hers that aside from all her devoted spit and polish, neither she nor any of her hardworking predecessors had the means to better maintain the house inside and out to its original mint condition. In her mind, the merchants and bankers and other enterprising pioneer families who'd settled in the area after seeking to make their fortune indirectly from the gold mines surely took enormous pride in building their homes.

One hundred and sixty years or so later and many of the proud, well-preserved, iron-front buildings that were raised in her four-block central residential and commercial area were still in existence — living history no less. And Adamaria was all too aware that her charming and modestly-sized, historic hometown was likely to continue to attract an increasing wave of well-healed newcomers in search of a more bucolic life. So many she'd heard of had tired of the fast-paced rat-race in San Francisco and similarly, an extortionately-priced Silicon Valley on the Peninsula to the south.

Real estate agents were forever sending her thick, glossy postcards and other forms of inquiring mail. She'd received at least two or three marketing mailers already that month tucked in amongst the dwindling numbers of Christmas cards. She suspected they knew somehow from public records that she had no mortgage or bank loans on the house.

Adamaria was as likely to sell the old place, cash drain though it was, as she'd be talked into making a move to the moon. And she was about to impart as much to the slick-haired, clean-shaven, eager young agent of change, who had subsequently managed to sneak up and scale the wet porch steps under the cover of a Sell Fast real estate company's logo-printed umbrella. Mr. Stickfigure had sprung back to life despite her mental machinations otherwise. He greeted her stony-faced reception on her doorstep with a set of sparkling white teeth and the same, smooth, practiced doorstep pitch she guessed he'd made a few minutes earlier to an equally immovable neighbor.

"Hi, I'm Phil and you may have seen me around. I've sold several homes in this part of town this year," he said. "You'll have seen my signs in the neighborhood for sure."

A glaring Adamaria refrained from accepting his outstretched hand.

"And, if you've a minute or two to hear more, I'd like to briefly share my showcase system to make a home like yours truly shine in next year's market."

Adamaria rolled her eyes.

"Sky-high home-sales don't impress me any," she replied, refusing the flyer he'd emphatically attempted to thrust into her hand. Rain drops dripped from its glossy, holiday-design. From the distance she kept as she stepped back, Adamaria registered its red and gold imprint of baubles and ribbons framing its festive year-end pitch. Despite having found herself ever the more cash-poor, the sink hole of her finances was her problem to deal with, she maintained, not his, or anyone else's. And she reiterated as much.

"I might ask, where we gonna go? Tell me that," she snapped. His smile waivered, an indication that he'd already received a similar response from her neighbor.

She'd said the same to Gracie each time she'd recycled yet another listing-request letter or flyer touting some previously unimaginable closing price on their block. And besides, Adamaria was more than a homebody, she'd be the first to admit — she'd slowly, over the years, become somewhat of a hermit — a regular Grinch if she said so herself. He should consider himself lucky she'd even answered her door.

"Do me a favor," she said. "Go home. And don't come back. If I see you at my door again, you'll be sorry. You hear me?"

Because she so cherished each and every quirky, vintage feature of her home, its fifth-generational legacy now with her grandkids living under its roof — its crumbling, cracked plaster walls, sagging ceilings and all, it was easy for her to forgive its lop-sided looks and difficult nature, the layers of history that gathered in its dusty, hard-to-reach corners and the friendly ghosts she sometimes wondered if she willed back into existence. No amount of money would persuade her otherwise.

She shut the door abruptly in the salesman's face. Though she'd not given him a chance to elaborate on his pitch, in truth, she didn't entirely blame the ambitious young fella for trying, for prospecting for a new year in a place that was surely out-pricing his own age group. But Adamaria was attached beyond measure to the house on Liberty Street. She was bonded to such a degree anyone unaware of its lineage might have been mistaken in thinking she'd actually had a hand in having constructed it herself.

Adamaria had never been all that handy in the fix-up department, preferring a kitchen worktop, or a garden trowel and a quiet spot of needlework to what she'd considered man's work, at least until there wasn't a man around anymore.

Still, there was a solid predictability, an ever-constant stability about the old place despite its escalating irritations and concerns. Aside from Gracie and the girls, the house was Adamaria's identity, her entire sense of belonging and usefulness. There was an impending sense of her own mortality wrapped in its slowly decaying layers.

Hands on hips, she turned and scurried back to the comfort and warmth of the parlor, holding tight to her belief that all she had to do to stay put, to provide a safety net for her family was to stick to her routine, continue to spin as many plates in the air as she was able and maintain things as close as possible to how they'd always been.

Over my dead body, she muttered, considering its sale. Don't get me started.

As long as she was able to hang on to the property, keep on patching it up, she was sure that everything else would fall into place. This house that had anchored her family for multiple generations afforded her, Gracie and the girls a sense of continuity, of belonging, that was priceless. Nobody could possibly buy such an assurance no matter how hard they tried to take it away from her.

# CHAPTER THREE

# SOAP BUBBLES, SHADOWS AND DAYDREAMS

Gracie was almost done with the putting away of their festive lunch. She'd nearly jumped out of her skin at the sound of the doorbell when she dropped a piece of Adamaria's time-worn Christmas dinnerware into a basin of soapy, pine-scented water.

"Jeez." She retrieved and inspected the undamaged plate from the suds. Her reaction had shaken her. The sudden alarm had startled her, though the subsequent tone of the benign conversation she caught between her mother and whoever it was at the door served to keep any further concern at bay.

Get a grip on yourself she urged as she forced the knot in her shoulders to relax. Ever since the first time she had felt the back of his hand, the fight-or-flight instinct had taken root and it was hard to shake. It crept up and cornered her when she was least expecting it. Something as innocuous as a doorbell ringing still set her off. She was forever looking over her shoulder.

It was evident that Gracie had indulgently squirted far too much dish soap into the bowl. She took a deep breath to calm herself and proceeded to blow an impressively sized, shiny bubble into the cool air of the kitchen. Gracie considered hand-washing dishes to her mother's high standard a tedious task as a rule, yet, that afternoon, as she'd lingered at the steamy kitchen window overlooking the back yard, the younger of the two women was grateful for the chance to lose herself in her more comfortable daydreams for a little while longer. The warmth of the sudsy water felt luxurious in her hands.

She'd promised herself not to give in to the creeping paranoia that had kept her hostage the past couple of years. Being lost in her own free thought was of far more appeal. Her face glowed a gentle peach-color in the dimly-lit room as she switched direction and pictured a second face beside her in the reflection of the window, not as she'd last seen it in person, as a teenager, almost a decade ago, but that of Julian's more recent, pleasing headshot and photos, the refamiliarization of his reassuring smile she'd gleaned from his fairly limited social media.

After extra-carefully rinsing off each piece of dinnerware in a second bowl of clean, cool water, she mindfully set the last of the plates onto a dry kitchen towel draped over a wooden draining board that was positioned beneath the original pie cooler inset into the wall.

A washed-out image of Raymond's cold, white face was in direct contrast to Julian's beautiful, black skin. She tried not to compare, to even put an image of the two men in her mind at the same time, but it was hard not to.

She'd been half-listening to Izzie and Rosa overhead. Her energetic daughters had been racing endless laps of the upstairs hallway, delighting in one of their rowdier games. A tad too much so, she considered. This was her mother's house after all, a fact of which she was made frequently aware, and though Adamaria was strict in her enforcement of her afternoon downtime, at least on weekends and holidays, it didn't feel right for Gracie to stifle the little ones' natural exuberance on Christmas Eve of all days.

She shook her head from side-to-side and a slight, defiant grin flashed back at her in her reflection. They'd catch it for being so playful and rambunctious, she and her girls. A walk into town would calm them, she figured. The rain would curb their energy level for the next few hours until it was time for bed.

Christmas was a risky time to submerge oneself in nostalgia and what-ifs and if she wasn't careful, she feared she'd find herself in a pity-party for one. In fact, Gracie had taken considerable pains to focus on the future and not on the problems of the past, especially during the holiday season. Her sole vision was that of a new life, one without Raymond. She had stifled so many of her own feelings in order to follow her mantra of looking forward. Yet in the days running up to Christmas, she'd sensed an inkling that a little more of her natural, open-hearted optimism was beginning to resurface all on its own. Maybe, she figured, she'd reached the point when her past and future would find a way to connect.

The sense of duty she'd taken on since moving back in with her mother with her own two little ones had weighed on her considerably. There'd been no ladder for her to climb up and out of the deep well in which she'd landed. Her self-worth was in short supply when she'd walked out on her marriage and she feared she'd entirely lost her identity. But she'd had her mother's support, her physical health, her relative youth, her work and most of all, her love for her girls to give her that final push out of the door.

Self-care had never been much of a thing in her mother's world. And the manifestation of the suffering Gracie had experienced before and after the separation had morphed into something that looked to her increasingly like Adamaria's sidekick, her shadow. She'd concentrated her full energy on the needs of the children, her mother's relentless meal routines and housekeeping, the never-ending requirements of the tired, old house. It had been easier at first to simply let go of herself and submit, to become invisible.

Outside influences had posed a danger not worth the risk. Gracie had lost all interest in the casual social life of her coworkers and the few friends of her age still living in the area. After a while, most of the well-meaning, post-separation invitations to get her back into circulation, the pot-lucks, back yard barbecues, movie dates and drinks stopped trickling in. She'd kept in touch, barely, with a handful of friends, but she'd locked all access to such a degree that anyone looking to reach out had to navigate a narrow pipeline of communication via the trusted few.

She'd kept going, wading through more chaos than she would have ever deemed possible in what she considered such an unexceptional life. It had gotten better, there were pinpricks of light in the darkness, more and more so and Gracie's perseverance, backed by her mother's, was finally paying off.

Follow your intuition, she counseled herself, as she studied her face in the window. Her propensity for patience and her subtle sense of humor combined, made for a resilience that she was thankful to still recognize within herself. She leaned in for a closer look, raising her eyebrows and sticking out her tongue, as she rubbed a clear, round circle in the glass with the ball of her fist.

Here's to all that, she declared. One way or another, a necessary stage of hibernation had come to an end. Gracie was ready to get back out in the world, one step at a time in order to reclaim her dignity.

"Lighten up a tad, girlfriend," she instructed her less-than-convincing reflection. "It's just one drink."

# CHAPTER FOUR

# COMPANY ENOUGH

"Dirty weather, indeed," Adamaria muttered, as she turned to take another look at the steadily degrading outdoor scene. The afternoon had taken a turn for the worse. Denser, darker rain clouds closed in. She walked back over to the fireplace and stoked the dancing flames, casting aside any lingering irritation toward the audacity of the young man at the door. She shook her head, willing the holiday to unfold as quietly and uneventfully as possible.

Gracie interrupted her mother's concerns, nudging open the parlor door with a narrow, slender shoulder and, after peeking her head into the room, she searched the shadows in the lowering light. Her eyes settled on her short, stout, hands-on-hips mom, as the older woman basked in the warmth of the fireplace.

The flickering of the blaze bathed the room in a dancing, crimson-colored glow. And within this comfortable scene, Adamaria's profile appeared to conjure the familiar shape of a pleasingly plump, little robin. Half bird, half human. Robust of breast and replete in a frilly-edged, red and white holiday apron tied at the waist over customary seasonal black slacks and red sweater. Her mother's barrel-shaped body held itself in balance on a pair of twig-like legs ensconced at the feet in fluffy carpet slippers. Considering their last name of Uccello (a Northern Italian medieval pet name for a human who looks like a bird) the irony of their affectionate, avian-memes wasn't lost on Gracie. Her mother had nicknamed her Birdie the day she was born.

Crackling wood hissed and spat cheerfully in the grate. A bundle of fresh rosemary that mother and daughter had carefully tied into leaves of dried sage the previous evening was tucked into the outer edges of the hearth, omitting a sweet, lingering scent.

"It's raining cats and dogs out there, Ma," Gracie said, her eyes fixed on the fire. "We'd best make a run for it before it gets nasty."

Adamaria jumped and tutted as a couple of fair-headed, mini-tornadoes burst into the room, narrowly missing their mother. Pink-cheeked and smiley-faced, the girls were so tightly wound, their sudden entrance startled their grandmother. She wished she had at least an ounce of that energy.

"Pop goes the weasel," she said. She burst into a peal of belly laughs, as she regained her composure. Their spontaneity did make life more fun. The two of them frequently reminded her of the hand-wound, battered tin Jack-in-the-Box toy she'd played with as a child.

The sisters were still Santa believers, she'd assumed, seeing as every nerve of their small bodies appeared to relish the anticipation of nightfall and all that Christmas Eve would bring. However, she was reminded of Rosa's distrust of strangers and the smaller child's recent reaction to Santa's arrival on the riverbank during the Downtown Merchant's event remained a concern.

As a consequence, Santa's impending visit was cause for their nervously counting down of every last second until bed time. Adamaria crouched down to better gage the mood. She narrowed her gaze into the black-rimmed pools of her milky-skinned granddaughters' forget-me-not eyes.

These were undeniably her soon-to-be-former-son-in-law's eyes that looked back into hers, only with none of the disdain and disrespect she'd come to expect from him. She caught her breath, briefly. Blue as blue could be, only his, she recalled, were rather more of a hawkish, steelier, grayish-tone.

Besides this, the girls had also inherited Raymond's hair color, though Adamaria expected it might very well darken a shade or two as they grew. Their flaxen curls only added to an adorable double act as the sisters snuggled side by side in the comfortable space beneath her bosom.

Come to think of it, Adamaria doubted Raymond had ever appeared so sweet and innocent as his young daughters when he himself was a boy. She couldn't recall having ever seen a childhood likeness of him. She patted the girls' backs with her age-spotted, work-worn hands as she swept away any more negative thoughts of their regretful patronage.

They clung on to her a moment longer, these sweet young things who were affectionate, energetic and mischievous only to a degree in Adamaria's mind that well-adjusted children should be. For the most part, she considered them happy and content, despite the emotional upheaval of having been separated from their father at such a tender age. It worried her, endlessly, all that they had seen and heard, their propensity for suffering in silence, though she for one, steered clear of so much as mentioning his name around them.

Gracie on the other hand was more transparent, claiming that any pain and loss was worse when hidden. And so, whenever her daughter spoke of their father to the girls, which wasn't all that often, Adamaria attempted to hold her tongue. No matter how much it irritated her, when it came to her grandkids, she was careful to keep her notoriously strong opinions to herself in the event that the unsavory subject of Raymond arose.

She gazed lovingly at her granddaughters. The world was all so simple at their age. At least she believed it still so. The situation would inevitably become more complicated to explain as they grew. As older parents, she and Aldo had struggled to keep up with their daughter's world. Recently she feared she understood it all less and less.

And yet, both women had been fully united in their collective lookout for any and all tell-tale behavioral issues in the girls after Gracie had finally plucked up the courage to leave. She'd returned to her widowed mother's house when the oldest child was barely out of preschool.

"We're goin' out on an adventure, Nonna," Rosa yelped, spinning on the spot as she released herself from Adamaria's embrace. "Splish-splash, sploshin' all the way to the store."

"Won't you come too?" asked Izzie, pulling at her sleeve, sensing her grandmother's reticence.

"No, not this afternoon Bella," Adamaria replied. "Your old Nonna has a bunch of chores to finish up before supper. And besides, it's dirty weather out there. I'm sorry we never had the sense to finish the last of the shoppin' yesterday."

Though the girls had delighted in their early, frequent visits to their grandparents' house, Adamaria had been conscious from the outset that it had been a major adjustment for all three generations in their coming together under one roof permanently and in such regretful circumstances. It was down to their father's inability to control his anger, to manage his life.

Fortunately, as it turned out, the arrangement was proving every bit as beneficial to herself as it seemed to be for Gracie and the children. Truth-be-told, Adamaria had never fully or even half-way adjusted to an empty house after Aldo passed. The sound of children's voices, their myriad routines of daily life and her daughter's largely gentle company were a god-send as far as she was concerned. Differences of opinion aside, she knew full well that families, old and young, have a tendency to drive one another crazy, but at the end of each day, Adamaria convinced herself with all her heart that for her family, like most folk what they needed most in life was one another.

# CHAPTER FIVE

# A PAIR OF
# CANARY YELLOW RAINCOATS

"Won't you two stand still for a single second?" Gracie urged, as she chased her giggling children in circles around a stiff, high-backed, couch. Her patience had waned with all she had on her mind that afternoon.

The formal, plum-velvet relic of a couch was centered, throne-like, atop a jewel-toned and partially threadbare Oriental rug set on the sheen of a freshly polished vertical-grain Douglas Fir floor.

Adamaria and Gracie had taken the trouble to roll up the parlor rug prior to the arrival of the Christmas tree to give the room what she considered its once-a-year pre-holiday deep spit and polish.

Gracie pivoted on her red and green striped, fuzzy-socked feet as she grabbed and held on to a double set of flailing, feather-weight arms, each of which she painstakingly inserted, one at a time into the four tunnels of sleeves of a matching pair of canary-yellow raincoats. The girls were growing in leaps and bounds, it was evident to her and Adamaria both, as Gracie made a mental note to keep an eye out for the next-size up in a replacement raincoat for the older child in the after-holiday sales. Rosa would be ready for her big sister's hand-me-down by the end of the winter, she wagered. Thankfully, there were several good resale stores within walking distance.

"If you keep on with your racin' around for what's left of the day, you two rascals will soon find yourself flat on your backs on the floorboards," Adamaria warned, wagging a stubby finger. "Look how nice and shiny it is, all spic and span for Santa's inspection."

She had swept, vacuumed and mopped after making up a pail of her long-favored homemade solution of olive oil, distilled white vinegar and a few drops of Lavender essential oil that she dissolved in a gallon of warm water. Her concoction had worked wonders on lifting the lingering grime that built up over the year. She'd given the floor a final pass with a clean, damp mop to remove the residue of the cleaning solution.

Such strenuous tasks were proving harder now than ever on her bones and she wondered how many more seasons she'd be able to manage.

"Santa's muddy boots are gonna make a big ol' mess." Rosa said, a look of genuine concern crossing her sweet, young face.

"And the reindeer!" Izzie added. 'That's a whole lotta hooves on the roof."

"Never mind all that. Santa will have 'em tied up real neat on the porch if he knows what's good for him," Adamaria stifled a smile. "And we'll have no more of you two little misses slidin' around on my shiny floorboards, thank you very much. There's been quite enough of that for one day by the sound of things." She looked down at the floor and lowered her voice so as to reinforce her efforts to teach her granddaughters their inside manners. "These here boards have been around a long 'ol time, longer than you, your mother and myself put together and I intend to see that they stay this way, at least until you two get married."

"You mean, go off to college, Mom," Gracie corrected. "These girls have it all in front of them."

It truly was a good deal of heavy, physical work, keeping the old place up, the inside cleaning alone (and it was ever more daunting to Adamaria by the year). And yet at the same time, the dozens of invisible ties connected to the calendar of items that required her attention served to anchor her at home.

When she herself was in grade school, Adamaria's mother and father had never once suggested that she should fly the nest for any other reason than to marry. It had been a different time entirely and yet Gracie's correction gave her pause to think. Where would life have taken me if I'd been given the encouragement and support to have continued my studies, she wondered? She glanced around, wistfully. What would have become of this old place, of her? It had been taken for granted that she would look for domestic work of some kind, straight out of grade school.

She'd never participated in any aspect of the Swinging Sixties. Even after Adamaria had gradually worked her way into a sensible career in book keeping (having stumbled into discovering a strong affinity for the balancing of household accounts), not one person, family member, mentor or otherwise had encouraged her to explore her options, take on any further formal study or exams.

Times had changed. She looked over at the girls, all buttoned up in their shiny rain jackets and full of hope and promise. Though she was grateful that her Gracie had elected to stay close to home while she studied for her teaching credentials — her daughter spoke frequently and encouragingly to Izzie and Rosa of their adventuring confidently out into the wider world someday. Gracie talked of university in such a way that the girls were being raised to picture and strive for far more than their elders in their explorations of their future selves.

"Don't even think of headin' out with anythin' other than rainboots on your feet," Adamaria cautioned, ever-practical, as she glanced down at two sets of small feet encased in their dusty, slippery red tights. Button-like black eyes narrowed under a pair of rimless spectacles. Her bushy, white eyebrows curled into a curious caterpillar shape.

"Is that a hole at your toe, Miss Izzie?" she asked. "Good gracious, didn't we just pick out those tights at the dollar store a few days ago?"

"Don't be a spoil sport, Nonna," the girl replied, sticking her nose in the air. "And you have a hair on your chin."

"And don't answer back to your elders," Gracie intervened. Her children were real people with real feelings, she believed, and although their playfulness was healthy and essential, she drew the line at disrespect.

The one thing Adamaria the elder appeared to gain more of each time she checked, given the unforgiving aging process — was a disagreeable resurgence of facial hair. Her once-lustrous head of blue-black curls, though still not lacking in body, was by now an alabaster white, a cotton-candy cloud that floated on top of her head. A mass of chalky strands had simply multiplied over time until the white had taken over. She wasn't all that bothered however for she was reasonably at peace with her matronly looks even if she did have to pluck a stray hair from her face every now and again. It was her belief that there were far too many other troubling aspects of life to take precedent over vanity.

Adamaria reached a hand to her ear and, as she was in the habit of doing so several times a day, she automatically pinched the closure of one then the other of the small gold earrings with their tiny diamond insets that she'd worn day-in and day-out without exception since Aldo had presented them to her. He had hand carried the earrings back from Italy as a gift shortly before they'd married, the one time he had returned to his home country after he had immigrated to the States. These belonged to his late mother, her one set of earrings, crafted in a traditional design with tiny diamond stones in the center of their delicate, circular shape.

"It's all good, Ma," Gracie replied. "We've thick socks to keep us warm." Gracie was petite, but still a good head taller than her mother as she lingered in the frame of the open front door. Her smooth, olive-colored skin-tone had lost its peachy luster from the steam of the dishwashing water. And yet it radiated something Adamaria hadn't seen in her daughter in a long time. Aware she was being watched Gracie tied her long, dark, wavy hair into a low pony tail.

And Gracie, in turn, paid noticeably close attention to her mother as she stepped back toward her into the darkening hallway. She looked into her mother's same round, almost-opaque, black-pupiled far-away eyes that both she and Adamaria had inherited from the maternal line. Gracie thought her mother appeared a little piqued as she stepped forward to meet her. She wrapped her arms around her mother's thick waist and pinched the soft pad of skin at her hip.

"Don't fret so, Ma," Gracie urged. "We're not made of paper." As far as she was concerned, the afternoon's bracing weather offered an opportunity to shake things up a little, wear off some of the holiday hubbub that had built up in both herself and her offspring over the past few days. The girls would need their sleep if they were to avoid a melt-down the next day. And what she wasn't about to admit to her mother was that she, too, had developed a serious case of her own butterflies given her set of semi-discreet plans for the evening.

All she'd confided to her mother thus far was that she was meeting up with an old high school buddy for a glass of holiday cheer. Julian — her first love, in truth, was back in town from southern California, visiting his parents. And he'd invited her to catch up with him.

"Only after I've tucked the girls into bed, read them a story and made sure they've set out their pillowcases for Santa," Gracie had assured, downplaying her excitement as best she could when she'd the broached subject with her highly-protective mother just the previous evening.

Adamaria, who had made a valiant attempt to feign her own disinterest by keeping uncharacteristically quiet for once, had declared it would do Gracie the world of good to get out with young people her own age. "It bein' the holidays and all."

Now she wasn't so sure. And as she rallied Izzie, Rosa and Gracie back toward the door, Adamaria glanced briefly at her reflection in the gilt-framed mirror that hung over the entryway console. She did a double-take. Her face that looked back at her appeared pale, more so than usual for the time of year. The all-familiar wrinkles and lines she had come to terms with some time ago sagged ever more steadily at the jawline.

Years of grievin' and the stresses of late no doubt catchin' up, she consoled herself, shrugging it off.

She ran her fingers through her short-cut, frugally self-styled hair with its helpful volume of curl at the crown. You're tired is all.

As she turned on the heel of her slipper, she pointed an arthritic finger in the direction of an orderly boot and umbrella stand positioned by the front door. "Mind you don't go catchin' a chill," she instructed her gaggle of girls, shaking her head in a series of side-to-side, bird-like switches, the hallway light catching the tiny stones within the small, gold earrings as the younger women of the house took off on their errands, closing the door behind them.

Adamaria lingered alone in front of the mirror, gawking at the process of a pair of visibly sagging earlobes. This disconcerting imposition on her modesty was yet another of the less spectacular elements of the human body that continued to advance with her years. Her earlobes, she could see, had stretched to a rather unflattering degree.

She raised her hand to her eye. "What ya gonna do?" she asked. The gold wedding band that Aldo had slipped onto her ring finger the day they were married reflected in the glass. Its twinkle was reassuring in the moment as she considered the amount of loss she'd suffered. She'd had the ring resized twice over the years, though Aldo had taken pains at the time to be sure he'd picked out the correct size for their wedding. It had been his first, her second, church-approved marriage however, on account of Adamaria having been widowed at a young age.

Adamaria turned her back to the door as she twisted the ring two times around. "Te dua per sempre," she whispered into the shadowy void. "Love you forever." Dear Aldo.

A vision of her once-slender self, walking down the stairs in the simple, cream-colored skirt-suit she'd worn for their wedding was one she allowed herself to indulge in every now and again — it was like a shaky old camera reel that spontaneously rewound in her head, the matching ivory-silk petaled headpiece stored in a hat box in her bedroom reappeared in detail. There had been no veil. Adamaria had never expected to be blessed with a second love after losing her first. Aldo had been her proof everlasting of the heart's capability of renewal.

She remembered the morning of their Valentine's Day wedding as if it were yesterday. They had invited few guests given that it was her second time at the altar and Aldo was still in mourning for his mother. It was her mother who had served the family an intimate, yet flowing, sparkling-wine wedding luncheon in that very house —in addition to the bubbly, there had been several delicious courses: anti-pasta, ravioli, meat that was butchered weeks before and hung to cure in the kitchen, salad, cheeses and fruit, followed by bowls of sugared almonds and a show-stopping, though modestly-sized Italian cream and liquor cake custom ordered from a bakery in San Francisco's North Beach Italian district.

Adamaria recalled the cake-topper, a family heirloom of an old-fashioned porcelain bride and groom that she'd later insisted Gracie and Raymond incorporate into the homemade red velvet wedding cake she'd prepared for what had all too soon proved a sadly dysfunctional union.

Now she was having no trouble in putting two and two together on the matter of a Gracie and Julian reunion, no matter that it was being framed by her daughter in such a casual way. Still, Adamaria had given a degree of blessing merely by keeping her mouth shut. Hadn't she learned to mind her own business by now? Didn't she already have enough to fret upon?

Adamaria had never intended on being malicious or hateful in her reproach to the Black boy back then. If she had only thought better of it, the bias Gracie had accused her of, before the ghoulish Raymond had come along and insidiously inserted himself into her daughter's life.

And now, all these years later, if she hadn't learned her lesson well enough already, she fought the temptation to interrogate Gracie with regards to Julian's impending reappearance.

Stay out of it, nitwit, she chided herself as she headed back toward the parlor. Her need to control everything and everyone around her was exhausting. What was it that Gracie had quoted the other night from a dog-eared copy of *Pride and Prejudice,* a book she'd been obsessed with since high school and devoured again any number of times in the past couple of years?

Oh yes: Keep your breath to cool your porridge. Or something along those lines. If she was to be respectful of her daughter's autonomy as an adult, she would need to work on that.

# CHAPTER SIX
## PUDDLE JUMPING AND PANETTONE
## LAST OF THE HOLIDAY ERRANDS

Gracie held one of each girls' warm little hands in hers, a child on either side as they strode along the slick, rainbow-colored sidewalk. She'd abandoned her umbrella on the porch as it was too cumbersome to handle with three. The hoods of their rain jackets would suffice if they hurried.

She felt her mother's watchful eye on her back from Adamaria's favored position behind the parlor window, though Gracie refrained from giving in to an urge to turn around and wave. It had all become a little much — Adamaria's well-intentioned, yet continual hovering. Her officious nature. And her mother's fixation on a return to the 'perfect' pre-Raymond past was more than slightly suffocating at times.

It had been Gracie's strategy all along to leave one or two of their holiday errands undone in order to escape her mother's suffocating nosiness and fussing for a while.

She'd tried volunteering for more of the daily domestic chores, updating methods of how and when they went about it all, but her strong-willed mother simply refused to let up.

By then, there was little traffic and very few other people out and about on foot. A flushed-faced couple in their teens scuttled towards them, entwined in a lover's knot beneath the cover of an extra-large, see-through bubble dome umbrella, that kind that featured in black and white photos from the 1960s. Gracie smiled at the image as she and her daughters stepped aside to let them pass, though the cute young couple only had eyes for each other. A round, curtain of rain thrummed off the taut, plastic sides of their substantial canopy, streaming thin poles of water onto the asphalt which in turn twisted and funneled into a roadside drain.

Gracie caught sight of a scrawny looking kid, a boy — he was cradling a small dog partially under his sweatshirt as he sat, huddled for meagre shelter under the eaves above the Veterans memorial plaque affixed to a brick building by the Rectory, along the far side of the church.

"What an afternoon to be out," she remarked, quietly, so only the girls could hear, shivering as she tightened her grip on her daughters' hands. She steered them around the corner onto Western Avenue.

"Why was that boy sittin' out there in the wain?" Rosa asked, a little too loudly. She frowned. Her mother shook her head.

"I don't know, babe, maybe he's waiting for someone. He'd best be heading home, in truth, though, shouldn't he?"

Gracie let go of Izzie's hand, briefly as she felt in her pocket for the crumpled, ten-dollar bill she'd discovered when she'd put her jacket on — it was just enough to justify the expense of another small gift for her mother. She was tempted to turn back and hand the money to the kid, but, despite their struggles, her desire to lavish Adamaria with something impulsive, though inexpensive was stronger in that moment than sharing what little she had with a stranger.

A string of clear colored commercial holiday lights swayed precariously above the street with a subtle click-click, dancing in the wind and the rain, lighted stars flapping against the lamp posts. The sky was gloomy with a dense cloud covering that hung wearily above the muted lights.

"It's pretty, look . . ." Izzie exclaimed, stopping to gaze at the lights. Grace thought she'd seen a better display of holiday sparkle in years when it hadn't been a wash-out this close to Christmas.

"We'd best get a move on, babes, or we'll be soaked to the skin by the time we get home," she cautioned, though in the back of her mind she wondered how she'd manage to make it through several more hours of nervous angst before her meet-up with Julian at their chosen venue, the old Speakeasy at Volpi's. She hesitated to think of it as a date as she and her daughters ducked their heads against the rain and continued on.

Gracie concentrated on the tasks at hand. It would not do to daydream so excessively, especially when out with her kids. And yet her heart skipped a beat at the mere hint of her love life taking even the slightest of a positive turn.

The downtown stores would shortly close shop for the holiday weekend. Gracie and the girls rallied along the street, through the packed parking lot and into the still-busy late-coming crowd in the market to pick up her order of a tub of fresh Dungeness crab salad. After patiently waiting in line, rainwater dripping from their jackets into a series of tiny pools on the linoleum floor by the register, the children were happy to be rewarded with a candy cane each by the friendly young cashier — a fresh faced teenager wearing a neatly-pressed apron over his button-down shirt and khakis. His little sister had been a favorite student of Gracie's the previous year.

"Merry Christmas, Diego," she said, as he handed her the tub of crab salad he'd taped shut. She'd brought along a fold-out nylon bag, her favorite, the one she'd bought in the city years ago that colorfully depicted the Golden Gate Bridge, sea lions and various scenic icons of San Francisco. "Give my best to Alma and your folks."

The three of them took a left turn at the other end of the lot. They narrowly avoided the spray of a passing truck before crossing the street and walking through the parking garage that opened up to an alleyway connected to Kentucky Street and a narrow walkway leading down a concrete stairway into American Alley and Putnam Plaza beyond. There they passed a water fountain which bubbled over with a mysterious red foam.

"Why is it wed?" Rosa asked. "The water."

"Someone has messed with it, silly." Izzie replied, wise to the world after having seen the fountain overflowing with an effusion of blue bubbles during an especially warm week the past summer.

"Food dye and washing detergent," Gracie guessed, laughing as she tugged the girls forward, along Petaluma Boulevard. "It's an old trick. Though don't even think of trying this at home."

Their last mission was quickly accomplished. They collected a tall loaf of Panettone sweet bread loaded with candied citron, lemon zest and raisins from the festively-decked, fairy-lit bakery storefront.

There was barely a soul in sight within the bakery café it being closing time. It was a contrast to the scene on busy weekends, when locals and tourists alike, on the hunt for its famous brick oven breads and pastries packed the indoor dining space. Gracie looked around as she paid. It must be nice for the place itself not just its people to take a breather over the holidays, she thought. She had taken special care to pre-order her mother's favorite sweet bread the previous week. It was one of her contributions to their holiday table and took a chore off her mother's list of home baked goods.

Back when Gracie was the girls' age, Adamaria had busied herself preparing several loaves of Panettone in the busy days before the holiday, one for the centerpiece of her own family's breakfast on Christmas morning and the rest as gifts for neighbors.

Gracie remembered, wistfully, how much she'd looked forward to helping out with the wrapping of these aromatic treats, encasing them, after they'd cooled, as did the bakery, in big, square sheets of crinkly cellophane tied with strips of red, white and green ribbon.

It conjured a wonderful and nostalgic scent memory as she headed back out of the door, her girls on either side, the three of them stepping into a shower of pearlescent rain drops. Welcoming thoughts of the lemony aroma of the distinctive sweet breads that had wafted so luxuriously through the old house on many a winter's day filled Gracie's head as they strode along the sidewalk. Adamaria had stopped baking the breads over time, in large part due to the moving away or passing of many beloved neighbors and then, finally, after Gracie's dad died, she'd given up on them altogether.

Still, Gracie looked forward to biting into a thick slice of the fluffy, fruit filled bakery-bought version she carried in her waterproof bag, an agreeable substitute to her mother's homemade when slathered with a sticky layer of rich, plum jam from one of the jars she and the girls had helped prepare and put away in the pantry during the summer.

"Best pick up the pace," she instructed the girls as she envisioned a second slice for herself, a small holiday indulgence, which she would unabashedly dunk into a double shot of thick, hot, sugary espresso poured from the stove top percolator.

The fact she was to see Julian again in person after so many years was a much bigger deal in Gracie's own mind than she knew what to do with and she was thankful for the distraction of her last-minute shopping. What she'd chosen not to share with her mother was that she and Julian had in fact been chatting for months, almost every night in fact. At first by text messenger, then, after a couple of weeks, in the still, quiet hours after eleven, when Adamaria had retired for the night, they'd progressed to taking turns with voice calls.

It was during one of these conversations, not long after they'd remade their initial reconnection that Julian had mentioned he was headed to his parents' home in Petaluma for Christmas.

"It would be cool to hang out," he'd suggested, casually. He was quick to let her know it would be a short visit at best, what with the long drives north and southbound from his apartment in the south. His work commitment, he explained, had ramped up after his recent promotion as a deputy district attorney.

Gracie had assured him in turn that she'd be pretty tied up herself what with the holiday, her girls and her mother, given that it was just the four of them. "There's no ditching my family for more than a stolen hour or so over Christmas."

"Well then, wanna grab a beer? Christmas Eve?" he'd suggested. And then, after she'd hesitated at the other end of the call: "Toast the end of a decade a week early? 2020 coming at ya."

Gracie had been encouraged that he'd thought it through sufficiently to ask if her mother would be agreeable to watching her kids after their bedtime. This thoughtfulness showed her he had at least the basic comprehension of her responsibilities as a mom. "She'll cover you for a couple of hours, right?" he'd asked. "You deserve a beer by the sounds of it."

"It's a little more complicated than that, Julian." The last thing she wanted was to come across as defeated by phone, though she'd felt compelled to explain, in short, how nervous she was of any slight possibility of running into Raymond.

"It's not that I'm gonna give him the power to control me for the rest of my life," she confessed. "But for now, all I need to do is to steer clear of him so that this damn divorce goes through." She'd taken a breath. "After that I'll be done with it, with him, for good."

Julian had appeared unperturbed, understanding in fact, especially given his line of work.

"I've a good idea as to some of the bullshit you've been through, Gracie," he said, frankly. "And you have my word, I'll not let Raymond within ten feet of you on my watch. A little Christmas cheer is all. A couple beers at most and I promise, I'll see you home safely."

"I can look after myself," Gracie replied. She'd laughed, self-consciously. The beer she could do without, but that wouldn't matter. She pictured a glass of something bubbly. "I'm a grown up, Julian. I don't want to disappoint but it won't be Gracie in her prom dress who shows up at the bar!"

"You'll always be Gracie in braids and her favorite Hollister tee," he replied. She imagined his smile at the other end of the phone. It was the warmth of his genuine nature that she'd first been drawn to and here it was after all this time, making a dent in the exterior of the stubborn, metallic element that was deeply lodged in her heart. "You can't have changed a whole bunch," he joked.

"Oh, you'll see for yourself," she'd answered. "I'll let you be the judge of that."

"In so far as marriage and kids and all the nine yards, well, yeah, you've most of us beat on that," Julian remarked. "But, hey, you're still plenty young enough to start living your life any which way you want."

The concept of living life, as in having fun was alien to her. Her life had been nothing but hard work since soon after her marriage to Raymond. Gracie held her phone at arms-length. She couldn't help but take his last, light-hearted comment the wrong way.

"Just so you know," she'd warned, attempting to make light, all the same. "I'm not all that desperate to get out there – whooping it up." As soon as the words were out of her mouth, she wished she hadn't said them. She sounded like her mother in making the assumption that frivolity and partying was all he'd be after.

"Hang on, that's not fair," Julian had taken a few seconds to reply. The tone of his voice indicating that she'd hurt his feelings.

"All I meant was that you and me meeting as old friends for a couple of beers is not anything more than what it is. A chance to catch up. Have a laugh. That's all."

Truth being, deep within her bruised and battered heart, Gracie did not want it to be all it was between them. Far from it. She'd smoothed it over, agreed to meet and the date was set.

The girls stopped to look at a Christmas display in the window of the hardware store — an assortment of whimsical garden gnomes decked out with thick streamers of silver tinsel draped over their arms, the colorful group nestled in a fluffy bed of fake snow. Izzie best liked the one perched on a toadstool, reading a book. Rosa pointed at a gnome with butterflies on his shoulder. He was holding a watering can in one hand and a toad in the other. Her small, round fingerprint left a smudge on the glass.

Hadn't Gracie poured her heart out over the many late-night catch-ups she'd shared with Julian? And he had listened, patiently, for hours, having responded with all the appropriate answers to soothe and appease. Was it wrong to hope that something more than their past connection was firing a spark between them? Wouldn't he have been completely turned off by now if not? As she gazed, glassy-eyed at the garden gnomes a worrisome new thought struck her that maybe it was pity that he felt, nothing more. Was she a fool, she wondered, to have dared to latch on to the glimmer of hope that the heart-thumping connection they'd once shared was somehow still intact?

# CHAPTER SEVEN

# DIVE BAR STALKER

Raymond stuffed his cold, bony hands into the pockets of his battered-old military-style utility jacket that clung to him like a second skin throughout the colder months.

The jacket was patchy in places, its camo-printed water-resistant coating had been heavily tested over the years. He felt a trickle of warm sweat drip from the bottom of his neck and run the length of his nubbly backbone. It settled at his beltline at the bottom of the grimy t-shirt he wore beneath its thinly insulated inner lining. The layering-effect was successful only in smothering his body's ability to adapt as he'd dodged in and out of doorways downtown, deftly trailing his estranged wife and daughters at the tail end of their holiday errands.

He hated feeling so zipped up and physically confined, just as he hated the uncomfortable situation that he found himself in now and for a second Christmas in a row. Perspiration steamed beneath the damp, cloying layers.

Raymond took some degree of satisfaction in the fact that chance had been close to perfect with his timing that afternoon, for he had just happened to exit the bar across the street from the bakery when his eyes were unexpectedly drawn to the familiar figures of Gracie and the girls. He'd clapped his hand across his mouth, stifling a long, deep and painfully loud gasp of surprise, followed by several awkward intakes of breath, as a mess of damp air settled into his lungs. Instinctively, he ducked his narrow shoulders into the shadows of a side alley, maintaining a safe enough distance to remain undetected as he trailed the three of them back to the house.

Raymond was careful. Extra careful. If any one of them had turned and seen him at any point, his game was up. There was always something unpredictable with how their little brains had operated, he recalled. It stung that he hadn't seen his kids this close in months. Raymond's heart beat fast and loud like a drum, its pulsating rhythm buried beneath his outerwear. A hard, cold, sensation ripped through his forced composure. It was the recognition of how much they'd grown and how much he'd missed that hurt most.

Earlier, he had parked his truck two blocks from the church and walked another couple into town to sit at the bar and then shoot a little pool on Kentucky. And after an hour or so of that, he'd sidled down Western Avenue and across Petaluma Boulevard to see what was shaking inside of another of his frequent watering holes.

The dive bar mood had been comfortingly festive in a dimly lit fashion. Three or four beers had put him in a fairly relaxed state. His plan was to sidle on in to the Children's Christmas Eve Service at St. Vincent's Church come late afternoon. He remembered how Gracie and her mother had taken Izzie over to the church that first Christmas, back when she was a newborn. He'd berated his wife afterwards that she'd been crazy to think the kid wouldn't scream the place down. Raymond had preferred to stay put and work his way through a good half bottle of his version of the holy water. He'd been right about that outing, as he believed he was right about everything, or most things, anyway.

This year however; he had made a concerted effort before heading into the bars to hit up the toy store nearby. In his hands he carried two large gift bags, inside of which, swaddled in sparkly tissue paper, sat a pair of collectible toy ponies in boxes with clear plastic fronts. Pricey for what they were, he'd thought. The teenage girl who helped him at the counter said she hoped he had his vehicle nearby, or an umbrella at least. He'd shrugged the rain off, assuring her he would stick to the sidewalk under the awnings.

On his way downtown, earlier, he'd stopped off at the beauty store in the strip mall. He pictured the small, red-ribbon tied gift box he'd left on the floor in his truck. It contained a small set of Eau de Toilette and matching body lotion. It was her favorite, Gracie's, at least back in the day — Dolce and Gabbana, Light Blue, Casual and Breezy, as the jargon promised, like a Sicilian summer, or at least how Gracie used to say she imagined one to be. The sales assistant had doused a thin piece of white card in a heavy mist of tester. He'd been taken aback by the strength of its familiar bouquet — an eerie mash-up of cedar, jasmine, apples and something like amber which aroused a conflicting jumble of emotions. He considered himself smell sensitive. Which was upsetting at times. The first summer they had been together, he recalled, sentimentally, had been all about that charmed, sun-soaked aroma. After she found out she was pregnant, it changed. A jarring new odor — dry breast milk, kid vomit, everything.

And it had come to this, in a few short years, him trailing her and his kids, like an animal, tracking their scent.

Raymond decided he would keep his distance, stick to his plan and take a gamble on her not ruining his kids' Christmas with yet another refusal to let him see them.

# Chapter Eight

# A Murder of Crows

Bundles of smoking sage infused the toasty parlor with a heady, woodsy scent, transporting Adamaria to remembrances of holidays past. Her weary eyes swept that which had always been her favorite room with a sense of quiet satisfaction. It was cozy, festive and, she was quite sure, impenetrable to the intrusions of the outside world.

Gracie had taken the girls to a Christmas tree farm on the edge of town during the last week of school. Though Adamaria had been apprehensive that the farm would've surely been out of decent trees so late in the holiday season, Gracie had been fortunate to find the very last of the pre-cut Douglas Firs. It had stood there, wistful looking, as if it were waiting for them, Gracie described it, afterwards, as having been propped upright against the redwood siding of the tree farm barn. It was short and round and slightly lop-sided, which was most likely why it had been left there in Adamaria's mind, a reject, unclaimed. Yet Gracie had hauled it home happily and at a bargain, which made both she and her mother happy. They had no one to impress other than themselves after all. The tree had personality and it suited them fine.

Izzie and Rosa were tall enough when standing on a chair to reach the tippy top of the quirky-looking tree. Adamaria reminisced fondly on the four of them having spent a festive evening playing an assortment of scratchy holiday songs on Aldo's rickety record player. Much to the children's amusement, she'd encouraged the sing-along, her octaves as horribly out of tune as ever, but enthusiastic nonetheless. First it had been Tony Bennett's *I Love the Winter Weather,* followed by another one of her favorites, a duo with Placido Domingo of *The First Noel.*

Together, the women and children had adorned the tree with armloads of aging strings of scarlet and gold beads, red ribbons, multi-colored lights and a cardboard box-load of once-shiny, glass baubles, many of which had lost much of their luster over the years. As was their family custom these past two Christmases, the youngest, Rosa, had been given the honor of placing a faded angel topper from Gracie's own childhood on the tip of the top branch.

Adamaria turned from the fire and stepped back over to the window. The children's presence in the house never failed to chase away any lingering spirits, at least during daylight hours. The absence of their energy reopened a void into the past. A slow, creeping feeling of sadness and loss threatened to wash through her. She could feel it in her bones. Still, the soft reflection of twinkling lights on the inside of the rainy windowpane served to produce sufficient a comforting effect to soothe her melancholic mood.

Blue lights cast back in soft-gray-tones and the red lights warmed and intensified, in large part, she figured, due to the changes in the lenses of her eyes having begun to yellow with age. She paused, allowing the colors to wash through her, making a mental note to look into cataract surgery during the coming year. Another thing she had put off, what with all the trouble with Raymond. This son-in-law and aging business were a double nuisance that she could do without.

A real Christmas tree was a significant, yet worthy expense in Adamaria's meticulously tallied books and one that had come as a welcome gift to Gracie when the tree farm owner had offered it at half price. "Given how close we are to Christmas and the tree bein' a little less than perfect," he'd claimed as he'd netted the tree and tied it onto the roof of Adamaria's decade-old Subaru which Gracie now drove almost exclusively. Gracie and the girls had returned with the tree and twenty-five dollars in folded notes to put towards one or two of the more expensive grocery items for the holidays — the Panettone bread for one.

Rainwater had revealed itself, having seeped beneath the sash of the crumbling window frame — moisture blown inwards that afternoon by the wind beneath the porch overhang.

"House rich, cash poor," Adamaria declared as she mopped the leak with a fresh, dry towel shaken from the neatly folded pile she'd washed and dried amongst many other tasks that morning and stashed on the floor, behind the drapes.

Adamaria was damned if she was going to give up on the old place in her lifetime, leaking windows not the least of its problems.

Somehow, it'll all work out, she promised, as if in homage to the house itself as she jammed a second towel along the ridge of the damp, swollen frame. I should've given Gracie a dollar for the lottery, she reasoned. Solve all our problems in one.

Outside, in the falling rain, a choir of jet-black crows perched on a power line, their beaks wide open in a winter's song. They were, she was sure, the same clever, social birds that had kept her company during the long, dark months she'd been alone in the house. Adamaria had pet-names for each of the 'murder of crows' that lined a utility wire running parallel to the porch in patient anticipation of her periodic benevolence. Much to her neighbor's chagrin, she mostly threw her frequent-flyers leftover sourdough breadcrumbs from her kitchen, although she'd noticed the hungry hoard would obligingly eat most things, especially favoring the unfortunate roadkill they took an impressive deal of squawky pleasure in clearing.

These sleek, smart birds returned her generosity with a convivial greeting on the rare occasions she left the house, mostly on foot. Their collective call, a loud, raspy cacophony was something to look forward to on the occasions she headed out and returned home from her weekly errands.

"Ciao," Adamaria called from the other side of the windowpane, waving her short, stocky arms in greeting. The birds scattered and dispersed in response to her movement, settling into the branches of a tall Sycamore tree. Safe in the knowledge that her feathered friends were better sheltered from the rain, Adamaria moved back to the now blazing fire where she lingered. She indulged herself as she played a turn of Frank Sinatra's *A Jolly Christmas* on the turntable before lowering herself down in the center of the couch. She closed her eyes and attempted to relax a little and enjoy the peaceful moment. Slowly and deliberately, she lifted her tired legs to rest on a small footstool, her dear late mother's original and once-striking bluebird needlepoint design now faded and close to threadbare from its decades of use.

The last of the holiday preparations rotated in list form in her head, despite her fatigue. Unable to unwind, Adamaria submitted to the mulling over of the disquieting subject of her daughter's imminent date.

Mind your own knittin', woman, she chided, as an oblivious Ol' Blue Eyes belted out a distraction to her campaign of concerns with a rousing rendition of *A Merry Little Christmas Now.*

Look where it got you last time, Adamaria warned, as the pleasant holiday music did little to stifle and silence the loud and persistent voice that pressed on tirelessly like a kitten's sharp paw clawing at her mind.

Her Gracie, twenty-nine! The years had passed in rapid procession since her daughter was in high school. Adamaria attempted to calm her thoughts with a short series of deep, determined breaths. She conjured a picture of Gracie's dear face. Then and now. In her mind, there was a romantic, distinctive look of the old-Italy about her daughter, not in any ill-fitting, old-fashioned way, but rather more of the dark, peasant-charm which Gracie exuded, petite yet robust — what her own mother had described as a look of the fields in her. And while Adamaria held tight to the hope that Raymond had not completely destroyed her overall innocence, the sweetness and integrity of her daughter's nature, she prayed that Gracie had learned her lesson in how to steer clear of the bad ones.

Adamaria opened her eyes and searched for the ever-present, all-seeing eyes of her own late-mother, Valentina. Give me strength, she pleaded. It was Valentina's stern, color-tinted photographic portrait, presiding over the right side of the fireplace that grounded her at times like these. Her mother's likeness was anchored to the wall, her familiar square face, flanked by snowy-white hair, the same colorless mane as Adamaria's own, only the older woman's was tied back in a thick braid and frozen for eternity within the confines of a raised oval, dark wood frame.

At least her mother's spirit, she believed, was content, it had found peace, moored as it was beside the portrait of her equally stalwart husband, Adamaria's father, Emilio. Adamaria's beloved Aldo only partially balanced his in-laws in his solo position, his framed portrait hung at the same level as her parents only on the other side of the fireplace. She couldn't help but consider him out of sorts, gone too soon. He never would have wanted to have left her first. One day, inevitably, she knew her own likeness would hang there beside her Aldo, finally, fully balancing the four, though she had no intention of adding to the wall of spirits just yet. On the mantel itself, there were smaller, framed photos of Gracie as a child, the three of them, Aldo, she and Gracie together in a formal studio portrait taken when Gracie was around six alongside an assortment of baby and toddler photos of Izzie and Rosa.

Adamaria had married Aldo a decade after his cousin, her first husband, Gino, was killed in a helicopter crash in Vietnam. The helicopter had been preparing to land troops for a jungle patrol in a bush clearing. Everyone on board the Huey died along with her Gino. She'd been all of twenty-one back in '71 when she'd been widowed the first time. She had learned, later, that Gino's Huey had been one of almost half of the 12,000 US helicopters that served that war and were lost.

What had she known of marriage, she asked herself? She'd barely gotten to know him properly. It had taken Gino's first cousin, an immigrant from the same steady, hard-working and determined, Swiss-Italian stock to convince her to marry again. There had been much talk of it amongst both families. She'd wanted nothing to do with it. For the longest time, she had cut herself off from her friends and retreated into her grief. That it had taken Aldo eight years of waiting patiently through the appropriate mourning period and then some in order for him to persuade her to give him a chance was testament to the both of them. The last thing she had needed was to experience such a devastating loss a second time. And dear Aldo, in his equally headstrong way of reckoning, fully believed that he was the one to change her mind. He couldn't have known he'd also go before her. It had been worth it, she figured. The sorrow.

"Capo tosto," he'd affectionately referred to her throughout their surprisingly happy marriage. "Hard head."

"Takes one to know one," she'd reply, tapping his balding skull in turn, though she'd be grateful for the rest of her years for his rock-like persistence and she had never had cause to regret having come around to a second match from the same bloodline.

Adamaria maintained it had been her decision after all was said and done. Ah, the old ways, she considered, releasing her more maudlin remembrances, that afternoon, as she maneuvered herself into a comfortable position on the couch. She and Aldo had been lucky. It had been a good deal less complicated than matchmaking today. All that online business people did now. Meeting up with strangers. It had worked out fine for them without any other options. Hadn't she been content to stay home and take care of him and the house and the baby that came much later?

She often wondered how many kids she and Gino would have born had he not been taken so soon. It was never meant to be. Though Gracie was Aldo's child, through-and-through. She may have made a fuss with regards to her father's stubborn ideas and old ways as she'd entered her teens, but they'd adored one another and were devoted as a family nonetheless.

Adamaria was determined to explain it all away to herself in a simplified fashion, both then and now, the attitudes they'd shared that Gracie had gone so far as to condone as prejudice —it was just how things used to be, in her own mind, the way of the world, but Gracie wouldn't have it. There had been some uncomfortable scenes. Yet she was never nearly as stubborn-natured as her mother and once she'd made her point, Gracie would let it go for a while, though it had become clear to Adamaria they had never fully resolved the unpleasant issue of their accused injustice against Julian. And, as she was growing more aware by the day, it remained an uncomfortably large elephant in the room between mother and daughter.

Adamaria told herself that all she wanted was the best for her daughter, past, present and future. As in an uncomplicated life. Her own pregnancy with Gracie had been unexpected after all, a wonderful surprise after a series of heartbreaking miscarriages. Gracie had finally arrived, as if by a miracle, a decade into their marriage, some eighteen years after Aldo had first set his eyes on the widowed Adamaria as his bride.

The minute she'd held her tiny newborn daughter in her arms and gazed down at her soft, round, dark-as-midnight eyes framed as they were with their long and lustrous eyelashes, Adamaria had claimed the girl was a gift from God. "Cherubino," angel, Aldo had agreed. Graceful as a dove. Her Birdie. She had vowed to protect her as long as she lived.

"Well, may the good Lord look out for my little Birdie tonight," Adamaria mumbled, appeasing any lingering guilt as she stretched out her stiff and swollen legs and rested them on the footstool. Just as she had herself, Gracie would need to learn to trust again sometime. Only Gracie would know when that time was right. And when the right one came along it was nobody's business but the two of them, least of all Adamaria's. She'd learned that much. She consoled herself that she no longer had any issue with Julian other than the fact he lived at the other end of the state.

After she wedged a plump cushion into the small of her back, Adamaria reached down to pull out a throw from a basket beside her feet. A gift from Gracie the previous Christmas. It was plush to the touch, the color of a full red wine. She sighed as she spread the soft fabric across her lap.

Her mind drifted. Her Gracie had been such a beautiful bride. She reached over and picked up a small, delicate brass frame, its contents a cameo photograph of Gracie — a head and shoulder bridal portrait, in black and white. Adamaria repositioned the image on the side table by her armchair. She thought about the larger, framed photograph of the small wedding party that she'd removed from the downstairs hallway after Gracie had made her escape. Adamaria remembered the pains that she'd taken to expand her daughter's simple white gown in an effort to disguise the bloom of an unexpected pregnancy that she and Aldo had been so determined to keep amongst themselves. At least until after the wedding.

And to think, as she reflected further, her tempered guilt resurfacing by the light of the fire, Raymond's having not been a Catholic, or much of a prospect from the outset had been regretfully so much lesser of an issue for them as Gracie's parents than the color of the first boy's skin. Her cheeks flushed as she faced the truth that she'd tried so hard and for so long to push aside. She had been horribly wrong, they both had. Come to think of it, she could barely name a single soul born outside of her own neighborhood (folk with largely the same, predominant European heritage of the area), whom she or Aldo had ever freely invited into their home. Julian had never been given a chance.

Adamaria closed her eyes and forced herself to further reflect. She believed now that she and Aldo's reasoning had been more in their heads than their heart. He had been a good man, yet, hadn't he, her Aldo? And she'd truly never considered herself an uncompassionate woman.

If my husband was any more guilty of bias and ignorance than me, then it wasn't entirely his fault, she reasoned. And the irony was, as Adamaria continued to pick at the past, her Aldo had suffered a long-lasting insecurity as an immigrant himself. It was as if he'd clung onto his own deep-seated need for identity by rejecting another, she figured. Why had she not put this together until now?

Her late-husband's primary desire had been to belong, she deduced, looking back on it. Hadn't he been threatened by other, more established men, a few with anti-Italian sentiment of their own, at work, at church, in the bar? Those insecurities had likely remained buried deep, their whole married life. And, American-born, she'd simply swept them under the carpet.

She would have liked to have let herself off so easily, now. Back when she was a girl, at home, at school, in church, why, all the folk around her had been predominantly white or whitish, she recalled — if her own olive southern Italian skin tone could be described as such. She asked herself, whose fault was it that I've barely traveled, never even left the darn country? Her folks had never dreamed of her marrying outside of their Italian Catholic community.

Adamaria had been exposed to little other than the ranch culture she'd grown up in. Despite her Gracie's protestations as she herself had grown older, enrolled in university and become a little more worldly, Adamaria's heritage had, until only recently, forged within her an iron-cast view on what was socially acceptable and what was not.

"It's no excuse these days to keep on saying that you're from a different time, Mom," Gracie reprimanded her, frequently — word for word. It was all so confusing to even try to get things right without offending someone. She'd meant no harm to anyone. And yet it had been foolish of her to continually refuse her daughter a more willing audience on the subject.

Adamaria fretted anew. What if Gracie took a notion to pack up with the girls and leave her silly, small-minded mother and the old house behind? Her head swirled, none of it any consolation to her on Christmas Eve afternoon when all she really wanted was a nap.

Her eyelids fluttered and she forced them shut. She jostled around for a more comfortable position. Aside from all her flaws, what she needed and desired above all else was to feel useful, to remain relevant in her family's life. This much was clear. The house, her daughter and granddaughters— they were who she was, her entire identity. She meant no one any harm.

Could she grow more flexible in her thinking, more accepting, she asked herself, more mindful of others? Like it or not, she felt her time of influence was passing. Best she learn to change.

Warmth gradually tempered Adamaria's waning angst as flames from the fireplace cast long shadows over the rug. The wood crackled and hissed. The room's enveloping heat lulled her into a steadily-satisfying level of repose.

She drifted off, comforted by the onset of the one thing Aldo had cherished, aside from his wife and daughter and later, his darling granddaughters — Christmas with the family. Adamaria conjured up his last holiday spent, blessedly, as it turned out, regaling his daughter and small grandbabies with colorful tales from the old country, his lively stories and song accompanied by a characteristic range of expressive gestures. He'd sung so much better than she, she recalled, articulating his melodious range with his sinewy arms.

So thoroughly content they'd been at their humble holiday table, it warmed her heart to think of how their small family would linger long after the meal was finished, playing games and sharing stories. It was Aldo who had insisted on keeping many of the traditions of his homeland alive.

Adamaria dozed a short, blessed while before being awoken with a start. She'd dreamed she'd lost the use of her arms and legs. It was a clear sign, she feared, as she reached down to make sure her lower limbs were intact and still attached, that she was losing her grip.

As hard as it was for her to release herself from a lifetime of parsimonious behavior, the rigid mindset and routine that came along with it, she resolved at least to put some effort into the prospect of what Gracie referred to as lightening up. In the meantime, however, she had supper to think of.

How she missed the juicy, whole, Dungeness crab Aldo would bring home, freshly-cleaned and cracked after a misty Christmas Eve drive out to the wind and fog-whipped shores of Bodega Bay. He'd several old friends, mostly all gone, who'd fished the Sonoma County waters for business and pleasure. Though he was afraid of the ocean himself having never learned to swim, there was little satisfaction he savored more than walking through the door with a whistle on his lips, the score of a bag-load of live pink crab on-ice in his arms.

Now that it was just Gracie, the girls and herself, a modest plate of fresh crab sandwiches would have to suffice.

She smiled as she recalled how the little girls had made a dent, earlier, in the contents of a platter of her favorite, iced and sprinkle-coated Wandi angel wings — delicious deep-fried sweet dough ribbons, the traditional powder-sugared bow-tie pastries her mother and grandmother before her had lovingly created each Christmas. Much to Gracie's chagrin, they'd gobbled down three-apiece after their lunch.

Adamaria had craftily squirreled a batch of the Wandi wings away in an airtight container she'd hidden under a kitchen towel on the counter —this would make for an adequate supply of treats for the next day or two, depending on how strictly she rationed them out. Gracie didn't approve of sugar. Adamaria, however, was not nearly so strict with regards to a little treat here and there, especially at Christmas. Some things she refused to adhere to . . . fully. And that was one of them. If their Nonna wasn't able to spoil the girls with a cookie or two, then who would?

# Chapter Nine

# One Last Chance
# to Change Her Mind

Darkness was Raymond's only friend, silent and trustworthy — its vacuous, all-encompassing presence a comfort to him. That afternoon, its cloak of obscurity folded itself in, much to his relief, a little before five p.m., its darkness keeping him hidden a little while longer.

He almost lost his balance as he slid on the slippery green algae that coated the shady sidewalk, a danger zone for the unfortunate few such as he who were, for whatever reason, out and about on the streets at that hour on a rain drenched Christmas Eve.

Raymond righted his step as he huddled in the shadows between his mother-in-law's house and the church. He braced himself for the smell of wet wool, of damp coats and hats, sweaty, hand-knitted scarves and mittens — the solemn, suffocating sensation he'd endured the few times he'd been subjected to the smoky incense of a Catholic Mass. The one consolation ahead, he assured himself, if it wasn't for the weather, was that there'd be far fewer folk out, the polished wooden pews otherwise packed like sardines for the kids' Christmas service.

The muted streetscape was deserted but for the occasional blur of a passing car. Raymond couldn't imagine anyone in his right mind giving up the comfort of his fireplace, a holiday-stocked liquor cabinet, a soft couch, a bag of chips and salsa and a working cable for the stuffy confines of the drafty and cavernous old church. He raised his tired eyes as if in prayer to the dark, cloud-covered sky. A heavy gloom had eclipsed the tops of the tall trees that lined the street. It was as if the world was closing in on him.

His face was a luminous shade of pale gray in the soft glow of a streetlight. I'll never know, he bemoaned, whatever it was I did to be shut out like this. The watery, gunmetal blue of his bloodshot eyes narrowed and fixed on the radiance that emanated from the parlor windows.

That same morning, he had decided that it was the day for Gracie's last chance to change her mind. And so, this was it. The past couple of years had come to a head and he was convinced that she would cave. He was confident that this time he would win her over into allowing him at least a first step back into their lives. It would be a start. The rest he'd work on later. Surely, he believed, she wouldn't be as cold-hearted to deny him his rights as the kids' dad indefinitely. He had done the right thing by her when she told him she was pregnant the first time and the second.

"How dare she shut me out in the rain, refuse me again?" he muttered.

Raymond's initial plan was a simple one. He would slip out to his truck shortly before the end of the kids' service and gather up the gift bags he'd stashed inside on the passenger seat floor. He figured he'd be back in time to wait for them to file out on foot with the crowd at the bottom of the church steps.

If he played his cards right, Raymond calculated, if he was able to display a sufficient degree of humility, maybe, then just maybe, she'd relent and he'd be invited into that claustrophobic, musty old-pit of a parlor to sit by the tree — to watch in the warmth of the fireside as his daughters opened the gifts that he'd so thoughtfully picked out for them.

Who knows, he romanticized, his belly rumbling, one of 'em might even go so far as to offer him a bite to eat.

His stomach churned, ever more loudly. He knew full well he was pushing it with the food fantasy, but if there was one thing he had to admit when it came to his bitch of a mother-in-law, it was the old girls' cooking. How he'd missed the heavily-laden foil takeaway trays of Sunday left-overs Gracie had brought home — stuffed to the brim with Italian food, meatballs, sausages, all kinds of pasta dishes he had taken for granted and wolfed down on a regular basis.

If worst came to worst and Gracie dared be so cruel and cold as to reject him right there on the church steps of all places, he would be forced to take his calculated plan to the next level. He had it all clearly worked out.

Raymond's fingers were stained by his near-constant chain smoking, weed mixed with tobacco — American Spirits. He slipped his hands from his pockets, lifted them toward his face for closer observation. His hands, like the rest of his body were by then chilled to the skeletal bone. Any routine in his rudimentary meal schedule had bitten the dust with the torment of his abandonment, the result of which had reduced his form to so little flesh cover that he felt the cold damp of winter far more miserably than during the days when Gracie had been around to take care of him. Food, since, was merely a function and no longer a priority. He worked to placate himself as his mind rotated through its various woes and anxieties.

His stomach, however, continued to advise him otherwise. It growled, a deep, hollow echo as he tortured himself pictured seated before Adamaria's typical holiday spread — some kind of pasta, followed by a garlicky, lemony leg of lamb roasted the perfect shade of blush, left to rest on a carving board and served with the juices poured over the top. There would be dessert after, for sure, he imagined. What he'd have given in the moment for a homemade biscotti dunked in a mug of strong coffee, laced with an over-generous glug of whatever was left of Gracie's old man's liquor cabinet.

The kids, his girls and their cruel, selfish mother had appeared to him to be way too content and happy-go-lucky for his liking. He wrapped his arms around his narrow torso for comfort. How it had stung — their smiles and laughter as they'd emerged from the brightly-lit bakery, gathering themselves and their Christmas shopping into a tight, heart-shaped-huddle under Gracie's embrace. His heart had lurched into his throat as he'd walked from the bar. He'd felt it sink and turn itself inside out as the three of them skipped and splashed the few blocks home ahead of him, totally oblivious to his somber, gutted presence even as he'd lurked in the shadows by the side of the church, watching their every move to the top of their grandmother's porch.

Damn it all, Raymond cursed, his hands re-emerging from the bottom of the frayed lining of his pockets. "It's that salty ol' witch who's to blame for all of this, poisonin' Gracie against me."

He was, in that minute, acutely aware of there being no one in the world left to look out for him other than his own old man and he was not much good for a whole lot of anything. It was an unfair playing field in his opinion, Gracie having the old formidable hag on her side. He sucked in a lungful of cold, damp air and drew a shaking hand across his chiseled cheekbone, a further reminder of his scrawny, sorrowful state.

His pair of damp jeans sagged miserably onto a sharpened set of narrow hip bones. He hauled them back up with one hand as he slicked a long, thin streak of stringy, sallow-colored forelock behind his left ear, with the other. He narrowed his eyes for a closer look across the darkened street. He felt a brief stab of regret in that he hadn't washed his hair that week, a lesser concern that his appearance had taken an unfortunate dive along with his pride.

It's gonna be chill after this, he promised himself. Hella. Raymond felt his spirit inexplicably lifting, despite the miserable conditions he'd found himself in that afternoon. It's me who's in charge now. They'll see.

# CHAPTER TEN

# GNOME TALES
# AND A PINK POINSETTIA

Adamaria's neck rested at an awkward angle on her shoulder. Her chin nestled into a roll of flesh above her collar bone. She'd nodded off a second time during the last throws of gloomy daylight and, aside from the collective glow of the fire and the Christmas tree lights, it was almost completely dark by the time she awoke, snug as she was indoors, shielded from the sheets of rain that were by now steadily assaulting the windowpanes.

It was the sound of the key in the front door that had broken her slumber. A thoroughly-soaked Gracie and the girls scurried inside with the last of their holiday purchases tucked under their arms.

Squeals and giggles bounced off the hallway walls as the children plonked their puddle-wet butts onto the lower stair for the tugging off of rainboots and removal of wet socks. Adamaria shook herself to, rallying what was left of her dwindling energy. The stormy weather had evidently failed to dampen the excitement of her grandchildren.

The parlor was prone to more than the occasional draft during the winter months in several spots that she was never quite able to fix. On cue, a gust of wind snuck in from under the built-in cabinets either side of the fireplace. Cool, damp air snaked around Adamaria's thick, stockinged ankles at the bottom of her pants as pink-cheeked adventurers burst into the parlor, brimming with renewed energy after their bracing expedition.

Adamaria made a mental note to tackle the offending gap in the exterior siding before the winter was over. Another priority line-item for her ever-growing fix-it list. In truth, she knew the house would never be entirely weather-proofed without the expense and considerable trouble of replacing the siding and reinsulating its walls. Its decrepit windows were in desperate need of replacement and the whole house begged for a long-overdue interior and exterior painting. She'd watched in a mixture of awe, envy and part disdain as substantial renovations had been carried out to a daunting extent following the past year's sale of a nearby neighboring property.

Sink hole, she said to herself, with regards to her home's ever-steady decline.

Adamaria shook off what was left of her nap-induced inertia. Slowly and deliberately, she rotated the lead weight of her head side-to-side above her stiffened neck and, after a series of crackles and snapping ligaments motivated by all that was still left to do, she unfolded her hands from her lap and smoothed down the bunched-up fabric of the apron she'd omitted to remove. She'd regret it later on, she feared, for her nap would likely interfere with a solid overnight sleep.

It was her late mother and her Nonna who had instilled in Adamaria's body clock a highly peculiar alert when it came to the onset of evening. She'd been indoctrinated to be wary of the dark from an impressionable age. Her people, the early ones who'd come from the old country, had held firm to their folkish belief in the night spirits that were said to linger on the street after dark.

Ever since she was a wide-eyed little girl, Adamaria had known, in her heart that these fantastic stories were little more than folktales and yet she still couldn't quite bring herself to block the customary fear, followed by a jolt of satisfaction, a deep sense of relief in the knowledge that her own little family was back home safe by nightfall — especially so since they'd been soaked through, as the afternoon had by then turned into a wet and howling early evening.

Glittery, glass baubles swayed in the breeze from the parlor door. Adamaria watched, transfixed, as a length of red, shiny ribbon that was pinned to either end of the mantle swayed back and forth, cradling the cherished few handwritten holiday cards that friends and family still sent in the mail. One of the cards, the only one to depict a traditional, glittery scene of the nativity, the old-fashioned, religious type that Adamaria favored, floated gently in slow motion in the heat of the fire to land, several seconds later, face up on the hearth rug.

"Pick that up, please, Bella." Adamaria directed Izzie, the oldest of the girls, as the child stood before the hearth, warming her small, pink hands at a safe distance from the robust flames. Adamaria was aware of a dull ache in her hips. "Heavens, look at the state of you."

A pair of formerly bouncy ponytails lay flattened from the damp excursion, rats' tails that lay limp and lifeless and dripping rainwater down the back of the girls' matching holiday hand-knitted sweaters.

"Come here," Adamaria admonished as she squeezed water in turn from each girls' hair into the cup of her hand. She tipped the droplets into a plant pot on the side table. "Get on upstairs with me this minute and I'll draw you a nice, warm bath. The last thing we need is for you two to go catchin' a cold."

"Ouch, that hurt," Rosa cried, twisting around, a look of indignation on her flushed, round face.

Gracie stepped between them. "Mom, you're over reacting again. It was harmless fun is all. A little puddle jumping and a head of wet hair never hurt anyone."

"We're okay, Nonna," an adamant Izzie joined the debate. "Don't be mad with Mommy. It was fun."

It was not lost on Adamaria that all three generations in the room that evening had been baptized in the very church that presided over the offending puddles that pooled by its great stone steps that led to the courtyard fountain.

"Holy water at least," she conceded, tutting again, her tongue tapping on the dry roof of her mouth.

"Come on, Mom," Gracie urged, as she carefully peeled off her damp sweater, revealing a long-sleeved, lace-trimmed, t-shirt that hugged her figure beneath. "Chill out. It's Christmas Eve. We're excited is all. We'll be fine."

One of the few things she had managed to keep from her mother while living in close quarters was the tattoo of a tiger's head that she'd splurged on having inked in glorious full color over her left shoulder blade. She'd sat for the tattoo in a small, blind-shuttered parlor in Petaluma on a rare summer's Saturday afternoon that she'd had to herself when Adamaria had taken the girls for ice cream and the movies. A former classmate from high school had been booked up for weeks but

61

he'd had a cancellation that day and had fit her in at late notice. In her mind, it was nobody's darn business but her own. So far, she had managed to hide her prized tiger from her observant offspring. She knew full well they'd not be able to keep it a secret for long. Adamaria, she was sure, would have had a fit if she'd broached the subject beforehand.

Gracie herself had no regrets. It felt good to have a secret. So accustomed was she to having her dirty laundry aired what with all the court hearings and with such little privacy at home. The tiger was hers and hers alone and something fierce to hold onto that had come after Raymond.

"What are we to do about the children's service?" Adamaria asked. "It'll be too late to make a dash for it by the time these two l'il elves are out of the tub."

Gracie glanced over at the antique banjo-shaped chiming clock that she'd taken a minute as she usually did to rewind that same morning. "Sorry Mom. I guess we're gonna take a rain-check, literally, this year."

Adamaria gazed longingly through the parlor window one last time. The silhouette of the church was softy illuminated by interior lights that shone through the stained-glass windows.

"If I'm still awake, then maybe, if the rain slows later, I'll head on over for Midnight Mass — if that's alright with you, dear." It was her way of letting her daughter know she was not at all happy with the break in tradition.

"I promise I'll be tucked up in bed well before eleven, Mom," Gracie replied, ignoring the bait. "You go if you wish." She had every intention of keeping things short and sweet with Julian. She'd not risk putting him off by acting too eager or overloading him with information he didn't need to know. She wouldn't over-stay her welcome, she told herself.

"And maybe, if we're all done with breakfast, we might walk over together for the morning service," Adamaria posed a further suggestion, pushing a little too hard for compliance in Gracie's mind as she looked her mother in the eyes, returning the challenge, a battle of wills. In Gracie's experience, the girls would be way too squirrely to sit through a Christmas morning service when all they'd want to do is relax and play with their gifts.

"Let's see what shakes up." Gracie said. She smiled and looked away. She didn't have the energy to negotiate, to explain her reticence. She was not at all sure she was able to think past the evening and her fast-approaching much-anticipated reunion with Julian. She still couldn't believe she was going to see him again, in person.

Adamaria huffed and puffed and bustled as she corralled the girls upstairs for their bath. The wooden stairs creaked under her weight. Stairs were becoming hard for her. Gracie lingered in the hallway where, after she'd made sure that her mother was out of sight, she retrieved a good-sized, pink, poinsettia in its foil-wrapped pot that she had stealthily shoved into the coat cupboard earlier.

Nothing says Christmas like a nice poinsettia, she reminded herself with a grin. It was one of her mother's favorite sayings each December only it hadn't escaped her notice that Adamaria had failed to buy one that year. She tucked the plant discreetly into a large bag she had recycled from a random but well-meaning assortment of holiday gifts given to her by her students at the start of winter break.

Adamaria was extremely proud of her green thumb even if she had let things go in the yard. Gracie knew she far preferred house plants to flowers when it came to thrifty gifting, devoting a good half hour each day in tending to the assortment of thriving potted and hanging plants that were positioned throughout the house. She was fond of orchids and was forever rotating around a dozen or so in and out of various sunny window ledge spots according to their stages of periodic bloom.

Gracie knew her mother would reap far more mileage for the money spent with many months of extended enjoyment and satisfaction in keeping this new addition alive. To think that people tossed them out after the 25th. What a crime! And this prime specimen had been enticingly marked down, it being Christmas Eve and late in the day at that.

Upstairs, Adamaria filled the deep, cast-iron claw-tub three quarters full with warm, soapy water. She prided herself in being extra generous with the water level and the bubbles, it being Christmas Eve and her granddaughters having been outside so long in such nasty conditions.

Adamaria was mesmerized by the small bubbles as they floated to the top, expanded and joined together, rainbows of soapy film that reminded her of the fuss Gracie had made about the brands of bubble bath it was okay to use when she'd moved back home. She'd had her feelings hurt as she'd reluctantly disposed of several bottles of bubblegum-scented, drug store bubble bath, the kind Gracie had reveled in with glee as a child. She felt a sentimental twinge for the days when nobody had batted an eyelid at a mountain of extra-soapy, highly fragranced bubbles in the family tub.

Gracie had taken pains to explain how it was no longer the thing to do to soak the kids in what she categorized as 'fake stuff, synthetic chemicals and dyes' and Adamaria hadn't forgotten how she'd felt more than a little patronized at the time, watching, speechless, as her daughter had simply swept aside the brand-new bath products she'd purchased for her grandkids and placed them into her mother's hands.

Adamaria's mind returned to the here and now as she turned off the water faucet, still secretly missing the good old days of Pink Camay soap bars, Mr. Bubble and the silly-putty-like Silly Soap that a much younger Gracie had out-and-out adored.

Gone were the bubbles up to the ears, though the girls had never known what it was like to jump into a bathtub that billowed with the foamy, frizzy, cheap, soapy suds of old. They seemed happy enough to jump into the warmth of a tub filled instead with lavender and rosemary-scented, hypoallergenic bubbles and an awaiting basket of Gracie-approved bath toys — an environmentally-friendly ocean animal sea set from last Christmas they had yet to grow bored with. This evening the girls were content to slither around in the tub as long as the water retained its heat, wiggling around like a pair of baby seals, splashing and giggling as their grandmother kept a close watch.

Adamaria welcomed the respite of perching her body on a vinyl-covered stool positioned beside the tub. It was padded in a pink and yellow flowery fabric she had fixed up herself beneath a sturdy, waterproof covering. She listened with one ear as Gracie climbed the stairs and turned the squeaky brass knob of her bedroom door, a shrine to her youth, more or less unaltered since she'd left home to live with Raymond.

"Tell us the gnome story, Nonna," Izzie begged, looking up from the orange plastic sea urchin she turned over in her small hand and plunged into the deep.

"That old tale again?"

"Yes," the girls chorused. "Please. Oh please."

Once, Adamaria had made the mistake of mentioning the gnomes — more of her family's folklore, in front of Raymond. She would never forget how he had chastised her for filling his daughters' heads with what he'd crudely called "her gnarly crock of old-world shit." — foolish and superstitious he'd declared. She knew full well what he'd thought of her. He'd gone so far as to make the ridiculous accusation that she was some kind of sorceress, a wrinkled old crone. He'd insulted her on numerous occasions in such a manner, well before Gracie had left him.

"Very well," she said, pushing aside a particularly nasty vision of Raymond's sneering face. Adamaria placed her papery hands with their squat and neatly trimmed nails in the center of her lap. "Gnomes are teeny, tiny, flutterin' creatures," she said. "They make it their business to scurry around the countryside and sometimes here in town, teasing unsuspectin' big folk like you and me by ticklin' our feet when we're fast asleep."

The girls, their dark, wet eyelashes glued together by small clusters of micro-bubbles, held their breath in unison as they leaned toward her, two sets of pink elbows resting on the ledge of the bath.

"And then what?" Rosa implored.

"Well, what do you think?" their grandmother asked. "They've certainly been known to pull the sheets from beds, to tip over a glass full of milk, sometimes water and worst of all, wine. They'll blow a pile of paper clear off a desk. Expect nothin' but a muddle when they're around."

"Is that all they do?" Izzie asked, her wide eyes like a set of blue saucers.

"Why, their meanest trick in my book is to pull a chair out from underneath just as some poor ol' unsuspectin' soul such as myself sits down." She pretended to topple from her stool.

The girls laughed uproariously, thinking this about the funniest stunt they'd ever heard. "Ouch. Has that happened to you, Nonna?"

"No, I can't say that it has, but I do make it my business to keep an eye open for them at all times," Adamaria replied. "I won't have those pesky gnomes, pullin' hair, pinchin', or reachin' out for any of their mosquito-like-stings in my house." Adamaria gently pinched each of their soapy forearms as she widened the pools of her round, black eyes.

"And if you should ever see one for yourself," she added: "why, then, he will most surely be sportin' a bright red hood on his head. It's this funny little hood that you must be certain to seize. Remember. Be absolutely sure to pull it clean off his head. This and only this will make him stop his mischief."

"But won't he be mad with us?" Rosa asked, her small, rosebud lips all a quiver.

"Oh no," Adamaria reassured, reaching back out to soothe her soapy wet arm. "Don't you worry. A gnome without his hood will surely beg you for it back."

"Rosa's scared of gnomes," Izzie said, her freshly scrubbed little face slightly crumpling. "And Santa."

"Silly child," Adamaria replied, resting her hand on the child's wet head. "You asked me to tell you the story. There's truly nothin' for you to be afraid of. These little gnomes, they may be naughty, but they're playful and they've never once been known to do anyone any serious harm."

"Pwomise?" asked Rosa.

"Cross my heart," their grandmother replied. "And as for Santa, he's a saint. Now, out of the water with the pair of you. Let's dry you off. And next time you're lookin' for something that you think you've lost, ask yourself: Was it me, or was it one of those pesky little gnomes?" She winked at each girl in turn. "And if you should be lucky enough to grab a hold of a red hood, well, legend has it, if you give it right back, the grateful little fella will lead you directly to his buried treasure."

Adamaria wrapped a warm towel tightly around each child in turn as they chattered excitedly about what the treasure might be. She robustly towel-dried each head of hair, one after the other. "Gold and silver and unicorns," Rosa suggested. "Diamonds and rubies," guessed Izzie. "And bags of candy canes."

"Now, let's get into those nice new pj's your momma picked out and head downstairs for a bite of supper," instructed Adamaria, softening her voice. "There'll be treasure enough for tonight. The sooner it's bedtime, the sooner Santa and his reindeer will be makin' their rounds."

# Chapter Eleven

# The Pillowcase Switch

Gracie half listened as her mother chitter-chattered with the girls in the bathroom. She was standing barefoot on a rag-rug in front of an ornate, heavily-carved mirror that was fixed to the wall above a heavy-set vintage dresser in her room. The sturdy old furniture had been in the house since her grandmother's day. It too was built of precious redwood and, like the fireplace mantle, had, at some stage, been stained a darker shade of mahogany brown.

She'd taken the time that morning to launder and press a pair of black velvet skinny jeans which she now wriggled into over her one good set of lace underwear. She couldn't remember when she'd given this much thought to her appearance, layer by layer, though she couldn't help but feel a little foolish in the act of dressing up.

It's not like anyone needs to know whatever the heck it is you've got going on underneath, she assured herself as she smoothed the crease in her jeans. Still, it made her feel pleasingly grown up for the first time in ages.

The Victorian dresser commanded space directly across from a cast iron bedframe that cradled the same, old, slightly lumpy mattress that she'd slept on (aside from the miserable Raymond years) since she was a kid. She caught the reflection of her neatly-made single bed in the mirror as she carefully removed one and then the other of a pair of delicate, butterfly backs from the thin silver posts of her sapphire-stud earrings. These Gracie tucked into a compact velvet box that she slipped into the top drawer of the dresser.

She tuned back in to her mother's storytelling and her daughters' unfettered laughter in the bathroom. It was comforting to hear these old, familiar tales that she'd grown up with told over and again despite her frustrations with Adamaria's fanatic insistence in keeping the old ways alive. She reminded herself how important it was to remain open to the better parts of tradition, of her parental heritage. While so much of it appeared more and more irrelevant in the digital age that they were living in, today, there was a richness in it, yet, a connectedness that came with her mother's tales, a cultural thread she knew she should in turn, attempt to preserve. Besides, her children's laughter heightened the lingering relief she felt in having escaped their being continually shushed by their father.

Nothing her mother did or said to irritate her on a daily basis had ever come anywhere close to the state of unrest they'd been forced to endure with Raymond. It had been all-out silence or shouting for years — one or the other with him. Besides, she figured, Adamaria was showing signs of improvement of late when it came to hearing her daughter out on the occasions in which they had voiced differences of opinion. And Gracie was thankful for this. She knew in her heart that they'd find a way to make it work, to be there for one another.

And yet, stuff and nonsense filling the children's ears, she chuckled, raising her eyes to wave a wand of thick, black, lengthening mascara over her already ample eyelashes. She leaned in to wipe a stray lash from her lid, catching sight of a rare glint in her navy-black eyes. "That's enough of that," Gracie reprimanded her reflection, smiling as she slipped the mascara wand back in its case.

The sapphire earrings had been a gift from Raymond back when they were newlyweds. Gracie had found out later that her mother had loaned him the money on his request that first Christmas shortly before Izzie was born. She'd also discovered through further extrapolation that Raymond had failed to pay Adamaria back so much as a penny on the loan. The stones brought out the blue tint of her dark eyes and for that reason Gracie had continued to wear them. Besides, if her own mother had essentially paid for them, then why be rid of them?

Still, Gracie's cheeks flushed with the indignity of the last material reminders of her soon-to-be-ex. She needed more than ever to be free and clear of him. There would be nothing of Raymond about her person to tarnish the evening. Gracie pulled open a second drawer and rifled through a pile of neatly pressed and folded shirts and tops. Though she had her mother to thank for routinely taking care of the family laundry, it guilted her to think of having piled so much extra work on Adamaria, a stickler for commandeering and ironing just about everything that came out of the washing machine. Gracie had given up fighting over it. She'd been too busy cooking that morning to have noticed Gracie's own efforts in the laundry room.

She slipped her arms into a soft, form-fitting, dark pink and black checkered flannel shirt and set about strategically buttoning it to reveal only the slightest glimpse of the black lacey trim of her bra which she then promptly reconsidered by fastening an additional button.

Gracie was deep in thought of her reunion with Julian as she brushed the knots from her rain-damp hair. She didn't have time to wash it, so instead, left it to fall in loose and heavy, humidity-induced waves onto her shoulders. A quick rummage around in her jewelry box unearthed a pair of hammered silver hoops. The slightest dab of clear lip-gloss was all she'd allow herself to add to her scant, barely-there makeup routine. Don't go looking like you're too stoked to be out, she cautioned herself.

The poinsettia was now safely tucked under her bed. Submerging herself on the edge of her mattress, she pulled on her socks and a pair of black, leather ankle boots with heels before she leaned over to retrieve two small boxes from the back of her bedside drawer. The boxes she set on her velvet and satin quilted bedspread, their lids flipped open so as to run her finger once more over their matching contents: a pair of short silver chains bearing child-sized silver heart-shaped lockets — the girls' first pieces of jewelry, aside from the Italian-gold crucifix necklaces that Adamaria had gifted them on their baptisms and which Gracie kept tucked away for safe keeping until they were older. This Christmas she had also squirreled away a small stack of new, early reader chapter books, chosen from the girls' wish-lists from the school's holiday book fair. There'd be packs of colored pencils, new sharpeners and metal pencil tins with bright, sparkly unicorn designs to open up in the morning, alongside thick pads of multi-colored paper that she tucked into a pair of identical pillowcases that matched an empty pair the children were ready to hang from the foot of their bed frames.

The pillowcase-switch had been a useful parental time-saving trick Adamaria had taught her. No scuffling around in the dark doing Santa's work in the dead of night when she would be better off tucked up in bed and fast asleep herself.

She hid the stuffed pillowcases under her bed, either side of the poinsettia and well out of the reach of mischief should the girls be up and about investigating before she returned.

Oh girl, what *are* you thinking? Gracie asked herself as she took one long, modest last look at herself in the mirror. Best get real. And don't get ahead of yourself. She questioned why in the world she was even half-way considering stepping into another relationship.

"Gracie," her mother's voice interrupted her thoughts. Its deep, gravelly-tone traveled from the foot of the stairs. She pictured two sets of feet in fuzzy bunny-slippers padding in the hallway behind their grandmother. "Ready for supper, Birdie?"

"Be down in a sec, Ma," she called, as she headed over to the now vacant bathroom, brushed her teeth and dabbed the tiniest drop of rose-scented perfumed oil she kept in the medicine cabinet on the insides of her wrists and onto the bare skin at the back of her ears. Gracie had mostly given up on wearing any kind of fragrance after the girls were born, but this, a gift from kind parents of one of her students, she could do. The expensive oil smelled to her like a rose garden in bloom — feminine and nostalgic and not at all as if she had slathered herself in anything too seductive or obnoxious. Subtle. That was her vibe. It felt good to be going out. Thrilling almost.

# CHAPTER TWELVE

# O COME ALL THEE FAITHFUL

Raymond refused to accept having been thwarted again. He'd been so sure they'd show up as he'd slumped in the far side pew, his beanie pulled down low on his forehead so as not to give himself away. The congregation launched into the opening verse of *O Come All Thee Faithful* followed by what he considered an interminable and dreary rendition of *Once in Royal David's City* as a gaggle of snotty-nosed, pint-sized nativity players tripped down the aisle, coughing and sneezing merrily into the pews.

He scanned the crowd. No sight of his wife and kids — or her mother. A young family with three little rug rats as he considered them had squeezed in beside him, the smallest children balanced on their parents' knees, the oldest of the three, around Rosa's age he figured, sat between her mother and father. He glanced around to check if anyone was looking at him. The mother, who was no older than he and formally dressed for the occasion, hair and makeup just so, gave him a quizzical glance. He felt her judgement and returned his gaze to the church bulletin, the edge of which he used to clean his fingernails.

When it came time to greet those seated around one another, the children and their parents in the pew in front turned and appeared to look right through him. He sat stock still and refused to turn around himself for fear of prematurely coming face to face with Gracie.

Raymond felt an emptiness and hollowness in his core. His self-pity served to illuminate the soft light of the stained-glass windows, the glow of the advent candles. He allowed himself to sink into a strange, dreamlike state as he reluctantly submitted to the comfort of the music and the interminable singing of carols.

In the end, Gracie, her mother and the kids were a total no-show as far as he could see, despite his having hedged his bets on their annual routine. Casting aside any small degree of benevolent spirit he had somehow managed to absorb, he skulked out before the offering after forty-five minutes-or-so of his suffering.

Raymond failed to notice a scrawny looking teenager sulking around in the foyer, a boy, who was tired, hungry and cold, searching for a convenient space to hide out after the service. The boy had a small dog tucked under his sweatshirt, the wiry tail of which periodically uncurled around his hip.

"By yourself?" an underdressed teenage girl who had followed Raymond out of the church asked when she had found herself face-to-face with the boy. She had a high ponytail scraped back from a broad forehead that revealed a heavily made-up face. She had deftly escaped the confines of her extended family for a breath of damp air.

The boy turned, shyly, looking anywhere but directly at her. "Na. My dog, here, he's with me."

"Oh. Cool," she replied. "Well . . . gotta bounce . . . have a good one."

"Yeah, you too," he said as he headed out of the church doors a minute or so behind Raymond. He would, he hoped, find some dry place on the church grounds to hunker down for the night after filling his stomach as best he was able with water from the drinking faucet. Too bad there wasn't any food to be had.

# CHAPTER THIRTEEN

# ONE MORE SLEEP

"You smell like summer, Mommy," Rosa was the first to notice the effort she'd put in as Gracie reached down to fasten the tie on a small, cotton apron she'd wrapped around her daughter's middle.

"It's your namesake, babe — rose."

Izzie squirmed when it was her turn for an awkwardly-starched apron tied around her soft new pjs. "Why do I have to wear this dumb thing?" she asked as she pulled at a red frill trim that Adamaria had sewn onto the store-bought craft aprons. "I'm too old for it."

"You know why, Iz," Gracie replied, fastening a second tie. "You two are a pair of messy little pups and these'll stop any spills from spoiling your cute new Christmas jammies. I want to see you looking all nice for a holiday selfie with me by the tree in the morning." She'd picked the pajamas out at a consignment store for next to nothing, justifying the splurge, nonetheless, since she generally frowned on one or two wear items. She'd been unable to resist, as they'd been barely worn by the unknown children of someone with far more cash to splash given the rate that children grow.

"It's not me who spills — it's her..." Izzie stomped her feet in protest, pointing at her little sister. Rosa blew a raspberry at Izzie, who, in turn, waved a spoon before her sister's face.

"Hush," Adamaria proclaimed, putting an end to the squabble. "Takin' pride in our appearance shows our good manners and character."

Gracie settled the girls at the kitchen table. She had diligently followed her mother's request to ready it for a simple, festive supper after she was done with the dishes from lunch.

She'd chosen a dark green from the stack of vintage holiday linens her mother had lovingly collected and embroidered over the years. In addition to this, Adamaria had placed herself in charge of decorating the formal dining room table as was her custom for the once-a-year big event of the family's Christmas Day dinner and Gracie had known to leave the dark red holiday linen set for the 25th.

Gracie thought it all a little precious, if not overkill for days on end but she kept the peace knowing how much these things meant to her mother. The tables would be decorated afresh all the way through to January first. Even the tree was non-negotiable. It was kept up each year until Epiphany on January sixth.

"All you need now is a bite or two and a glass of milk to help you sleep," Gracie assured her daughters as she served them each a crab-salad sandwich consisting of an oven warm roll filled with the pink, moist meat that they'd collected from the market that afternoon.

It was Gracie who had deemed the modest crab rolls their latest Christmas Eve mainstay. Besides, she'd assured her mother, the confusion of dressing a whole cracked crab would be far too time consuming given that she was planning on going out after supper.

"All that melted butter — I can't very well head out stinking like I've been out on a fishing trawler all day," she'd implored, humorously, the flush of her cheeks a give-away as they'd assembled their shopping list earlier.

Besides, there was already plenty to keep Adamaria occupied in her keeping of at least several key elements of an old-school Italian Christmas.

Though Adamaria tired easily, it appeared to Gracie as if her mother's hands and her body propelled themselves on autopilot during the holidays. Preparing for the annual festivities that December hadn't failed to transport her mom back to the happy days with Aldo.

Gracie had failed in her attempt to talk Adamaria out of making a brandy and espresso-drenched Tiramisu that morning, in his memory, for their Christmas meal on the 25th.

"It's way too much for one day, Ma. You outdo yourself," Gracie reminded her mother as they settled down at the kitchen table. "Plus, Tiramisu is hardly a dessert for kids. Biscotti and your Wandi wings would've done in my opinion."

"Try tellin' that to the children of Italy," Adamaria replied, hands on hips, brushing aside her daughter's all-too predictable concerns on the subject of too many sweets. "There's no harm in a small slice. Crab is one thing to cut corners on, but your father, God rest his soul, would insist that it simply wouldn't do to go without a Tiramisu."

Adamaria took a sip of her favorite crisp, cold local Chardonnay from a small glass tumbler she'd poured for herself with supper. Her eyes pooled and glazed over as she glanced at the half empty table, conjuring the dear faces she so missed, the laughter and banter and the heaping platters of foods.

Gracie held her hand over her wine glass as the girls steadily munched on their crab rolls, all-the-while intent on kicking one another under the table. None of them had noticed that they had sat closely together. They'd left an empty space where Gracie's father had sat.

"Back when I was your age, we never went without a dish of wild boar ragu with our holiday supper," Adamaria launched into one of her favorite reminiscences — the hunting the men had prided themselves on, her grandfather, father and both of her late husbands included.

"What's a boar?" asked Rosa.

"A pig, duh!" Izzie poked her sister's arm. She puffed out her cheeks and snorted. The children goaded one another, having lost interest in their grandmother rattling on about her childhood.

"That's a topic for another time, Ma," Gracie intervened, as she stood and pushed her chair back in order to clear their empty plates, putting an end to the evening's lesson of their Italian American culinary heritage.

"Drink your milk girls, it's almost bed time."

The wine had loosened Adamaria's tongue.

"He knew just where to find a pack of rampagin' boar— not to mention the mushrooms he doubled down and hunted durin' the rainy season," Adamaria continued to reminisce, colorfully, oblivious to Gracie's readiness to move on with the evening. She'd had no qualms in the incorporation of her late husband's gifts from the wild in her winter soups and sauces and richly flavored stews.

"I wouldn't take the risk with wild mushrooms now," she said as she held on to Gracie's arm as her daughter left the table with a pile of dishes. "Though what I'd give for a basket filled with meaty ol' Big Caps, a fresh haul of the nutty-flavored Porcinis your father brought home. He knew what he was doing out there."

Gracie pictured her young self, standing with her mother at the kitchen sink, meticulously cleaning, drying and slicing a haul of prized Porcinis.

"Sure, Ma," she replied, a spontaneous smile forming at the richness of the memory, though she was growing more anxious to move on with her schedule for the evening. "I guess I had no idea how special it was at the time."

How much wine had her mother consumed, she wondered? Adamaria's face exhibited a wistful, sentimental expression — the raising of eyebrows in a certain way, her eyes glossing over as she gazed longingly into a far-away space.

"The Porcinis came in at least a couple times each winter," Adamaria went on, sharpening her focus as she refilled her glass to the brim and subsequently wiped a tear from her eye with the corner of her napkin.

Gracie was concerned that her mother's maudlin tendency to romanticize and reminisce was about to escalate and at length with any more wine.

She stuck the cork back in the bottle and switched topics. "Let's help Nonna light the candles, shall we, girls?"

Squeals of delight chased away the last of the lingering images of a giant wild boar running amok along the forest floor. The children leapt from their chairs, free at last, and darted into the parlor.

Gracie followed. She stoked the dwindling fire and placed a large log into the center of the embers. Adamaria ambled in behind them and proceeded to light a long match from a decorative box on the mantel as Gracie lifted Rosa with both hands around her narrow waist. The older woman placed her hand gently around her granddaughter's chubby little fist and guided it toward the first of the brand-new set of sturdy red candles lined up in a row of four and nestled in glass holders on the mantel. Izzie was tall enough and old enough to be trusted to strike a match without assistance and, in taking her job very seriously, she carefully lit the second two candles under close supervision of her mother and grandmother.

"There, now doesn't that look festive?" asked Adamaria. "You know what's next?"

"Mary and Joseph," Izzie replied, pushing ahead of her sister to reach down beneath a side table where she retrieved two small, hand-painted ceramic figurines to add to the nativity scene — a stable with three kings, shepherds and animals in place around an as yet empty wooden manger.

"One each," Adamaria instructed, as she purposefully removed the slightly chipped figure of Joseph from Izzie's hand and placed it into Rosa's.

"When you wake in the mornin', the newborn baby Jesus will have joined them," Adamaria informed. "Well, I never," she added, patting the side of her head as she looked around the room. "We darn near almost forgot about Santa's midnight snack."

"What's he like best?" Rosa asked, earnestly.

"Carrots, of course," replied Izzie, who was old enough to remember. "For the reindeer. And for Santa, a glass of milk with one of Nonna's Wandis will do."

After they'd assembled the snack in the kitchen, carried it carefully back into the parlor, Izzie propped a hastily scrawled and carefully folded note that she'd scribbled on behalf of the two of them by the side of the plate. It was time for teeth cleaning, face-washing and bed.

Gracie supervised the last of the evening's bathroom activities in order to avoid a rehash of any further hunting tales or night-time gnome antics at such an advanced hour.

"Go potty before your bedtime story and then it's lights out for little people," she announced cheerily as she pulled back one after another of a pair of dark green, quilted-velvet coverlets draped over a set of narrow, twin beds. "Time for two little live wires to settle down."

She had wallpapered this, the smallest of the bedrooms, the one at the front of the house closest to the stairway, herself, with Aldo's assistance. It had served as a box room until the first of her girls was born and their grandfather had taken it upon himself to clear it out of its decades of stored junk for his grandchild to have a room of her own whenever she came to stay. Little did any of them know it would serve as a permanent base before Izzie and her little sister were able to tie their own shoe laces.

Gracie had picked out a woodlands theme wallpaper, washable and pre-glued for easy application. The ceiling was high and she had employed the use of a ladder from the back shed which her father had held on tightly to, she recalled, upon Adamaria's insistence, to keep her from tipping over should she have wobbled. The paper's blue-black background was decorated with densely colored foliage and flowers which gave off the impression of an autumnal forest at night.

"Your choice," her mother had remarked at the time. "A little dark for my taste."

Owls, squirrels, bunnies and birds populated its wooded expanse. Gracie was delighted with the end result. She would have never known the room after its budget transformation had she not been the one to have tackled the decorating. It had held up well. The girls loved it. A room of their own that was snug and magical.

Raymond had, without complaint for once, assembled a vintage pair of narrow twin beds with wooden frames which Adamaria had picked up for a song from a yard sale in the neighborhood soon after her second granddaughter was born. The only thing Gracie had added after she and the girls moved back into the house was a set of salvaged, live-edged wooden shelving on the side wall above each bed and a shared, yard-sale bookcase which she had stenciled with a leafy tree motif. The girls had all of their soft toys and dolls lined up along the shelving, surprisingly neatly, in rows according to size. It was almost as if they were at a picnic in the forest, seated side-by-side on a bench looking out into the room.

"Why are you wearin' makeup, Mommy?" Izzie asked, ever direct and to the point. Rain pounded against the windows.

Gracie hadn't planned on informing the girls she was going out that evening in most part for fear of having to over explain herself. On second thoughts, she figured it was best to avoid an untruth. Children always knew when something was out of the ordinary. The last thing she wanted was to create any stress or confusion from the outset when it came to her rekindling whatever it was that was happening between herself and Julian.

"Nonna will be right here, downstairs, listening out for you. Mommy is gonna visit with an old friend for a very short time."

"But you never go out at night," Rosa was upset and was pulling on her arm. "And it's waining hard."

"I know," Gracie replied, employing her calmest, most reassuring tone of voice as she held her youngest tightly and lay down beside her. "But it's Christmas for mommies too and that means a treat of spending time with another grown-up."

"Nonna's a gwown-up," Rosa pointed out, wriggling free of her mother's arms. Gracie could feel her daughter place her hands on her tiny hips, as she lay there, indignantly. "And she's not goin' out."

"Duh," Izzie replied. "She means she wants to hang out by herself with her buddy."

"Like a play date?" Rosa asked. "With your friend?"

Gracie was now intent on wrapping up the debate. "Not exactly," she said, patting Rosa's head as she opened a dog-eared copy of *A Night Before Christmas*. "As a matter-of-fact, I do have one or two buddies you've not yet had a chance to meet. There's an old friend who I haven't seen in a very long time. But enough about that tonight."

After she finished reading, Izzie took the book from her mother's hands and tucked it under her pillow. Gracie flicked on the moon and stars nightlight that was plugged into the wall before she reached down to dim the bedside lamp with its toadstool shade that sat on a small table between the two beds. The nightlight would give off sufficient enough a glow as to guide the girls to the door of their night forest room should either of them need the bathroom during the night. They quietened down, sleepy-eyed as they were and, surprisingly in their mother's opinion, neither of them asked for another story, let alone pressed for more details on her outing.

Gracie tidied a small pile of dog-eared Christmas books that were scattered on the nightstand. Her mother had stored a box of books back from when she was a kid. It had proved a treasure trove of precious story-time-escape after Raymond held most of the girls' books and toys hostage as well as their change of season clothes after she'd left him, along with most of her own personal stuff.

She had simply left it all behind in the end and not looked back. Gracie moved toward the two, long, narrow windows at the end of the room. The thrum of the rain dulled as she drew a heavy, moss-colored velvet drape across a pair of sheer under curtains adorned with a flock of colorfully-embroidered butterflies. The girls had picked these out when it had been time to replace a sun-shredded previous set. The rain-distorted glow of a street light illuminated the slip of a space on either side. She glanced around the small, darkened room and was reminded once more of her gratitude to the coworkers whom she had confided in, those who had rallied after she'd split with piles of hand-me-down clothes and shoes, boxes of toys and a generous gift card that had just about covered all of their basic clothing needs.

The last thing Gracie had intended was to become a financial burden on anyone, least of all her mother who was barely making ends meet on her own. Gracie's legal fees alone made for living life on a monetary precipice. She'd felt like she was dangling over an abyss by one arm much of the time. And yet it had been worth it. There was never a day that passed when she had looked back and regretted her decision.

God, I wouldn't wish this mess with Raymond on anyone, she consoled herself, silently, as she tiptoed out of the room, taking stock on how far she had come and yet, still no final resolution in sight.

"Good night, Mommy," Izzie whispered so as not to wake her sister, who though pretending to be fast asleep, was, in fact, listening nervously for the sound of reindeer hooves on the roof. "Love ya to the moon and back."

Gracie peeped around the door.

"Love you to the moon and back and all around the universe as well. Shush now, babe. Don't you worry about a thing. It'll be Christmas morning when you open your eyes."

"T'is the night before Christmas," Izzie declared, theatrically. She had tucked the book under her pillow as she was accustomed to doing in her belief that she may absorb the story in her dreams. She stifled a yawn and turned to one side where she scrunched her eyes closed and willed herself to sleep.

# CHAPTER FOURTEEN

# TABLE FOR ONE

Raymond's interior and exterior jugular veins pulsed, a thumping sensation in the thin hollow at the back of his eyes. As he swung his truck a sharp right the contents of the gift bags shot out and spilled across its littered floor. His anger propelled him to accelerate speed. He winced, his face contorting with indignity and shame — the fresh humiliation he'd endured in church.

His heart pumped with frustration and a fuse-blowing anger. Why was he still on the outside looking in?

Gracie walked toward the window, drawn to him, in his mind, as if by Raymond's own will. Yet, as far as he could see, she did not appear to be aware of his presence, having failed to spot his truck as he slid it into a freshly vacated space left free by departing church-goers directly across from the house. From this new position, Raymond was briefly able to watch her every move. He killed the engine just as Gracie drew the drapes — not so much against the onset of nightfall, he assumed, rather more an impenetrable shield between them, blocking him out.

His hollow stomach turned inside itself. Though she appeared to him as unreachably alluring as ever, he refused to be hoodwinked into believing that her coy, innocent looks were not more devious and deceiving.

Raymond stewed in righteous self-assurance. He would break her resolve — before it was too late forever, for all of them.

How he hated her. How we wanted her. He thumped his forehead. Was it hate? Or was it love? All he knew as he stared out into the dark was that it was the love that he had for her that he would turn around to somehow find a way to break through the venom, the loathing and the hostility he so battled within himself. He was willing to bet his life on it

— her life on it. Such was the strength of the hatred and passion that coursed through his veins, arousing inside of him a stronger, half-strangled, almost murderous emotion he'd yet to experience to such a cripplingly painful degree. He had his flaws, he could accept that, but didn't everyone? His conscience assured him that almost anyone would be pushed to such extremes given such an outrageous and unjust punishment.

Raymond forced himself to take a moment to think rationally. He inhaled a series of turbulent, greedy breaths in an effort to regain control of himself as he gripped a tight and sweaty-palm hold on the wheel. After a couple of minutes, he resolved to move forward with Plan B —though he'd need to wait it out an hour or two after the lights went off upstairs. Only then would he act. That way, Raymond plotted, his kids would not be forced to be witness to his taking back of what was rightfully his — their mother. It would be Gracie first. He would start by removing his wife from her mother's overbearing clutch if it was the last thing that he did.

Raymond leaned back into the cracked leather driver's seat that was held together with strips of painter's tape. Gracie was about to find out what a danger it had been to ever dare think she could leave him for good. He'd see it through if it was the last thing he did.

They would start again from the beginning, he vowed, as he scrunched shut his bloodshot eyes and pictured her face. Someplace inside, he still believed in her, despite the nightmare of the past couple of years that she'd put him through. All he had to do was to convince her she'd been wrong.

It's her goddamn mother who's gonna pay for all she's done in aidin' and abettin' this whole fuckin' deal, he promised as he lit a fresh, fat joint. He took a deep hit of weed, before he set it clumsily into a spilling-over ash tray. This he followed with a generous swig of Jack Daniels from a half full bottle that he'd stashed in the glove compartment.

"Fuck 'em all," a red-faced Raymond roared, as he hammered the dust-covered dash board with his bony, blue-white knuckles. "Fuckin' ruined my life."

What had he ever done but adore her, he further bemoaned? Protect her from her sly-ass, meddling mother? "Bitch don't deserve me. I don't deserve none of this," Raymond raged outwardly in the sanctuary of his vehicle. The whole cab shook in tune with the jagged rhythm of his agitated state. Hadn't he taken her to court enough times already? Six times if he was counting right over the past two years. And what had Gracie done when he had filed for custody of his own damn kids, he asked himself?

Sat there, the calculatin' she-devil, not once lookin' me in the face. Cold as ice she was, he recalled, as he'd been reduced to near hysterics one time, humiliated. Bawlin' my eyes out in front of 'em all.

In his mind, the judge who'd slapped the restraining order on him had no idea what this woman and her goddamn mother had put him through, put his kids through. He hadn't forgotten how Gracie had out and out refused to read the dozens of desperate notes he'd left her on her windscreen while she was at work. She'd blocked his messages on her email, changed her phone number, gone so far as to return every single letter, card and gift he believed he had every right to send to his daughters, unopened. Why hadn't the judge seen that they were the ones who were suffering, him and the kids?

If she had been even a tad more reasonable, agreed to meet and talk, to hear him out, Raymond was convinced he would have won her back by now. Sorry-not-sorry but shit should never have come to this, he fumed.

It had taken every ounce of self-control within him to restrain himself from confronting her in the street when he'd spotted her outside of the bakery with his girls. The regret of how he'd held himself back choked him up. He might have just as easily shoved her clear out of the way — grabbed his kids and made a run for it. Would have served her right, Raymond was sure of it. If he was to be continually deprived of his daughters and on Christmas especially, then why should she not be given a dose of her own bitter medicine? He wished he'd taught her the same painful lesson she had put him through had he thought for a minute he could've gotten away with it.

Raymond rolled down his driver-side window a slither. The windows of the truck cab had fogged up, blocking his view of the house. He shook the liquor bottle and, after taking one last, languid pull of his joint, he ground it into the ashtray and downed another swig of the little that was left of the smooth, smoky, syrup that burned the back of his throat.

The rain fell heavily now. He half opened both driver and passenger seat windows anyway.

Gracie reappeared, as if by his summons, a porch-lit apparition. Only this time she was outside of the house and zippered back into her rain jacket, hood down and her hair loose. He watched, transfixed as she lingered under the carriage light by the open front door. Raymond perked up as he wiped the inside of the windscreen with the back of his sleeve. He checked the time on his phone. He must have dozed off, he figured.

He watched, eagle-eyed and suspicious as she stepped out onto the lamp-lit porch and shook open an umbrella.

Well, well, what do we have here Sherlock? Raymond asked himself, rubbing sleep from his eyes as he watched Gracie make her way down onto the slick sidewalk, umbrella in hand. She slid the hood of her rain jacket up over her head with her free hand and then paused, unaware, as she tucked her long, loose hair into the back of her hood.

"Interestin'."

A moment later, without further ado, she strode off before his eyes at a quickened pace, heading back in the direction of downtown.

What are you up to, Little Miss Innocent? Raymond questioned, ugly sensations coursing through him as he turned the ignition key and started up the truck. His shrewd eyes narrowed, accusingly, better ready to pounce. Something inside him stopped him from leaping out of the truck and accosting her right there in the street. He knew he had to lag far enough behind so as not to alert her to his trailing her a second time that day. Follow her lead, he instructed himself. Let the unsuspectin' bitch give herself away.

The stores had shut by that hour, it being Christmas Eve. She had no friends that he knew of who lived close enough for a visit on that night of all nights. He had seen to that. Unless she'd branched out on a new social life that she'd managed to keep hidden from him, Gracie heading out alone meant one thing to him and one thing only in his accusing mind. Perspiration trickled down his back.

"I shoulda known it," Raymond spat and cursed into the dark void beyond his windscreen, "I shoulda goddamn guessed." Fury rose — a coating of thick bile in the back of his throat. It was as if an invisible fist had tightened on his windpipe. He coughed up a chunk of phlegm and spat it out of the window. "Cheatin' whore."

Raymond slammed his foot on the gas and careened around the corner, almost tipping the truck on two wheels into a side street that he knew would conjoin with the route that Gracie was on.

Dipped headlights reflected on wet asphalt as she turned the corner onto a sodden river that was East Washington Street. And yet, given the cover of the dark and the distorted view in the downpour, Gracie remained oblivious as to Raymond's truck creeping behind her along the block.

His vehicle crawled to a stop. Raymond pulled his beanie low over his forehead and slid from his seat, all the while pinning his eyes on his wife as he positioned himself under a tree on a damp square of grass that was cut into the sidewalk across the street. She was headed in the direction of Volpi's — the family-style Italian restaurant with its Speakeasy bar where they'd celebrated their birthdays together a few times.

He considered himself territorial about places they'd been to as a couple. This was one of their places. He remembered how Gracie's mother had described how she herself had waited alone many a time as a kid in her daddy's old truck, by the former grocery store-turned-restaurant, all the times her pa had stopped in for Italian staples — bread and cheese, salami and the like.

"It used to take the ol' boy twice as long to run an errand considerin' the shot or two that he'd take in the back bar with his ranching' buddies," Adamaria had recalled.

His remembrances turned back to the present as Gracie headed inside, only after she'd taken a minute to shake and fold up her umbrella. Like a hawk, he watched her every move as she gently lowered the hood from her head and shook out the thick, black waves of hair that in Raymond's furious mind, he and only he had the right to run his hands through.

What he wanted more than anything was to grab himself a tight fistful of that hair. He would yank the head of that woman who was still married to him, on paper at least, clear out of the doorway and back to the home they had made together before it had all gone bad.

Somehow, as irate as he was, Raymond managed to refocus on his breathing as he waited to make his move. He would give her time to make her way through the main dining room and, most likely, he wagered, into the small, windowless space at the rear of the building.

Nothing much had been done to the place in decades. And that's how folk preferred it. Vintage cans of tomatoes and olive oil were stacked in neat, nostalgic arrangements. The stab of a forgotten memory of a family meal at Volpi's back when his mother was still in the picture resurfaced, eclipsing the image of the last time he and Gracie had eaten there. He pushed this painful memory out of mind almost as fast as it had appeared. Raymond felt bad enough already and he was not prepared to deal with the added sorrows of his childhood. His mother's leaving had been a crushing blow made all the worse by Gracie's later betrayal.

A double treachery, he swore as he dodged a steady stream of traffic passing over the rain-soaked crosswalk. Outside the restaurant he peered through the holly and ivy of the painted holiday windows. Red-checkered tables were filled with animated groups of four, six, some up to eight or ten rosy-cheeked diners, their upper bodies illuminated by the candlelight of wax-dripped Chianti bottles — jolly-faced revelers tucking into their Italian family-style Christmas Eve supper under the twinkling strings of Christmas lights draped along the edges of the former grocery-store shelves.

Raymond shoved the door open with a clownish, sopping wet sneaker. He looked around the room furtively, the zippered collar of his jacket hoisted up over his mouth, as he attempted to diminish the visible space between the front cuff of his beanie and the rest of his face.

The restaurant was as low-key a time capsule of the Prohibition era if ever there was one. The Speakeasy bar at the back remained for the most part a hidden gem, ever-popular with the local crowd grateful for its authentic, Italian-American vibe and a distinct absence of day trippers and tasting room tourists feeding directly up from San Francisco into wine country. It had been six years since Gracie and he had sat together at the bar top counter by the tell-tale metal trap-door, the infamous escape route into the alleyway that had been long since been sealed closed amongst an array of fading newspaper clippings, jumbled hunting trophies and forever-frozen taxidermy. Adamaria had watched Izzie, as a baby so that the couple could have an evening out together without a car seat in tow.

Raymond felt the hackles raise on the back of his neck, a thin slither of skin beneath his shoulder-length hair where he'd gone so far as ink the letter G, set for all-time within a crown of thorns and roses. He'd come home with the tattoo as a stamp of ownership, a token of his love for her, on their first anniversary. What Gracie had not known, as far as he believed, was that this had been his way of atoning for having cheated on her the first time after they'd married. The sear of the needle he'd considered his penance. Debt paid. Done.

"Table for one? Or are you waitin' on others, hon?" asked a cheerful, curly-red-headed waitress with a warm, wide smile. Raymond sized her up with a rapid employment of his general standard of assessment when it came to women. He'd become especially drawn to those a few years older, the kindly, motherly types who promised to take him under their wing. All the more so since Gracie had walked out.

"Only me," Raymond responded. He made steady eye contact before glancing over her shoulder at an empty table set for two, positioned discreetly along a shadowy sidewall. "That'll work."

"Sure thing sweetie," she replied, with a noticeable swing of her generous hip as she swiveled on her sneaker-heel, menu-in-hand. "Wanna hand over that jacket? I'll hang it up to dry."

"No thanks. It'll be just fine on the back of my chair."

"It's pretty soaked."

"I said it's fine."

She was nice enough, he figured, easing up. Her eyes had twinkled at him mischievously and she'd checked out his ring hand as he'd reached for the menu. He'd stopped wearing his wedding band soon after Gracie left. Stuck it in the back of a drawer. He'd never seen the point in denying himself the benefits of having been stabbed in the back. And, now, if it turned out that Gracie was intent on attempting to play the same game, then Raymond believed he had every right to be on the look-out for comfort elsewhere. He'd found no shortage of one-night stands when he'd been in the mood. For all his festering anger, he'd had no issue in feeding his ego. His one gift in life he was sure of was his ability to lay on the charm, to reel women in, one after the other, like sport fishing.

This one would do, in a pinch, should something go wrong, which he promised himself it would not. They locked eyes a second time as she continued her hovering – her eyes were close-set, darting around him, like silver lightning, outlined with thin streamers of a darker blue liquid-liner for extra effect. He couldn't help but notice her heavy eyelids were slick with a goopy-aqua-blue eyeshadow that glistened beneath the curtain of a set of thick, black, obvious eyelash extensions.

"What'll it be, darlin'?" she asked. Raymond calculated she'd spent a good deal of her holiday tips on those lashes. Total waste of hard-earned money in his opinion.

"Give me a Coors and a bowl of pasta. Whatever comes outta the kitchen fast."

"You in a hurry?"

"Just hungry is all."

"In that case, I'd recommend the ravioli. Beef or cheese?"

"Beef."

He tapped his right foot, nervously, the squelch of his sock inside his sneaker muffled by the chatter and good spirits of the holiday crowd.

Raymond impatiently drummed his fingers on the red and white checkered tablecloth as he waited for his beer to arrive. A frail, elderly woman in a Santa hat and sequined sweater set, seated in a wheelchair at a nearby table gave him the once over as she fixed her watery eyes on his beanie. He twitched as she stared at the top of his head disapprovingly. What business was it of hers if he kept his wet hat on?

"And you can get lost," he said, as he shot the woman a burning look of disdain. She had no problem receiving his message and she immediately redirected her gaze first toward her equally delicate dining companion and afterwards, back down to her half-eaten plate of chicken piccata.

"I'll bring you some garlic bread, hon. On the house." The chatty waitress was back. Raymond decided she was possibly too pandering for his liking after all. "Looks like you could do with it if you ask me," she added, reaching out to touch his arm.

He hadn't asked her. Who did she think she was, making such a remark? He bristled. It pissed him off, the assumption that he was sad or pathetic even, unwanted, uncared for, unloved. He stifled an urge to shoot back a suitably curt response, instead taking a double take and thanking her with the same broad smile he generally employed to win over all of his women.

All he needed was his own wife, goddamn it. He was in no mood for any mindless game. And yet, if he played his cards right, Raymond reminded himself this one might be useful as a back-up, a confidence booster at a later date. If this chick thought him hot enough to flirt with, why the hell was he seated there alone?

His server disappeared into the kitchen, soon to return with a coy half-smile as she leaned over him, close enough for her cleavage to brush his sleeve with the delivery of the aforementioned plate of garlic bread, dripping with butter. He inhaled her scent — some kind of wintery flower-bomb that competed in a weird way with the garlic — rich and heady and vanilla-like, sweet, stinging. It would be like laying on a bed of soft pine needles with this one, he imagined.

"How come you're on your lonesome, sweetie?" she asked, stepping back, sensing his growing unease. Raymond was afraid that Gracie might, at any minute, discover his presence, blow his cover on his stalking her. The last thing he needed was a public scene, a showdown. And besides, he was hungry. First things first. He had to eat.

"Oh, you know. Family," he replied, raising his eyebrows and tipping his head to the side, dismissively. "Plans fell through."

"I hear ya. What ya gonna do? Shit happens. I see it all the time. Ain't nothin' wrong with eatin' out solo durin' the holidays. Or take-out, a bottle of somethin' strong and a workin' tv."

"Hey and a lot less of a price tag." Raymond played along, tapping his pocket. Her nails, he noted, were perfectly almond shaped, long and luxuriously polished for someone who handled so many dishes. They were alternately lacquered in red and white and green with tiny, sparkling rhinestones, candy cane motifs painted on each of her little fingers. She had a lot going on with those hands. He closed his eyes briefly and imagined the sensation of the tips of her glittering nails scoring into the thin flesh of his back.

Warm garlic butter dribbled down his chin. He'd scarfed a left-over half of a zapped super burrito at noon and nothing since. The bread hit his empty stomach and caused the lining to swell with the threat of heartburn. Once he was back with Gracie, he assured himself he would focus on eating healthy again.

Raymond licked his lower lip. He dabbed his mouth and chin with the corner of a starched napkin. He sprinkled parmesan over the dish of small packages of ravioli that appeared before him, topped in a marinara sauce just as a crowd of a dozen or so rowdy ranch hands funneled in through the door like a herd of young cattle heading in for their night feed. They moved, as one, in a cloud of steamy breath, all ruddy cheeks, camo hats and Carhart jackets, Wranglers and work boots as they made their way through the packed dining area and into the back room where they jostled and positioned themselves for the best spot at the bar.

The increasingly crowded scene made it so that Raymond was better set to take a closer look at who it was his wife was meeting without immediate fear of blowing his cover. The sound of festive greetings, a brew of laughter and loud, animated conversation — live accordion Christmas music emanated from the bar. Raymond pushed his chair back and stepped away from his half-eaten supper so that he might skulk and linger in the shadows by the restroom in order to scan the dimly lit speakeasy.

There, in the far corner, beside a green wall of patchy old taxidermy, several outdated, curling calendars and under a ceiling filled with yellowed, dollar notes, he zoned in on the familiar outline of his wife. She was perched, cross-legged on a barstool. Close beside her, too close, sat a sharp-dressed, preppy-looking Black dude. Raymond's pupils burned and constricted. It was immediately clear by the way that the pair of them were eyeballing each other that this was not the way that strangers set about a casual pick-up.

"Traitor" — he cursed, "I should've fuckin' known." How long had she been up to this, whatever it was?

Jealousy surged — an instant, inward fury hit with a massive punch to his gut. No amount of the anger management reconditioning training he had been forced to endure over the previous two hellish years was powerful enough to slow the degree of adrenaline, the sheer knock-out pulse that reverberated throughout his body. His breathing shallowed and his face flushed a dark blood-red. Raymond's muscles tensed into tight coils and his arms shook, his mind racing murderously.

Somehow, though he knew not how, he managed to restrain himself from punching a hole in the wall. "Save it," he swore, holding his fist in his other hand. His as-yet unidentified rival would feel the weight of his fury soon enough.

"You ok, hon?" It was his server again. The woman had stepped close enough, he feared to practically take hold of his thumping heart as it threatened to beat clear out of his chest. She touched his arm again, tentatively, her decorative nails catching on his sleeve as she trailed his eyes back toward the bar. "You look like you've seen a ghost."

"I .. I'm alright. Just need to pay up, gotta get outta here. Get some fresh air."

"You want me to pack up the rest of your food in a to-go-box, hon?"

"Yes. No. I mean, I'm done. Thanks." Raymond ducked into the restroom where she had no choice but to leave him alone. The last thing he needed was her fussing around, drawing attention to him.

Afterwards, he dropped a couple of twenties on the table. "Extra tip," he said as his sympathetic server continued to look him over, though in a quizzical, concerned fashion. "For your kindness."

"Merry Christmas, hon," she replied, with a shrug, resigning herself to the strangeness of some as he grabbed his jacket and maneuvered the wet wool of his beanie back down over his forehead.

"Yeah — you too. Have a good one," he replied and, propelled by the slow burn of stewing outrage, steamed out of the door.

# CHAPTER FIFTEEN

# SPEAKEASY

Gracie tucked a strand of hair behind her ear, fearing her nerves might give her away with the slightest jitter of her hand. Julian was perched close enough on the bar stool beside her but not too close to be intimidating. He was drawn to her scent, a subtle essence of powdery rose. Its old-fashioned fragrance, freshened all the more by rain water, hovered in a gentle haze at a level above the cloying bar-smell of stale beer, whiskey and Old Spice. The room was more brightly lit than either of them would have preferred given that there was no escaping the fact it had been a decade since they'd last laid eyes on each other.

The bar was a popular joint during the prohibition years, back when all the legit booze in the land was legally banned in the 1920's and early 30's. It had never gone out of fashion even after alcohol was made legal again. It was a fitting venue for a reunion. And here, now, was the guy who had stolen her heart in high school soon after he had transferred in during junior year from Atlanta, Georgia. And she was the home town girl that got away. This was fact and they each knew it. There was no denying it, even if it was a little corny, Gracie considered, but then, so much of her life had become a cliché, so why not? Who was to say that a relationship couldn't be uncomplicated if you simply gave in to it and trusted your most basic instincts?

Julian considered himself reasonably adept in decoding body language — just as he was good at reading a room. The way a woman played with her hair for instance, he found generally insightful, especially in an intimate setting such as this.

Gracie's frequent fiddling around with her runaway locks signaled to him that whether she knew it or not, she was intent on removing distractions, ready to focus her attention on the two of them. This in turn helped ease his own nerves. His eyes were drawn to several random streaks of silver — silken threads in the curve of an otherwise dark-colored hairline above her left ear. This subtle reveal of the gradual aging process served to make Gracie more real, more vital to him than if she'd taken pains to coat the hint of grey with color. No amount of cover-up would have made her any more attractive to him in that moment.

She was a natural. She had never been one to be overly self-absorbed in her appearance he recalled and it pleased him that she still wore her thick, dark shiny hair long and loose to her shoulders, just as he remembered it. Other than the few silver threads and the gently etched lines at the sides of the same dark blue eyes that had indelibly imprinted themselves on his soul, she had barely changed.

Gracie on the other hand was more than a little self-conscious, despite having warned him that he may not have fully anticipated this older, more lived-in version of herself. Try as she might to relax, she was perched so upright as to be uncomfortable. Her heart had double somersaulted as she'd sat herself down, flush-faced and she hadn't known what to do with her legs, her feet. She half-wished she was able to melt away and escape into the thick air of booze fumes, bar noise, music and warm bodies.

"Damn," Julian said, his lively, hazel-colored eyes smiling at her as he leaned back at the waist so as not to overcrowd her. "Gracie. Almost thirty. The both of us. It suits you."

"That's kind of you to say," she replied, meeting his steady gaze head on and breaking into a fast half-smile as she play-punched him, a soft contact in the space beneath his collar bone. "But look at you," she'd teased, jokingly, pulling her fist back before abruptly dropping it to her side. She kept her hands off him, but was unable to stop herself from giving him an overtly obvious, though tentative once-over. "Clearly, you've been letting yourself go, Julian."

She consumed him with one long swoop of her eyes. He was certainly in fine shape — trim, toned and immaculately groomed. The lanky college freshman she'd last set eyes on had long since morphed into a broad-shouldered, fully-fledged man. Julian's once unruly hair that she'd teased him about trimming so often was now neatly clipper-cut close to his head. Still so comfortably familiar, his smooth face was freshly shaven and at almost thirty, elegantly chiseled.

"Tad leaner for sure. Dropped the last of any lingering puppy fat a while back," he laughed, patting his stomach with a pair of broad and neatly manicured hands, an expensive-looking watch on his left wrist.

Gracie, emboldened by his self-effacement, held her breath as she reached out for his right hand and lowered her head to closer inspect a set of neatly trimmed fingernails. White, half-moons on a healthy shade of palest pink. She had not prepared herself for the chemistry they'd shared so long ago to reveal itself so soon. Electricity sparked and bolted from his hand into hers, a rapid-fire surge through the core of her arm.

"Yup, definitely lawyer's hands," she remarked, dead-pan, a forced, serious expression masking the pleasure she felt in his sheer physical proximity, his touch. "Darn it, Julian, your nails are in better shape than mine."

"Hey, it's called professional grooming!"

The nerves and tension she'd felt on walking into the bar were steadily fading. It was hard to hear one another over the din of the crowd and the onset of loud accordion music. Her back and shoulders relaxed. For the longest time, Gracie hadn't been able to remember what it was like to be with a man her age, someone who she'd felt anything close to comfortable around, to be able to be herself with. She'd been afraid to be over familiar with Julian after so much time had passed. And yet, in reality, it was nothing less than thrilling to be sitting there beside him, to recognize herself in his eyes. It was hard to contain her relief.

"Hey, do you remember those twilight drives we used to take out to the beach in my old man's truck?" Julian asked, raising his voice over an especially rousing rendition of *Jingle Bells* courtesy of the in-house accordionist, as much a part of the institution as the speakeasy itself. "I'd hoped to head out that way for a drive over the holiday if it hadn't been for this storm coming in."

"Oh yeah, the scent of bay and eucalyptus trees on the backroads. I remember Wilson Hill," she said. She smiled as she looked away, shy, embarrassed to reveal how she had held tight to the memory. "That view. It's still there."

"Some things don't change," he replied. It was his turn to blush, a rush of blood warming his face to the color of rich chestnut. Her eyes were drawn to a faint, pink scar beneath his left eye, an old injury from his high school sporting days. "Hanging out 'til the sun went down. Good times, Gracie."

It was, for the both of them, for one spine-tingling moment, as if their Christmas parting a decade earlier had never happened. The summer prior, before he'd headed off to southern California for college, was, as each of them was now acutely aware, fully-preserved in their shared pool of life's most delicate and precious, floating memories, an innocent, youthful picture unshattered by time.

Julian eased a thin, tan, cashmere sweater up and over his head. "It sure is warming up in here."

A bare stretch of shiny abs revealed itself above his beltline, the sight of which caused Gracie to take a short, sharp intake of breath. She forced herself to avert her eyes from the thin line of dark hair that ran from his belly button down to the top of a quarter inch reveal of his crisp, white boxer shorts. Julian effortlessly lowered his well-toned arms and tucked in his undershirt, a slimline, crisp white crew neck that matched his underwear. His choice of clothing emphasized his impressive physique and taut skin. It was a lot to take in. Gracie swiveled and settled her glance at a shelf of amber liquid across the bar. She ran her forefinger around the rim of her half-full glass of prosecco in as nonchalant a fashion as she could muster.

"It barely rained at all that winter if you recall?" Julian asked. "Unlike this one." She nodded. She remembered it all.

"Is it hard for you to readjust to the cold and the damp up in here in Nor Cal?" Gracie asked.

"A little," Julian replied. "But I could get used to it again."

She was clumsily unsure of the bar scene and equally uneasy with small talk and she felt the intoxicating effect of the bubbly. Her posture had softened. Still, Gracie scanned the room as she was wont to do in any public place. Rancher family siblings and a tight-knit group of friends they'd known from school, plus their family mechanic who was married to her hairstylist mingled with a host of local folk who had, she assumed, various guests in tow for the holidays. A cashier from the market raised her hand and mouthed hi. Gracie tried her best to avoid the kind of eye contact that would lead to any uninvited conversation, awkward questioning as to why she and Julian were out on the town together after so many years.

She leaned in. "Well, you certainly smell as good as ever," she remarked, thinking aloud, the words tumbling out of her mouth, unbidden except by the bubbles. "Not that I mean that as a come on," she added, with a nervous giggle. She could've kicked herself. She was usually so self-contained, so guarded. Gracie was afraid of blundering her way through the evening given the public proximity of it all.

"It's just that I've never forgotten your scent, always so clean and woodsy, somehow — so Julian. I bet I could pick you out in a line-up, blindfolded."

"Compared to?" Julian was intrigued. "Not . . . him. I mean, what do most guys smell of?"

"Deodorant. Cologne. Beard lube or motorcycle oil — my bad. I'm stereotyping, I guess. Garlic — beer."

"Well, I'll take the woodsy compliment, in that case," Julian laughed, his eyes lighting up as he leaned in slightly. "I'll be sure to tell my mother that I washed up well."

"Did you tell her who you were meeting? Does she remember me?"

"Yep. She always liked you. She says hi."

Julian had heard from an old school friend that Gracie was back living at her mother's. He'd floundered around a while before he asked her to check in and if it was okay with Gracie to pass along her contact info as he'd thought it would be fun to catch up. Julian had broken up with a girlfriend a few months earlier. Although he was not planning on launching into any kind of serious relationship so soon, he'd found it hard to deny the news that Gracie's marriage being over had sparked a renewed interest in what he'd always wondered might have been.

There had been little time in his law school and work schedule for casual dating. He'd inputted Gracie's number in his phone where it had sat for a week or two, burning a hole in his pocket. In the end, he'd texted her late one evening asking how she was doing. Gracie had responded the next day and with all of the ease of their teenage attachment, minus the romantic overtones, their initial back-and-forth dialog was surprisingly fluid. It had been a relationship based on friendship from the start and faster than either of them had expected, it was as if no time or distance had passed between them.

"Hot shot, handsome Julian," she'd jokingly texted back. 'Can it be? You've time for the likes of me?" She'd expressed her surprise that he was unattached.

"Not giving off the vibe to settle, I guess," he'd replied. "Had a lot on my plate."

"Tell me about it." Gracie had texted back, grinning from ear to ear for the first time in years. "I'd say you having set your eyes on the goal, put your career first and all and making it all the way into the DA's office doesn't surprise me one bit."

That night in the bar she was aware of an odd, but undeniable mix of half-agony, half-hope creeping in, taking hold, though she dared not think too far beyond the fact that the rekindling of their friendship was all it was. She headed to the restroom and stared into the mirror, her heart skipping a beat as she failed to convince herself that friendship was all she truly wanted it to be.

Their knees touched as she slid back onto the bar stool. She wobbled. A drunk dude in a camo jacket pushed past sloshing a spray of beer. She felt klutzy and stifled a laugh as a long-dormant sensation shot upwards out of nowhere, primal, a basic lust that seared through her thigh and pierced her gut like a gunshot. Julian felt it too, it was clear from their silence. He held her gaze. Neither said a word.

Gracie took a sip of her drink, concentrating on swallowing as she focused on not choking on the bubbles. She blushed again, intense heat radiating through her body as she felt the blood rush from the back of her ears and across her cheeks and over the front and back of her neck. A dark pink tell-tale tone settled on a resting point on the bare flesh at the opening of her flannel shirt. She held the palm of one hand over the warm skin around her collar bone, unconsciously slipping a finger beneath the bra strap at her shoulder over the tiger tattoo.

"As for me, well, I was an idiot, clearly — clueless," she burst out in a confession of sorts, bumbling. The prosecco had taken hold. "Stupidly settled for the first dumb guy who came along and showed me some interest, after you."

"I can't imagine you doing anything too stupid," Julian replied. "He must have had something going for him at the time — other than the fact he found you."

"Yeah, I try to tell myself he's not all bad at the core. I don't hate him, honestly, he's broken — his addictions, all kinds of issues he's tried his best to drown. I was totally taken in by his charm, his utter devotion at the start," she explained. "It's called love-bombing by the way — all bravado and charisma, reeling in an unsuspecting someone such as myself with way too much attention. Classic warning sign, I learned after trying my hardest to fix him when the cracks appeared."

"You would've met some other dude by now if it hadn't been him," Julian replied. "Chances are you'd have been happier, made a better match. Doesn't really matter when it comes down to it, does it? Nobody can change the past. We all make bad moves at some point in our lives. It's what we do once we've failed and figured what we really want for the future that matters."

"What do you want?" she asked, emboldened, suddenly. "Doesn't sound like you've made too many wrong turns along the way. I mean, Deputy DA? How long until you're running the department?"

"Well, I'm a free agent," he replied. "I can move departments when the time's right. I'm certainly not locked into So Cal, that's for sure."

"But you have a life down there — an awesome one by the sounds of it."

"In part. But my folks are here. I've no major commitments outside of work. Friends come and go wherever the work is. I'm not opposed to switching it up location-wise when I've figured out what comes next."

Gracie paused in thought. "I can't imagine what my life would have been like if I had left here the same time as you – gotten away from my parent's old-fangled ideals."

"It's not as easy as you think. Breaking loose. Living alone — occasional good roommate aside. I get why you played along with whatever it was they wanted from you. Kept the peace. After all's said and done, I'm not sure immediate career success is enough to make up for being so far from my family long term. I've been thinking of maybe moving back some day. My folks aren't getting any younger."

"Yes, but look where it got me, putting my parents first. Back then at least. Nowhere. I'm still going around in circles it feels."

"Well, I think it's pretty awesome that you're teaching. That's not nowhere. Ask the kids you teach. And you have your own little ones to be proud of, right? You've worked hard. If it hadn't gone down as it did, they wouldn't be here, would they, your kids?"

"Correct. As always, I'd suspect. And on that subject, Mr. Footloose and Fancy Free, I bet you've never even thought of having children? Being a daddy some day? I mean, doesn't it freak you out that we're the same age and mine are already in school?"

"No. To be honest, I've never given the idea of marriage or parenting much thought. Studying, partying a little in between and getting started with work has been about it for me. But you know what? No, it doesn't freak me out that you're a mom. It's more like you were meant to be exactly who you've become."

"Well, that's nice of you to say, but it's not much of a stroll in the park, single-parenting, take it from me. It changes a person — I may walk and talk and even look a little like I used to but I'm certainly not the easy-going, happy-go-lucky girl you once knew."

"From what I'm seeing, you've grown a pretty strong backbone. It suits you — being an adult and all!"

One thing Gracie was sure of was that she was way smarter, more self-aware and a whole deal more resilient at twenty-nine than she had been when she had last seen him and she felt a renewed sense of pride in her on-going fight to build a good, safe and rewarding life for herself and her daughters. Still, the thought of how she'd allowed Raymond to call the shots on their lives for so long was sickening. She shivered to think of him, out there, somewhere, haunting her.

"You weren't gonna see me that Christmas, at first. Remember?" Julian asked, changing the subject back to the two of them and their history. He'd felt the ice melting and his instincts told him it was not the time to hold back. "You'd written me that letter at Thanksgiving if you recall. Classic Turkey Drop."

"Ha! Dumpsgiving, right? Everyone warned me you'd dump me first if I didn't cut you lose," she replied. "It was all about self-preservation for me. I was stuck here with my folks and you were partying it up in some wild fraternity house at UCLA getting up to who knows what."

"But then you agreed to meet me in the park after dark that Christmas Eve."

"I needed to make it official. Closure. Stop you thinking I'd be up for hanging around pining for you for the rest of my life. Jesus, that was a terrible thing to do at this time of year."

"Brutal. Though, be honest with me, Gracie, did you never wonder in all these years, what might have happened if you'd never given me the marching orders that night?"

"Oh, I've wondered alright. But who do you know who is still with their high school date? Truthfully? I never imagined I'd be sitting here running off at the mouth with you, back here in town, tonight."

"And your dad? The fact you never wanted him to know the truth about us. How serious we were." Julian had always known what that was about, Aldo's blatant disapproval of his being Black.

"I'm pretty sure both he and Mom knew full well what was going on between us anyway. I moped around that whole winter, after."

"It must be hard for her without him."

"Yeah, they were totally attached at the hip, set in their ways the pair of them. Though I've gotta say, she's slowly coming around to the modern age since he's been gone. I dare say it's been a rude awakening having me and the girls show up; kids today and all that."

Julian pressed on in a gentle fashion with his questions. He asked if her parents had been supportive of her getting married.

"Truth be told, they were never overly enthusiastic about him," Gracie replied, as she laced her ringless fingers on the polished wooden bar top. She found herself wanting to tell him everything. "But there was no way on earth they'd have let me set about raising a kid as a single mom. And there was no debate as to my not having the baby. She part blames herself for a lot of what's happened, my mother, I know she does."

"How so?"

"In that she knows my settling for Raymond was not something that she should have pushed for. There was zero question of my not going through with any of it."

The truth of the stigma that had surrounded their dating one another stung him still, he realized, all these years later, no matter that they had been teenagers when they'd parted. He'd thought he'd dealt with it, pushed it to the side as one of life's many lessons. The fact that Raymond was white had been a defining factor in her parent's acceptance of a partner for their daughter, or in his case, their rejection. No matter that Raymond had been a lousy husband for their Gracie, her parents had approved of the match on face value. Julian had experienced this kind of unjust discrimination on and off for as long as he could to remember. The resurfacing of his having never verbally challenged the bias of Gracie's folks caused him considerable regret.

"And you?" Gracie asked, reading his mind. "Has it been better for you in southern Cal? I mean, more diverse?" She struggled to find the right words for his having left behind the whiteness of her provincial upbringing.

"In so far as my friends and neighbors, professors and coworkers, yeah. Otherwise, if you'd consider waking up every day wondering if it might be your last – like — maybe-a-cop-will-shoot-my-educated-black-ass today kind of reality, well, that's just something I've had to come to terms with all the more since living in a big city. It can happen anywhere though and it does."

Gracie looked around.

"I guess things haven't changed as much as we'd like," she remarked. "It's getting better around here but there's still a ways to go."

Julian said he'd noticed a little more going on in the downtown shopping district each time he'd been back. "Nice to see different folk and families. Though there's plenty of room for improvement," he replied.

"Being made fun of back in high school — my hair, my skin, my Georgia accent, the blonde-haired cheerleader chicks telling me I was good looking for a Black dude. It sucked to be singled out. I was a novelty here at best. I could count on one hand how many Black kids were in our grade. It was different with you, even if your folks didn't like you hanging around with me."

Gracie reached for his hand and gave it a squeeze. "It was different for me in every way on account of you being just about the smartest, kindest, funniest, least annoying dude in school," she joked, looking away and then back at him. "Not to mention the hottest guy on campus."

"Want another one?" he asked, trying not to show how good it was to hear how much she had admired him as he stared down into his empty beer bottle. He was encouraged by her last comment and he didn't want the evening to end. "Don't worry. I'll get the check."

Something tightened in her chest. They'd agreed initially that they'd split the bill. "I'm not looking for someone to take care of me," she shot back. Her defense mechanism had kicked in. She was unable to control it. Inside, she understood that she was afraid of losing what newfound autonomy she'd struggled to regain. Raymond had controlled her income to the penny. "I can look after myself."

"Hey, there's no need to get defensive, Gracie," Julian replied. "I'm feeling generous is all. It's Christmas."

The two glasses of bubbly she'd put away had tipped her sudden mood swing into overdrive. "What is it you want, Julian?" she asked, vulnerable, yet emboldened, adjusting her seat on the stool to face him full-on. "I'm not into casual these days — just so you know. We may as well be completely upfront with each other. If it's a holiday thing you're after, a Christmas fling for old-time sakes, then you're gonna be disappointed. And I'm not out for flattery or attention."

Julian looked crestfallen. How had he messed up so fast, he wondered? He took a few seconds to process what she'd said before he responded: "That's a bit of a rough take on me, isn't it? I think you know me better than that."

"I'm sorry," Gracie replied, deflecting the situation as she narrowed her eyes and checked the time on her phone. "It's the booze speaking is all. My pride is a little fragile at times. Let's wipe the slate clean. Pretend I never said that." She was embarrassed by her behavior but she knew herself well enough to understand that she had to be sure of him, to protect herself, her kids. "Time to say goodnight."

Julian insisted on helping her on with her jacket and walking her home in the rain. He wouldn't hear otherwise. Still, they maintained a slight, yet energetically-charged distance beneath the shared umbrella the few blocks it took to reach her house. Neither of them knew quite what to say after her unexpected outburst. It had been a bumbling end to the evening. Julian held the broad canopy of the umbrella steady above the two of them and kept his mouth shut.

"You can keep the umbrella for now," she urged, as they arrived at the foot of the porch steps. "Drop it on the porch before you leave."

"I don't want to impose any, but I'd really like to see you again soon, before I take off," he broached. "If that's alright with you."

"Maybe," Gracie replied, reaching up on tip-toes to kiss him fleetingly on the cheek. "I'll call you."

Julian lingered until she had closed the door behind her. The light from the hallway that seeped down the wet steps to where he stood was gradually extinguished. He felt like an actor playing out a scene from an old black and white movie as his brain raced to what he would write in a follow-up message.

After one last look at the house, he turned and headed back in the direction of his folks' place, sensing contentment, an idea that he hadn't been aware of what he was missing — hopeful for whatever would come next.

# CHAPTER SIXTEEN

# CAROL OF THE BELLS

Adamaria lay in the sleepy soldier position, on her back with her arms down at the sides, her legs straight out. She was wide awake, eyes staring up into the dark. A set of worn rosary beads were interwoven between her fingers. Her brain continued to run on supercharge despite the busy day's exertions.

She turned her head, tilting one hyper-alert ear after another at the familiar sound of Gracie's soft footsteps on the stairs. Maybe she'd surprise them both, she pondered, should she step aside sooner rather than later by giving her daughter the room to make some much-needed changes in their domestic set-up.

Gracie was respectful, quiet as a mouse, turning in, as she did most nights, without so much as a peep to disturb her old mom. And yet, Adamaria was concerned that she had created a something of a roadblock in her daughter's attempts to rebuild her life. Getting it right in parenting at her age was a little too hard to fathom.

The one thing Adamaria prayed for consistently each and every night was that her family would be spared any additional sorrow, that they'd remain safely out of harm's way under the sanctity of her roof. She muttered as much, out loud, in her third appeal of the night.

"Lord, hear my prayer. Protect us from all evil. And, if you do help me settle tonight, I promise I will shut my trap next time anythin' mean makes a run to burst forth."

She wiggled her toes. She was warm enough, cocooned under a set of heavy flannel sheets. Adamaria considered herself effectively encased, shroud-like, from head to ankle in her long, white, flannel nightshirt resplendent with delicate sprigs of green and red holly she had delicately hand-embroidered around its neckline and cuffs several Christmases ago. A multi-colored crazy quilt stitched by her own mother with remnants of old clothing lent an additional layer of cover to her thick, down comforter.

She'd timed the rickety, forced-air heating to turn off at bedtime — saving on the hefty utility bills that racked up through the winter months. The weather in Petaluma being temperate year-round, made it just about bearable for a hardy soul such as she and her brood to go without heat during winter nights. Layering was essential, especially when it came to bedding. Adamaria snuggled beneath her many covers, drowsy, yet unable to let go of her many considerations.

The pattering sound of rain on the patchy roof distracted her as she strained her tired eyes, fixing her focus on the shadows of the leaf pattern that surrounded the ornate, Victorian ceiling rose positioned directly above her bed.

Adamaria's mind wandered back to the Christmas before last, not long after Aldo had passed. It was then, in the midst of her sorrow and grief, that she had first confronted her son-in-law for his rumored infidelities and worse still, the undeniable mental abuse he'd inflicted on her daughter and in turn, her precious young granddaughters. What remained of his thin mask of forced civility had dropped and smashed like a porcelain plate into a million jagged pieces on the spot. There had been a terrible, menacing scene, during which Raymond screamed and shouted and threatened (as he had innumerable times since) that if she continued to brainwash his wife against him, he'd make absolutely sure that she would pay.

Flashbacks of the weeks it took for Gracie to leave him after that hideous incident, haunted her. Especially at night.

It's finally almost over, she consoled herself, working the rosary beads between her fingers. One thing is for sure that I'm real over him by now and I promise you, God, I'll never allow that sorry excuse for a man to spoil one more holiday in this house.

Outside, through the nocturnal, water-logged valley, the church bells struck midnight – each metallic toll appealing to her as some kind of beacon of hope. Adamaria lowered her eyelids and pictured the ruddy-faced priest in his crisp, gold and white vestments as he greeted the devoted in their departure from the warm, dry, candlelit church. Though

Gracie had arrived home as promised in plenty of time for Adamaria to have roused herself for midnight mass, she'd been far too sleepy and had taken herself to bed a good hour or so before the girl had returned.

Instead, she'd been content at first to reminisce as she lay in the warmth of her bed how she and Aldo had enjoyed many a midnight mass together, his arm around her as they'd sat side-by-side in their favorite pew. All the effort it had entailed was for the two of them to have stepped in time with one another, hand-in-hand, out of the door, down the porch steps and across the street. Somehow, since he'd passed, she'd lost interest in reinforcing her faith in person, especially when it came to going out after dark.

Adamaria was happy to make do with her humble prayers in the comfort of her bed. She'd basked a while in the glow of the colorful stained glass from the window at the top of the stairs as she'd turned in for the night. Besides, she was confident in her heart it was God and Aldo both who were right there with her in her act of battening down the hatches so as to keep her small, still-vulnerable family as comfortable and protected as she was physically able.

The last thing she was aware of before she dropped off was the haunting sound of the Smart Train whistling its approach as it rumbled into the empty downtown station, at Lakeville and D. A light, slumberous respite followed the sound of the train's passenger-less journey as it pushed on its tracks testing the train control and road crossing warning systems through the rain-drenched valley.

Adamaria's heartbeat, her breathing and eye movements had slowed. Her feeble muscles at last relaxed. She lost feeling in her legs as they twitched beneath the covers. Her brain waves had engaged the brake, her wakeful pattern at rest.

As mind and body slipped into a period of deep, restorative sleep, Adamaria's eyes moved behind her heavily shuttered eyelids, switching side-to-side at a rapid pace. Her heartbeat and breathing, having dipped to their lowest levels, periodically raced, arm and leg muscles slackening to the point of temporary paralysis.

She was a light sleeper, all the more so since Aldo had passed. This night proved no exception. Not an hour after dropping off, her re-charged brain cells registered the groan of a set of rusting hinges on the side-gate that led into the back yard. Instantly, Adamaria's eyes sprang open. The hinges, she was aware, were long-overdue for a deep cleaning with the bar soap she kept in a basin under the kitchen sink. She had been meaning to tackle that particular task for months, a year, maybe more. With a start, she flailed around amongst the bedclothes, wrestling to remember if she'd fastened the lock on the back door of the house.

As over-consumed as she had been with the last of her holiday preparations, she had let this and other, more important things slip. Plus, hadn't she been preoccupied with keeping an ear out for her sleeping granddaughters while Gracie was out? So much fussing about had thrown her off schedule. Try as she might, she was unable to recall if she'd taken her routine turn around the house before she'd retired for the night. Surely Gracie would've double checked that she'd locked up, she reassured herself.

Seconds later, she registered another ominous creak, this time, more like the cry of a night owl – though she knew it as the sound of the swollen back door as it squeezed to a close in its frame.

Adamaria bolted upright, shifting her weight against a pillow that was wedged in the small of her back. The melodic pattern of persistent rain tapped against the thin pane of her bedroom window. How she missed her Aldo and his old dog, Doc, as she nervously perched on the edge of her bed. Doc was the last of a series of gun dogs Aldo had trained up over the years. He had guarded the house with an unrivalled dedication, though he'd been a secret softie indoors, especially around the family.

The vulnerabilities of living in the center of town were heightened without a dog asleep on the mat and her husband now gone from her side. A couple of times since Aldo had passed, a vagrant had wound up making a bed for the night in the bushes of her backyard. There had been no real consequence to this invasion other than Adamaria uncovering evidence of an abandoned blanket and clothing, a stash of empty beer and liquor bottles. She'd later attached a lock to the back gate with the use of Aldo's old drill set but since Gracie and the girls had returned to live in the house, the lock had become more of a hindrance than a practicality. There was forever someone in and out with bicycles and trash bins and what not and she had gotten into the habit of letting it slide. The back door to the house, on the other hand, that was something she had never left unlocked before. Especially with regards to Raymond taking a notion to let himself in.

Raymond. The odds that he may have entered the house took root in the forefront of her mind. It was Christmas after all and his being kept from his kids would likely provide as good a reason as any for him to choose that moment to break his court order. She was never too sure as to the level of danger he posed. Adamaria stored a heavy flashlight in the drawer of her bedside table. She rummaged around in the dark, grasping its heavy steel handle as she launched herself from the mattress as fast as her reluctant body would allow. A sudden dizziness washed over her, followed by a wobbly sensation as gravity made its grab in pulling the blood down to her bed-stiff legs and feet. And yet it was Adamaria's stubborn, undaunted spirit that kicked her heart into gear. Her blood vessels set to work overtime, pumping vital fluids to her brain as she threw on her robe and marched, lips pursed, trembling ever-so slightly, in the direction of the bedroom door.

"What the devil?" she muttered, as she slid her feet into her carpet slippers and fumbled to tie the belt of her robe that had hung on a hook on the back of the door. Her sleep-swollen hands were stiff, the flashlight gripped firmly in their midst.

Adamaria considered herself a formidable woman, a solid force to be reckoned with. She prided herself on being in possession of a gutsy determination in lieu of any physical strength. She knew herself capable of taking on any adversary who dared to threaten her household. It didn't cross her mind in that moment to wake Gracie, to disturb her daughter's much-needed sleep. She could handle it she figured as she took a tight hold of the stair rail and tip-toed downwards in the cover of dark.

A slither of dim light from beneath the kitchen door guided Adamaria's path as she felt her way tentatively with her one free hand along the chilly wooden wainscoting of the downstairs hallway. The scent of the previous morning's sauce-making lingered — a familiar aroma of onions, garlic and tomatoes which had simmered on the stove for hours. It was the smell of home and it settled her nerves.

Maybe it's only Gracie, after all, fixing herself a little something to eat, she thought, calming herself. A cool draft wrapped itself around her ankles. She nudged the kitchen door with the toe of her sheepskin slipper.

Adamaria's sleep-weary eyes widened as she trained her focus. A faint glow surrounded the silhouette of what she first discerned as a small man standing by the kitchen counter – his back to her. A short, skinny, wire-haired mutt sat by his feet. The dog jumped to attention, turning to face the disturbance. The animal was clearly as startled as she was, though it didn't bark, but remained silent — watchful, assessing her.

It wasn't Raymond, that much was apparent. This fella was a good deal shorter than her son-in-law. Whoever it was had a baseball cap on his head, turned backwards. He wore a dark, drooping, oversized hoodie out of which emerged a small, scrawny hand burrowed deep in a container of Adamaria's homemade almond biscotti. Her hand shot to her mouth.

"What in the Lord's name are you doin' in my kitchen, helpin' yourself to my holiday goods?" she demanded, her lips pursed tight as she trained the flashlight directly onto the audacious young intruder. The dog gave out a low growl, yet he and his master continued to stand their ground, mouths agape, mirroring Adamaria, who had, by then, deduced that the stranger was in fact, not much more than a boy. A teen. And a young one at that.

"My goodness, what are you, thirteen? Fourteen?" she asked, her eyes scanning the counter top for evidence of the child's having pilfered more of her precious holiday provisions. In her ma's day there would have been homemade sausages, fresh pasta made at the kitchen table, hams, cheeses, trays of peppers and olives, bowls spilling over with grapes and melons covering every inch of that kitchen's surface in the sleepy hours between Christmas Eve and Christmas Day. These days, due to Adamaria's modest social security budget, the staples of her family's traditional holiday table were more scaled back and sacred than ever. She wasn't going to give any of it up to an intruder.

"S-s-sorry ma'am, we n-n-never meant to disturb. Honest." The child was clearly more alarmed by the sight of her than she of him. Biscotti crumbs clung to his trembling lips. "Alls I was wantin' was s-s-somethin' for me and Peanut here to eat."

"Yes, well, I can see for myself you're makin' yourself at home and enjoyin' the fruits of my hard-earned labor," she countered, her sharp eyes honing in on a small heap of crumbs on the countertop. Peanut returned to the half-eaten biscotti that the boy had dropped in the disturbance.

She watched, in equal parts indignant and intrigued, as the boy reached down and scooped up the shivering, scrappy looking, white and tan terrier.

"He's evidently soaked to the skin. As are you, otherwise, I'd be flippin' my lid about now."

"I guess so. Yeah." The boy paused before he nuzzled Peanut's smooth underbelly with his nose. A slow, disarming smile emerged.

"What are you going t-t-to do?" he asked, his pimply forehead furrowed under the shadow of his baseball cap with its faded Modesto Nuts logo.

"What is it that you were plannin' on?" Adamaria asked, her eyes fixed on the dog as he wriggled around in his young master's arms. What if the wiry, vermin-chasing four-legged creature lunged forward and bit her? She was more concerned about her nighttime encounter with the dog than his master.

"Is this scrappy little fella gonna pose a problem?"

The boy tightened his grip protectively around the dog's middle. "Not if you're nice to him."

"Really, is that so?" she replied, one bushy, white eyebrow arched. She stepped forward and deftly swiped one of the new dishtowels that she'd adorned with a set of gold embroidered bells from a small pile on the countertop. She handed him the towel.

"Well, why don't you dry the shiverin' creature off, at least?"

Adamaria's first instinct had been to call the police. As she eyed her cell phone in its charger on the tall wooden cabinet behind the boy and the dog, she recalculated her position. These days she was slow in her movements and making a grab for it and a subsequent call would require her being nimble of foot and wearing her reading glasses which were inconveniently tucked inside her pocket. She was slow with technology and the boy would have ample opportunity to push past her and escape, possibly even attack or injure her in some way.

Yet there was something about him that evoked a sense of dormant compassion within her, the grandmotherly instinct that was strong. She simply couldn't help herself, though she knew she should know better. His deep, olive complexion had drained to a greyish brown, a color which reminded her of the puddles in the courtyard across the street. Innocent-looking enough, but what was he capable of, she wondered? Her mind raced.

Old fool, she reprimanded as she reached to switch on the overhead light without so much as moving her feet. Don't be so swiftly taken in. He's nothing more than a common thief — no matter how small and innocent he appears.

After Adamaria set the flashlight on the kitchen table in a slow and deliberate a manner, she swiveled to replace it with a heavy, wooden rolling pin she'd set to dry on the counter top that morning.

"Whoa. You're not gonna hit me with that thing, are you?" the boy asked, a sudden frown forming above a pair of deep-spaced, almost elliptical-shaped eyes. A rainwater-green and blue, they were dotted with flecks of brown and framed by a pair of long, dark and delicate eyelashes clumped together by rainwater. The boy made no attempt to run or barge past Adamaria, standing her ground despite her bulky form in her layers of sleep attire and a sudden self-awareness of a row of metal clips that held her hair in place.

A pool of dirty rainwater puddled at his feet.

"So, first things first. Let me ask you this," Adamaria cautioned. "Why is it that you are here in my house and not at home with your folks? It's Christmas Eve for heavens sakes."

The boy hung his head, the last of the raindrops dripping from his eyelashes. It was either that or full-on tears. She couldn't tell. Was it all a cleverly orchestrated sympathy-inducing show, she wondered? She thought not. The pimply-faced youth appeared to Adamaria nothing more than skin and bones beneath his sopping clothes. He was cold, he was tired and he was hungry and thus sufficiently diminished in spirit to appear to be actually cowering, physically, in her matronly presence.

Adamaria looked down at his worn, checkerboard slip-ons. A hole frayed above his sockless, right big toe. She tried in vain to ignore a pull of tenderness that uninvitedly tugged at her tightened heartstrings.

"You simply do not break into a stranger's home and steal their food in the dead of night."

"I get it," he replied as he lifted his head to meet her eyes. "I n-n-never broke in, see. It was open. The gate. And the back door. You should be more careful."

111

"The nerve of it," Adamaria said. "Squeezin' through spaces, creepin' in. Whatever. You'll soon find yourself in deeper water if you continue to go around makin' a habit of this kind of thing."

"I . . . I told you already. We was needin' somethin' to eat, someplace dry to sleep, Peanut more 'an me. We don't want n-n-nothin' more, I swear."

Adamaria figured the poor mite deserved a chance, to be heard out in daylight at the very least. She decided without much ado to grant him a few hours to dry off and rest. But then, she feared, hadn't she been so wrong in doling out the benefit of the doubt before, the benevolent department hadn't been her strong suit when it had come to Raymond? Once bitten twice shy, for wasn't it she who had allowed the King Rat himself into her home?

She would never forgive herself for keeping it quiet after she'd heard from a friend of a friend that Raymond had a history of being a ne'er-do-well. A hint of violence. Adamaria had swept it aside as pure gossip at first. He'd subsequently married their darling daughter on her and Aldo's insistence after Gracie had discovered she was pregnant with Izzie. And her Gracie, her angel, her little Birdie, well Adamaria had not for one second imagined that Raymond would treat her daughter with anything less than the love and adoration she deserved. How horribly wrong she had been.

And now that the other one, Julian, was back on the scene after all that she had said and done to steer her daughter away from him in the first place, well, Adamaria was left with no choice but to regret her part in the whole sorry mess of the Raymond saga.

"I'd better have learned to judge a character by now," she said, as much for her own benefit as the child's. The boy looked at her quizzically.

It was not an easy task for Adamaria to sweep aside her petty insecurities and yet, here she was, the good, humble Christian woman she'd long considered herself, being called so suddenly and unexpectedly in the dark and stormy, early hours of Christmas morning, to spare a few measly hours of comfort and warmth for a stranger. And his dog. Adamaria looked them over again — a couple of lost souls if ever there was in need of her hospitality.

A shadow of soft-downy, whisker-like hair sprouted from the tight skin of the boy's cheeks and a streak of wispy, mouse-brown hairs lined his upper lip.

"Where've you come from?" she ventured. "I mean to say, I can't quite figure you out. I may not know anything about you but I hope, at least, that whoever your people are, you are more aware than you appear of the basics of what's right and what's wrong."

Adamaria looked him up and down, sizing him up good and proper, he believed, which added to his discomfort. And yet, he held himself steady and met her eyes straight on. She wasn't much taller than him.

"Can't see as I'm any much d-d-different to you," the boy replied, his head tilting slightly along with the dead-pan delivery of what had become his stock answer for an all-too familiar line of assumptions and questioning as to his specific stock. He knew what she was getting at, pigeon-holing him as an illegal. He could've come from anywhere south of the border, his brown skin would be all the same to her in her big, old relic of a house he figured.

"I was born here in C-c-california." he added, a slight smile of satisfaction punctuating the usual delivery whenever he'd been so blatantly profiled.

"Well, well . . ." Adamaria hesitated. "Whatever it is that I do decide to do about this breakin' in business, Mister, I'm hardly about to send you back out there in this storm, catchin' your death of cold on Christmas Eve of all nights."

She paused, hands on hips before pressing on with her further questioning. She asked how old he was and demanded an explanation as to why it was that he and Peanut were in need of shelter in the first place.

"And you'd best tell me your name," she said. "Let's get started with that."

# CHAPTER SEVENTEEN

# ZAT YOU, SANTA CLAUS?

Izzie's head buzzed with excitement. She'd awoken with a start sometime after midnight. The room was cold and dark, except for the faint, pearlescent glow of the nightlight. She scrambled from her blankets to the end of her bed and reached out her hand to investigate the lumpy contents of the pillowcase that had lain flat before she'd closed her eyes. She wasn't sure in the moment if she was relieved or disappointed that she'd slept through Santa's visit.

She weighed up her prospects of being undetected if she should dare to tip-toe in the chill silence of downstairs to check out the contents under the tree in the parlor. Maybe he was still there — Santa, lingering over the last crumbs on the plate of treats they'd left out for him. Something, she knew not what, had disturbed her in the midst of a deep and untroubled sleep. She'd never been brave enough to make a middle-of-the-night jaunt alone through the house and she wasn't at all sure she had it in her to actually follow through with her instinct to explore and investigate further.

First, she'd need to leave the safety of her warm and cozy bed. The room was slightly damp and unappealing outside of her bedcovers and she shivered as she withdrew her hand from the bulging pillowcase with its delicious, mystery contents awaiting reveal. Rosa snored softly in the bed across the room. She sat still and listened to the wind and the rain, heavy on the window pane.

If she had missed Santa, she figured she might still try tracking him on his route on her mom's tablet that was plugged in to charge in the kitchen. Before their afternoon game of make-believe, with their mother's permission, she and her sister had downloaded an app that showed the progress of his reindeer-driven sleigh as it careened around the globe and though it had been fun to follow his whereabouts a handful of times during the evening, she had forgotten about checking it one last time before bed.

Izzie was all ears. She thought she heard voices downstairs. Maybe it was Santa after all. What would happen if Nonna had been awake and she'd seen him, she wondered? Or what if Mommy had accidentally disturbed him on her way home? It was all very confusing. Was it allowed for grown-ups to see Santa? Izzie's active mind imagined faces — multiple sets of eyes lurking in the shadows of the woodland creatures of her bedroom décor. Muffled sounds and movements appeared to her to emerge from the hallway beyond her bedroom door. It was the storm, she assured herself, as she listened to it rap against the windows, though she couldn't help but picture the walls of the house come alive that night with all manner of creepy creaks and groans, whispers and moans.

Outside her bedroom window, behind the heavy drapes, trees swayed violently, dispersing twigs, leaves and small, sharp pieces of bracken into the night, tip-tapping at the glass as they raced past and swirled inwards, scratching the glass of the windowpanes. It was an eerie hour to be huddled in bed undecided whether to be bold enough to get up and explore or burrow down and will herself back to sleep.

She lay back against her pillow, slipping under her bedcovers and pulling them up to her chin. A faint image of her father's face swam before her shuttered eyes. Izzie hadn't seen him in over a year or maybe more and it was difficult sometimes for her to remember exactly what he looked like. She wasn't sure if she missed him much now or not. After her parents had separated, Raymond had been given visitation rights for a short time. It had been decided, by someone, Izzie knew not who, or why, that for their wellbeing, she and Rosa were not to see him, let alone spend time with him, at least for a while. Their mother never said much about him that she had heard and Izzie, in her own way, accepted that.

She thought about how she was different from other kids because of it. She and Rosa both. Most of their friends had moms and dads at home, or if they didn't live together, all of them under the same roof, the kids she knew of at her young age with divorced or separated parents appeared to spend equal time with both. That arrangement seemed fair in Izzie's young mind, though she'd grown used to the way things were in her own family and she didn't relish any thought of her parents reuniting.

"What's wrong with Daddy?" Rosa had asked, out-of-the-blue, a week or so before the holiday. "Why can't he come spend Christmas with us?"

Izzie's young heart sank in hearing her little sister ask such a thing, yet she was unable to put the right words to the sense of grief that they shared.

"He's not in a good place, I guess," is how she'd responded, trying to sound like a grown-up, not wishing to upset her younger sibling any more than necessary.

"Well, I have a gift for him," Rosa declared.

"You do? What is it?"

"Not tellin'."

"Why?"

"'Cause it's a secret."

"Okay, but if it's in our room, I'll find it."

"It's a picture book. I made it myself."

"Is there a story?"

"Nope. Just dwawings."

"Of what?"

"Oh, okay then. It's pictures of you and me and him. Doin' things, like playin' catch and fishin'."

"When did we go fishin'?"

"In the future."

"Oh."

Gracie had done her best not to belittle her daughters' feelings and confusion over their father's absence. Not wishing to add to it, she'd leaned in to the pain of separation and let them know that she felt it too.

Although she couldn't be expected to grasp the more difficult concepts, Izzie had a way about her in which she'd learned to compartmentalize the unpleasantness of grown-up failure. Instead, she focused on helping her little sister to see that their family, as in their mother and grandmother, she and Rosa were as normal a family as anyone else's.

And it was with this youthful spirit of experimental thought, her careful evaluation of evidence and analysis of life's mysteries, that seven-year-old Izzie reasoned it really wasn't all that likely that Santa would possibly make it around the world in just one night anyway.

Her bare feet beneath the bedcovers shuffled down far enough to touch the loaded pillowcase. Its weight was reassuring, calming, despite her revelations. She clamped her eyes shut and covered her ears with her hands as she pictured the light of Christmas morning, her little sister's excitement and, gradually, she slipped back into an untroubled sleep.

# CHAPTER EIGHTEEN

# SONGBIRD

"My name's M-m-mateo," the boy stuttered as he held out a small, cold hand in a gesture of formality that Adamaria had not expected. "I'm t-t-thirteen. It's been three days an' nights since we left the Central Valley."

Adamaria was not about to take that grubby little hand of his in hers until it had been given a good and proper scrubbing. He sensed her reluctance toward physical contact and dropped his arm to his side. His sunken cheeks flushed an indignant, dusky pink in reaction to her persistent interrogation. She watched, intently as he knelt down and placed Peanut gently on the floor.

"We was on our way north, to my auntie's place, to see my little sisters. Figured we should stop off 'round here while the rains pass through."

"So, basically, you've been on the streets? Alone."

"Well — at night we was covered, seeing as I kinda b-b-borrowed a tent. We slept under the freeways. Last night we found a spot under a bridge, down by the river. The wind that blew in earlier, it tore the whole thing up — r-r-ripped it clear off the ground."

Mateo described how he had sought the shelter of the church, that afternoon, an act of desperation after the loss of the tent. The pair of them, kid and dog, he explained, abandoned their huddling under the bridge when the rain came in.

"It being Christmas an' all. I figured on it being crowded in the church, so I snuck Peanut inside under my jacket. We sat through all the s-s-services." His eyes swept the kitchen.

"Did you not think to share your predicament with anyone? Someone at the church would have helped you, surely. You're only a child."

"Ain't nobody's business but mine. Besides, there's no way we're goin' back to where we came from."

"And where is back? Your parents' house?"

"No ma'am, they're g-g-gone."

"What do you mean gone?" she plunked herself down on a chair at the kitchen table so that she was able to more comfortably continue with her steady line of questioning. This might take a while, she reasoned. Surely the boy was far too young to be running loose on the streets alone? Who was looking out for him? Who had reported him missing? She'd heard of teenage runaways but this one was so very young, so small and vulnerable — barely into his teens.

Mateo wiped a clear stream of snot from his runny nose with the back of one hand while she retrieved her pair of eyeglasses from her pocket. She balanced their wire rims on the tip of her nose. The base of each of his slim fingers was etched with the letters that formed the words SONG BIRD — a rough self-inking if ever she'd seen one. His finger nails were chewed to the quick. He watched her as she spelled out the letters with her beady, black eyes.

"My mom, it was the special name she gave me — her little s-s-songbird she used to say — el pájaro cantor on account that I was always singin' some sorta song or another when I was small. Before."

Adamaria's agile mind pictured the image of a Mousebird, a soft, brown creature with hairlike body feathers and a long, scruffy tail flapping its wings. She'd seen a nature show once that featured these rare cockatiel-sized specimens. He was more of a Mousebird than a Songbird, in her opinion.

"What happened to her? Your mother?" she asked, thinking it a coincidence that this strange little bird had chosen to invade her nest.

"She passed, my mom. This time last year. It was Christmas Eve. My baby sister, she came too early, see. No time for a d-d-doctor."

"And you were there with your mother when this happened?" Adamaria asked, unflustered in her enquiry, although his story had grown increasingly troubling. She had suffered much loss herself and she decided, if he were speaking the truth, to tread carefully.

"Yes. The baby, I tried to help. I had to. My little sister an' me. We did what we could with towels and blankets. My sister ran for the n-n-neighbor, but it was t-t-too late."

"And where was your father in all this?"

"He'd been workin' the vineyards, see. Had an accident durin' harvest two months before."

"And where is he now?"

"He's dead an' all. They pulled him out of a p-p-plastic wine tank. He fell in while he was cleanin' it. It was the fumes that took him. My mom, she had no choice but to get herself ready for the new baby. She was freakin' out. Spent all the m-m-money we had on his burial. We was left with pretty much nothin'."

"But surely there was some kind of compensation?" Adamaria was aghast. "Your family is due some form of financial help, I would imagine. You said he had his papers? Your father?"

"Yes. We was legal an' all. All I know is the child protective services people, well, they came for us in the night, soon after the c-c-cops and the ambulance. They packed up all our stuff in big ol' black plastic trash bags there and then an' they took us, the baby, my little s-s-sister an' me."

"And so, let me get this clear. Your sisters are now with your aunt?"

"My mom's sister, she has 'em both with her an' her family up in Ukiah. I ain't seen 'em since."

"And why are you not with them?"

"My uncle. Her husband. He said no to takin' me. On account of him sayin' I'd be too much t-t-trouble for them to take on, c-c-comin' into my teens an' all. They have two of their own, see. Boys. He said that foster care would do better by me."

Adamaria pulled out a second chair. She motioned for him to sit beside her. "Well, that's a tragic story if ever I heard one," she said. "Am I to take it that you have issues with your foster home?"

Mateo's face crumpled. He looked like he was about to burst into tears, though he stifled the urge as he cradled his hollow, downy cheeks in his hands. He opened his mouth and took a long, deep, shuddery breath.

"So wrong, m-m-makin' me stay there," he replied, his heavy eyes resting on a tile on the floor. He took a second hefty intake of breath, before launching into a fast-paced diatribe of how it was the third foster home in a year that he'd run from and that this last one was by far the worst of the three.

Floodgates opened and closed. He sobbed intermittently, lowering his head into his hands. The valve of internal distress released and emptied months of pent-up emotion. He confessed, between stifled sobs, how he had hated being in care as much as he'd detested the last school that they'd sent him to.

"That's when it all w-w-went wrong."

He described, in his own words, how he had been taunted and traumatized by the other kids until he could stand it no more.

"Then I had a massive fight with my foster family's s-s-son, see — he's older 'an me an' he was forever b-b-beatin' up on me for not makin' my curfew, messin' up on chores — whatever it was I did to set him off."

Adamaria tutted as she listened and nodded her head. Each time he let out a fresh sob, she reached out her hand to pass him a tissue and pat him lightly on the arm. She certainly did not wish to overstep the mark by being too over familiar, or worse-still, coming across as condescending in her sympathetic response but there was nothing to be done but be kind and hear him out.

"It had gotten so bad, I figured I would either have to put an end to it all or s-s-start again on my own. Me and Peanut."

Mateo confessed how he'd left behind a handwritten note on the back of an envelope that he'd carefully construed to throw his foster family and ultimately, if they even bothered to inform the social services, off track.

"I lied. Told 'em I was headed s-s-south, over the border. Wanted them to think I hightailed it all the way to Guadalajara where my f-f-folks are from."

"And you don't think the authorities would consider you'd try to be in touch with your aunt and your sisters here in California, first?"

"My guess is that nobody gives a shit about m-m-me," he answered. "Sorry for the use of bad words, but I been so afraid of losin' anyone else, I n-n-never spoke of any of 'em to no one when I was in care." Besides, he added: "I been plannin' on takin' my time m-m-makin' my way to where they are so as to cover my tracks."

"Do you think your aunt may be persuaded to take you in this time?" Adamaria asked. "Maybe she's received some assistance from the occupational safety folk if there's been an investigation into your father's accident."

"I dunno anythin' about all that. I just wanna be sure the ninás are g-g-good. I wanna see them again, check they're ok, even if only at a distance."

Adamaria heard how he had hitchhiked his way over from Stockton, Peanut tucked into his jacket, a small backpack with the tent he had "borrowed" from his foster family his only luggage. He described how the two of them had taken a long, dreary walk through the graffiti-tagged streets of Oakland the first evening. They'd spent the cold, damp overnight under the freeway overpass in Berkeley before hitching a ride over the Richmond Bridge and across into the North Bay and into downtown San Rafael.

"Next day we hung out at a gas station near the freeway ramp headin' north. A dude in a beat-up work truck drove us as far as Petaluma. I ain't never h-h-heard of this place before."

"And Peanut?" Adamaria asked. "Is he yours, or did you take him on loan from your foster home along with the tent?"

"He's m-m-mine," Mateo replied, reaching down to pet him. "Only thing in the whole world that is."

Adamaria suggested that surely his foster family were not all bad if they'd allowed him a dog.

"They used him as a barterin' tool," he replied. The boy was wise for his years, she deduced, given all he had experienced. "I begged 'em to let me keep him after I found him as a stray. They was not about to give in 'til my foster Dad finally figured he'd have s-s-somethin' over me."

He explained how each time that Mateo had been in trouble at school or home, Peanut had been taken from him. Turned out, his foster brother was as mean to the dog as he was to Mateo.

"Kicked Peanut clear out the door a dozen times. I thought about e-e-endin' it all more than once," he admitted, avoiding her eye. "But I would never leave this li'l dude in their care. I would've had to f-f-finish him off first and I'd never, ever do that."

"Well, I'm sure Peanut for one is grateful for that," exclaimed an astonished Adamaria, almost, but not entirely lost for words. She gathered herself. "A boy your age – why, you've had more troubles to deal with in your short years than most folk in a lifetime."

Fresh tears welled in the corner of his mournful, young eyes. This curious old woman was the only person who had sat down and listened to him since his mother had died. He wanted to trust her but it was too soon.

"Well, you certainly have courage, I'll grant you that," Adamaria continued, sensing his distrust. Her mounting concern was fueled by the list of indignities the poor child had suffered. "I'd say you're a fighter, a survivor. And I can see how you've a good heart in how you care for your sisters. And this little four-legged fella of yours."

The kid would almost certainly have to deal with an entangled range of anger and abandonment issues down the line, Adamaria reasoned, but who would blame him for his misgivings, given the circumstances?

"Did you never complain to the authorities?" she asked.

"I went to the police department, once, when things were bad in the second place," Mateo replied. "The foster mom, she was s-s-spendin' my clothin' vouchers on her own kids. Cops told me I'd be labeled 'troubled' if I made a stink. I'd wind up in one of the big group homes."

Adamaria's heart sank further as she wrestled with his suggestion that he might not have made it had he remained in a system in which he meant so little to anyone.

"What made you so bold and determined to go it alone?"

"Like I said, thinkin' of my sisters an' P-p-peanut," he replied. "And being out of that house that I hated so much. Since I left, I think more about the good times back when we was all together."

His eyes lit up when he talked about his own family, time spent with them at home and outdoors. "We had a big 'ol garden out back in the last place. My dad, he loved it. He teached me how to grow all the good stuff — peppers, corn, tomatoes . . . he said I'd be the one he pictured makin' outside spaces for other people someday —as soon as I made it through school. We was always drawin' up ideas together, designin' pathways on paper napkins, any scrap of paper, that kinda thing, talkin' of how I'd soon be plantin' gardens and trees, buildin' shade spots for people to sit under an' enjoy."

"Well, I have to say," Adamaria replied. "That all sounds mighty fine to me." She noted his lack of a stutter when he talked of his dad and the time they'd spent together outdoors. The child had lost a better father than her own grandchildren had ever had. He had suffered an especially cruel fate to have lost both of his parents.

"But I thought it was all computer screens and video games you youngsters are obsessed with these days," she said, directing the subject back to the boy himself.

Mateo stifled a yawn as he clapped a hand over his mouth. His stomach groaned and filled the empty space in their conversation.

"There's all these cool design programs on the computer," he explained, his eyes coming back to life as he responded to her interest in the subject. "The one teacher I got on with, she s-s-showed me how to use 'em."

"Well, that's all well and good, I'm sure." Adamaria resigned herself to the child's more immediate needs, starting with the quelling of a series of rumbles that emanated from inside of his concave stomach. "But it's food you need first. So why don't you stay right here while I fix you and Peanut a bite to eat?" she instructed. It was her firm belief that any amount of upset was best eased by a hot drink and a plate of home cooked food.

"And after that, a nice, hot shower will warm you up."

Both boy and dog held their hunger at bay as she busied herself preparing and duly presenting them each with a plate of thick slices of buttery toast alongside a steaming mound of soft, sunny-colored scrambled eggs. They'd watched, transfixed, as Adamaria had stirred in a few thin slithers of pink from the small pack of smoked salmon she'd tucked away in the refrigerator for her family's New Year's breakfast fixings.

After they'd eaten, she set about making a pot of honey and chamomile tea, turning her back to give the boy and the dog some space and privacy. Neither was able to disguise how famished they were.

Noisy contractions of toast and scrambled eggs gradually made their way through empty gastrointestinal tracts. This proved hard to ignore in an otherwise silent kitchen. Mateo was acutely aware of the similarity of the growling sounds that his and Peanut's insides made as their two sets of intestines went to work on the perfectly fluffy pillows of scrambled egg, savoring each mouthful.

"Ain't ever tasted a scramble that wasn't all rubbery since I visited my grandparents in Gaudalajara for Christmas back when they were s-s-still alive," the boy said, after he had fully polished off his food.

"Free range in these parts," Adamaria replied, puffing her chest out with pride. Only the best eggs in her kitchen.

"Never guessed I'd wind up in another f-f-farm town," he replied. He'd taken note of the familiar sight of western boots and dressed-up ranch wear in the church congregation, earlier.

Adamaria sent him on his way to the downstairs bathroom as she swept up crumbs and shook linen over the sink.

Fifteen minutes later, freshly showered and encased in a set of soft gray sweats (Gracie's) that Adamaria had pulled from a heap of newly laundered clothes, a cleaner, warmer, dryer and no longer hungry Mateo lay snuggled beneath a blanket on the couch. Peanut sprawled blissfully in his arms, the both of them equally transfixed by the vision of a cheery, restoked fire. Christmas tree lights danced in the warm glow of the parlor completing the theme of the two of them having thought they had died and gone to some kind of old-fashioned holiday heaven.

Adamaria, as she busied about with a pile of extra blankets and pillows, announced that she would spend what was left of the night in the comfortable and suitably watchful confines of her armchair.

"Don't tell n-n-no-one I'm here," Mateo begged, his eyes drooping with tiredness.

"Whose business is it where you are tonight of all nights?" she replied. "Still, that said, there is no way I'm about to leave you and your pal, Peanut, here, unattended in my house. I'd suggest you close your eyes and get yourselves some rest. That's all you need concern yourself with for now."

She hovered, listening to the rain as it continued to fall in irregular intervals — soft showers interspersed with episodes of greater intensity. Adamaria took care to replace the soggy towel in the leaking window frame with a fresh one. It was to be a long night. She remembered that the back door was still unlocked and made her way out to the hallway to the back of the house to remedy the situation before settling down herself.

Never in all my days have I found reason to knowingly lock myself into my own home with a complete stranger, she thought, as she re-entered the parlor. She was not at all sure if she was in her right mind, after all as she did a double-take to make sure she hadn't imagined the whole episode with the boy and his dog.

"I ain't never had a real Christmas tree like this one," the boy replied, sleepily — as if it was the lights of the tree that had lured him in for the night. "Only ever a f-f-fake one."

"Well, we'll leave the lights on then, shall we, seein' as they'll aid me in keepin' an eye on you?"

"How will you sleep sittin' up?" he asked, his eyelids drooping as he sank further into the down of the pillow. Peanut was already fast off, chasing a dozen squirrels in doggy dreamland.

"Never you mind," she replied. Adamaria thought it best if she led him to believe that she slept with one eye open.

Before long, a concert of loud snores indicated that neither boy nor dog was faking having succumbed to sleep. Still, she looked over at her unexpected guests.

"I'm not much for sleepin', anyhow," Adamaria declared, as much to herself as to Mateo and Peanut. "It's over-rated. You'll find that out for yourself when you're my age."

# CHAPTER NINETEEN

# A BETRAYAL AND A VICTORY

Raymond's face flushed blue either side of his forehead and crimson red at the center, the colors of anger. His otherwise sallow skin was salty with perspiration. Back at his place, his family room without a family contained a sordid air with its stink of weed, stale beer and discarded Mexican food. It did little to calm his mood.

This was the same, once clean-and-tidy room in which Gracie had stored photo albums and her high school yearbooks, personal items she'd been forced to leave behind when she'd fled. Seeing as they hadn't been touched since, he knew just where to look for them, stacked inside an old wooden chest that doubled as his coffee table.

In order to do so, he bent over and with the back of his hand he swept off a week's-worth of empty beer bottles, coffee mugs and shot glasses. A large abalone shell filled with the stubs of many joints tipped and spilled its contents on the general grime of the rug.

Waves of anger and jealousy made for especially poor bedfellows given the level of chemical imbalance within his brain and body. Raymond kicked the chest, which directly resulted in an immediate sharp pain and a subsequent swelling to his right foot. He flailed around the room, cursing, all the while heaving armloads of Gracie's neatly organized memorabilia into a haphazard pile in the middle dip of a stained suede couch.

Raymond slumped back against a small, thin, throw pillow, one of a pair that Gracie had made up for him on an online photo site for Father's Day a few months before she'd left. Beneath a layer of crud, a collage was imprinted on the fabric, a now-faded assortment of photos of Raymond and his small, blonde babies.

There in the middle of the tossed pile of books, boxes and albums lay Gracie's senior year book. Raymond, in his fury, had honed in on a hunch that Gracie and whoever the son of a bitch was that she'd been drooling over in the bar were definitely not hooking up for the first time. It had flashed through him, as he'd careened the country roads like a maniac, how he'd forced it out of her, not long after they'd hooked up and shortly before she'd told him she was expecting. He'd been jealous as hell when she'd told him about her first time, her short history with men. How her folks had made it difficult for her to be with him on account of his skin color.

He didn't give a flying fuck who it was or what color his skin was, he swore to himself, for it was he, Raymond, who had claimed her as his wife. She belonged to him alone.

And yet the mere idea of another man's hands on his property, this minute, right now, after all he'd been through with her, was unbearable.

He'd given her a hard time back then when his jealousy had reared its ugly head and he would sure as hell do so again, he swore, as he pictured her delicate arms bruised from his grip. She'd pay for the torment she was causing the minute he had her back in his house.

Visions of Gracie, those same slim, olive-skinned arms wrapped around the smarmy bastard he'd spied in the bar, jeering over her shoulder, ridiculing him, Raymond, her husband. He feared his thumping head and the sharp stab of pain he suffered in the back of his eyes might very well rupture his blood-red ears. He struggled to focus as he rifled through the pages of her senior year book. It was she who had pushed him to the violent mess of emotion that had built within him. He smashed his fist on the page where a younger version of the dude he'd spotted in the bar stared straight out at him, all trussed up in full tux for his year book photo but the same man alright, still grinning from ear-to-ear.

"Asshole, tauntin' me like you own it. How fuckin' dare you?" he swore, spittle hitting the glossy sheen of the year book.

Raymond wrenched the paper clear out of its bindings. He reached down for his lighter and, with a shaking hand, set fire to the edge of the sheet, laughing, crying, raging in turns as the face of his rival crumpled and burned and settled in a hot flake of ash on the rug. He stamped out the embers with his left foot, the one that didn't send a shooting pain up his leg with each and every move.

I'll show 'em, he swore to himself, furiously shaking his fist at his reflected image, which lost no intensity in shaking right back at him from the mirrored blackout of the window. He should never have let it all get to this.

All of 'em, Raymond vowed. I'll teach 'em. They have no clue.

Somewhere in the back of his addled, unmined brain, the deepest part of his inner self, Raymond knew exactly what it was he was about to do and the extent he was willing to go to. He was perfectly clear that this was a major breech of the months of self-discipline he'd been forced to endure. The court had hit him hard. How was anyone who called himself a man to stop himself, he asked? His fury was all-encompassing – a measure, he convinced himself, of his undying love.

Meanwhile, Raymond's blood pressure lurched to a perilous new height. It peaked at a precarious level. Angry plasma battered his artery walls. The amount of weed and alcohol he'd consumed since he'd rolled out of bed that morning forced the psychoactive effects of his cannabinoid receptors, tiny spots on the neurotransmitter cells of his brain, to labor over-time in order for his body and brain to communicate, connect.

Raymond's very perception of time, touch, sound and sight was distorting, collapsing in on itself. The one external reality he was still able to grasp was the sound of the dull thumping of heavy brass hands — the belabored mechanics of his grandmother's clunky old pendulum wall clock that marked the hour of midnight with its dull, depressing chime. Before he knew it, it was 2 am as he continued to seethe and stomp.

And it was in the early hours of Christmas morning that the buzz of his having crossfaded large amounts of cannabis and whiskey elevated his internal level of distress to an entirely new level of self-denial.

Raymond's doctor had prescribed him an antidepressant after Gracie left, the effect of which, when paired with his continued use of his various substances of choice had created a medical crisis. Though it had been made clear to him by his doctor that this complex, interaction of multiple chemicals could be potentially fatal someday, it was far from his mind that morning.

Denial is a powerful foe, for though Raymond had already been diagnosed with the condition known as Serotonin Syndrome, he considered himself invincible. He paid no heed in the heat of the moment with regards to his escalating risk of high fever, seizure, shock, irregular heartbeat, unconsciousness, even and if he truly pushed it, death. Raymond's cognitive state failed to connect the dots to a sufficient degree for him to assess the direness of risk. He was unable to put a stop to it. The only thing in his mind was that he was ready at last to reclaim his wife.

Rain pounded on the windscreen of his truck. Frantic, he started up the engine. Blue streaks fell in thick, diagonal sheets before the beam of the headlights. It would soon be over, he promised himself, his law-enforced exile from his family. Victory and justice would be his. He was convinced. Raymond vowed afresh to quit the weed and the whiskey both once he and Gracie were back together. And with his vision of domestic Utopia in mind, he shed the final hackles of his restraining order. He swiveled his neck to reverse the truck on a bed of wet gravel as he slammed his aching foot on the accelerator pedal.

His was the only vehicle on the road, it being the early hours of Christmas morning and the conditions vile. An avenue of eucalyptus trees formed a dark and sinister tunnel of giant silhouettes across the deserted, heavily rutted lane that led to the slick and oily main road into town. Even the deer had taken shelter from their routine night-patrol.

The dashboard lit up as if in response to the empowerment within the palms of his hands as he gripped the wheel. Hot, fat, anger-fueled tears rolled from his eyes and down his sallow cheeks. He swiped them away with the back of his hand as an orchestra of synchronized thunder claps cracked and rattled the night sky. It sounded to him like a giant sheet of metal rolling back and forth above his head.

Exhilaration coursed through every last vein in his coil-sprung limbs. Raymond had not experienced anything remotely close to this pulse of sheer electric energy since Gracie had left. It thrilled him. And he was not about to risk his unbridled elation falling anywhere close to short.

A dramatic fork of lightening piqued his adrenaline. Ten minutes into town, a second, more extensive fork lit up the downtown intersection of traffic lights beneath the clock tower, flash-lighting a row of Victorian iron-front stores, shuttered cafes, a faintly-lit barber-shop and still-open bars in the same blazing wash of electric-blue and purple that saturated the crosswalk — now a shallow, neon river.

Look at that — beautiful, Raymond thought as he let out a low whistle. It was as if he had summoned the heavens to command such an impressive storm, a reflection of his own furious determination. "My will is your god-damn command," he screamed into the cab, laughing hysterically and raising the clenched fist of his right hand to the elements of the powerful night sky.

Raymond cackled and cursed intermittently as he slowed his speed, signaled and turned the wheel of his truck in the direction of his mother-in-law's place. His furor was greeted by the twinkling reflection of exterior holiday lights strung along the eaves of neighboring homes. Their cheeriness despite the weather conditions taunted him.

Gracie's bedroom was located at the back of the house. Raymond killed the ignition, shut his eyes and visualized the layout of the home to which she'd run like the weak child he considered she was. His girls, he tried his best to picture, would be tucked up cozily in the rickety old twin beds that Adamaria had insisted he assemble in the small room up front. Back then, at least, there'd been a roll-guard on Izzie's bed to prevent the toddler from dropping onto the floor in her sleep. How he'd hated his first born and later her sister being out of his sight for more than an hour or two, even then. Raymond's issue with his wife not pandering to all of his demands after the babies came along was complicated by his pathological need to keep them all in his clutches. Every so often, Gracie had made some excuse or other to stay over at her mother's.

He should have known that the two of them had been plotting her doing the dirty on him all along. Never again, he swore as he smacked his tear-soaked cheek bluntly with the back of his hand.

Raymond had the forethought to change into a set of clean, dark clothes before he left his place in the early hours. He had dressed carefully from head to toe, topping his clothing with a black, plastic rain slicker he'd rummaged around to retrieve from an unopened package in the garage to keep him dry as he crept around the side yard, sticking close to the house. He had no fear of anyone hearing his footsteps given the velocity of the rain. He reached over the top of the gate that led into the backyard and carefully lifted the lever. A large rat scurried out of the open passage, between his feet and into the side yard. Raymond squeezed his narrow frame through the opening, nudging the gate to a partial close.

The back of the house sat in darkness except for a faint glow from an exterior light on the neighbor's back porch. Its illumination, though subdued by the downpour, was sufficient enough to guide his path to the small shed in which Raymond gambled, from a long-past experience of fixing a problem with the flashing, contained an expandable, metal ladder. This took time to locate. Some efficient busy-body had tucked it neatly away amongst his late father-in-law's motley assortment of aged and rusting tools.

Earth around the wooden siding at the bottom of the house was sodden, swampy almost from excessive moisture. Raymond's first footing on the ladder's stout, perpendicular rungs revealed how shaky and fragile it was. By the time he was half way up, the ladder's anti-slip safety shoes had sunk into the ground on one side, tilting it to a degree that made it clear, despite his altered state, how precarious it was. Raymond swore under his breath as he figured, too late, that he should have tightened the hex nuts on either side of the extension before beginning his climb. He wasn't fond of heights at the best of times and in order to avoid losing balance completely, he remembered how his dad had forced him to clean gutters, as a boy.

He knew he had to maintain three points of contact, whether climbing up, down or somewhere in between. Two feet and one hand, he repeated to himself, over and over, nervous of the ladder sliding out beneath him as he shifted his weight. Somehow, by keeping his center of gravity lower than the top of its frame, his slight body weight and impaired movement was not enough to send the ladder sideways or backwards and he was able to climb exactly to the point where he had intended on the back side of the house.

The latch on Gracie's back bedroom window was of a vintage design and thus, it proved, as he'd wagered it would, laughably easy for him to release its rotting hardware. He had gone over this unlikely Plan B in his head countless times over the past many months. Though he'd been convinced he wouldn't need to take such desperate measures, here he was and he was relieved that he'd thought it through sufficiently. Raymond settled his nerves and smiled with satisfaction, a lop-sided grin. He commended himself on his wily masterfulness.

Within a matter of minutes, the inside walls closed in on him and Raymond dropped to his knees on a rug by the window. His heart beat like a tin drum. He sprang up by the foot of Gracie's bed and lowered himself over her sleeping form, clamping her slender legs in a vice-like grip.

Swiftly, he levered the full weight of his upper body onto hers, sliding one hand beneath her head and the other he placed firmly over her mouth. Her hair was splayed out around her head — a dark halo on her pillow.

Raymond's initial elation dissolved into a sobering state of minor shock mixed with his suspended disbelief at having gotten this far. The second Gracie's eyes sprang open, he released the back of her head and she felt the steely tip of his sheath knife prick her throat. Its sharp point was positioned with sufficient pressure to prevent her from acting on her first instinct to scream. She knew in an instant it was him. Her worst nightmare materialized.

Wide, terrified eyes darted from side to side, instinctually searching for any possible route of escape available. The only part of her body Gracie was able to move were her arms, which she flailed around desperately in a silenced attempt to slide out from under the dead weight of her husband's body.

Raymond repositioned himself, pressing harder with the cold tip of the knife. He lowered his gaunt face and placed his thin, blue lips onto her left ear. "Shut it and do what I say and you and the kids won't be hurt."

She dropped her arms to her side, palms up, an act of forced submission. Raymond released the knife pressure long enough to cut a length of duct tape from a roll balanced over his right wrist. He lay his head close to her face, his breath, heavy and stale with weed and liquor as he methodically worked to seal her mouth.

Gracie froze beneath his form. She worked frantically to calm her brain, despite her hard-wired urge to fight. Somehow, she was able to conjure the rationality she knew she would need amidst the panic and fear to process her limited options. She had known this was coming eventually. She had prepared for this.

Raymond cut a second strip of tape and, pulling her up by her slight forearms, he maneuvered them both so that he was able to secure her wrists across her chest. The sheet and blanket that had covered her lay crumpled in a heap on the floor. Gracie's short, pink, flannel nightshirt rose up over her thighs. Mesmerized, he stroked the flat, still-firm belly that had housed their offspring, lowering and placing the other of his stone-cold hands in the warm curve of smooth, flat skin that lay above an untrimmed triangle of hair. The nearness of her aroused him. She resisted him with all her might, violently arching her torso backwards into the mattress.

Raymond shoved her arms upwards, taking her small, round breasts into the palms of his hands. He lowered his mouth onto a pillow of soft, warm, flesh. His tongue teased around her nipple. Gracie bolted upwards, revolted yet strengthened by this sudden, repellant assault. Much to his surprise, she knocked him off balance with a rapid twist of her waist and the sharp employment of her shoulder as the only weapon available to her.

"I said, stop," Raymond hissed, smacking her on the side of her face. "Look at me." He raised his head and let out a dry, silent sob. "I need you, babe. Can't you see?"

Gracie rolled to her right. And mustering the last ounce of strength within her she wrapped her legs around his scrawny middle and gripped him by the knees. The rocking motion that ensued rolled the pair from the bed. They landed, entwined, with a thud on the hardwood floor.

# CHAPTER TWENTY

# A FIGHT ON THE STAIRS

Downstairs in the parlor, Adamaria stirred. The sound of a dull thump — a leaden body hitting the floor broke her slumber.

"You two stay here," she ordered the boy and his dog. Two sets of sleepy eyes met hers in the low light of the tree-lit room as she unfolded her sleep-heavy limbs and shuffled past their warm and comfortable makeshift bed, avoiding one of the buckets she'd set out to catch any leaks. The boy and the dog were half asleep still, disturbed more by her stirrings than the sudden, dull thud overhead.

"Oh my! Sounds like someone's taken a tumble," Adamaria announced, as much to herself as to her company. "Never you mind though, for there'll be no more addin' to any commotion 'til mornin'. No-one needs to catch a sight of you two 'til daylight. Then we'll have some explainin' to do."

It was technically already Christmas Day, though she'd had so little sleep she was in no mood to start the holiday any earlier than necessary. Adamaria hadn't given much thought earlier as to how strange the presence of her uninvited guests would appear to Gracie and the girls.

"A little more shut-eye would be wise," she muttered.

Upstairs, Raymond had rolled himself back on top of Gracie's body, effectively pinning her to the floor of her room. As he struggled to a kneeling position, he hauled her upwards from the waist so that they were face to face. He reached beneath her and hoisted her to a standing position, grasping the cold, exposed skin of her buttocks. The neck of her nightshirt was stretched over her shoulder, revealing the top of the tiger tattoo.

"What the fuck is that?" Raymond asked, yanking it down for a better look.

A hot, prickling sensation — pure fear, traveled the length of Gracie's spine in sickening, slow motion. Bile that was stuck in the back of her throat washed down her windpipe.

"Try one more move and our little angels in there, those kids of ours who've done nothin' to no one — they'll get an eyeful of what's comin' to their sneaky, cheatin' mother. Is that what you want, Gracie?"

It took more courage and composure than Gracie was aware she had within her to play him and she locked her eyes dead center in his. She forced an unblinking contact as she shook her head, vehemently side to side, all the while desperately willing her crumpled nightshirt to fall from its fixed position under her armpits. Gracie was dangerously exposed and more vulnerable in that moment than she had ever been.

"Don't worry. I've no time to mess with you," he could smell her fear, like a cat on the hunt. "Though hell knows I've every right. We're leavin', you an' me, girl," he whispered in Gracie's ear, his hot, damp breath a scourge on her skin. The saccharine tone he'd switched to sounded to her in her silent panic, all the more sinister. "Someplace we can get ourselves properly re-acquainted is all — in our own time. Nothin' bad's gonna happen here as long as you do as I say."

Fat tears welled in Gracie's eyes, a signal of her weakness in his hands and leading him to believe the fight was over. And yet she remained stone-cold clear in her own mind that she would focus her fight with a level head in order to maintain any slight degree of control over the terror he'd induced.

Play him at his own sick game, she counseled herself silently. Raymond, on the other hand, was all the more emboldened by the relative ease of having implemented his plan this far. His adrenaline had begun to slow, for he had her where he wanted her. Finally — well, almost. He'd deduced that emotional blackmail worked best when it came to Gracie. Whatever she'd done to destroy their family, messing up the kids by taking them and keeping them from him, he'd been absolutely sure she'd put the safety and welfare of their girls before herself when push came to shove.

Raymond scrunched a chunk of Gracie's hair in a tight ball in his fist, holding it firmly at the back of her head. She winced as he pushed her toward her bedroom door. She felt the pressure of the tip of his knife on the center of her spine.

"Someday soon we're all gonna be together," he promised. "Happy families. The four of us: the kids, you and me. Like it used to be. You'll see."

Gracie's immediate fear, other than her girls waking and being forced to witness what was happening, was not for herself, but for the safety of her mother. She still hoped he would do no physical harm to his own children, but she knew full well that Raymond loathed Adamaria and possibly even more than he professed his hatred for her, his wife.

She was acutely aware of how lightly her mother slept. Don't you do it, Mom, she willed, silently, as if she were sending a telepathic message directly into her mother's mind. Knowing that Adamaria did not possess even half the strength to take on the crazed figure of her soon-to-be-ex-son-in-law, there was nothing to be gained from having her involved.

Please, God. Please, please, please, just leave her be, Gracie manifested, over and over in her head.

Gracie told herself that if she did whatever it was that Raymond wanted, her time to fight would come, but only after she had made sure that the others were safe. Later she would work out some way to escape, even if she knew she was risking the sacrifice of her own self by allowing him to take her from the house. Gracie figured she had no choice but to play along, allow him to think she was compliant. She'd stopped struggling as she stepped into the shadows of the upstairs hallway, leading Raymond to believe she was moving willingly toward the stairway with him behind. She sensed a smugness in his strength, the pressure of the knife point. Pride comes before a fall, she hoped, gathering her senses. Be careful. Just wait.

What neither husband or wife had bargained for was the figure of the woman they'd assumed was fast asleep and tucked up in bed, manifesting itself in the shadows at the bottom of the stairs.

"Jesus Christ," Raymond let out a long, thin moan of disbelief. "Look who it is. Who'd have guessed she'd be up and about mannin' the fort at this time of the mornin'?"

Adamaria flicked a light switch, which shone an instant and jarring spotlight directly on the scene. Her daughter, bound and gagged, barefoot and scantily dressed, was balanced by her bare toes on the edge of the top stair. The hall chandelier flickered, on cue. Adamaria let out a violent, owl-like screech, her hands flying over her mouth at the sudden thought of her sleeping granddaughters.

"Quit your interferin', bitch," Raymond spat down the stairs. "Step aside. This is none of your businesses. I've come for what's mine."

"Not on my life," Adamaria shot back. She anchored her hands on her robe-encased hips and puffed out her chest as if it might expand to fill the space between them. Adamaria was fully fired up as she prepared herself for whatever he'd think to do next. Raymond and Gracie watched spellbound as she hopped from foot to foot, weighing her options. As she took a first, tentative step up onto the staircase, she voiced a prayer to the Madonna and signed the shape of the cross on her thumping chest.

"You out of your mind, woman?" Raymond glared down at her. He circled the flashing knife around from its pressure point in the center of Gracie's spine to rest at a fresh spot at the front of her throat. "Neither you or your goddammed prayin' is gonna stop me now."

Adamaria grabbed the ornate wooden newel at the bottom of the staircase and drew in one more deep, dramatic breath as she found her balance. She froze to the spot for another second or two before she propelled herself upward in a speed that both shocked and impressed her as much as the two who were teetering at the top. It was Raymond's turn to stare — stunned and open-mouthed for a moment in an almost comic, suspended animation as the barrel-like Adamaria launched herself toward him.

The force of her short, stout body knocked the knife clear from his sweaty grip and the pair of them fell backwards in a tangled heap of confusion taking Gracie down with them.

While this commotion was occurring, still, by some fortunate miracle of childhood wonder, the little girls continued in their candy cane dreams of oblivion, even with the onset of a shrill and sudden bark that let out subsequently from the parlor below. Peanut had sprung from his master's feet and leapt ahead of him into the hallway. Three sets of eyes looked down from the ground at the top of the stairs as the small dog appeared in the dim light of downstairs. Peanut's basic programming kicked in just in time to back her up. The little dog's learned experiences in the foster home had taught him a thing or two, Adamaria wagered as her mind darted in every direction.

Peanut had sensed the danger the second he'd registered the tenor of her voice in the hallway. He smelled it — the menace in the air. The hair on the animal's back rose into a visible ridgeline, his natural protective instincts honed entirely toward the human who had fed him so generously not a few hours earlier.

Raymond, who lay semi-trapped beneath the bulk of his heavy-breathing mother-in-law, locked eyes with the animal. The small, growling creature held himself in check in a rigid pose, readying to pounce with the next wrong move. The knife had dropped too far out of reach from Raymond for him to attempt to slide it toward him. He barely had time to brace himself as Peanut bared his teeth, snarled and then, quite suddenly, lunged up the stairs.

Peanut deduced that it was Raymond who posed the danger in the tangle of human limbs and torsos. The small animal nose-butted his unexpected full weight directly into Raymond's exposed left arm, releasing his jaws and nipping into his flesh, a first bite that barely broke the skin. Raymond let out a piercing yelp and, flailing angrily, propelled Adamaria to one side. Gracie slid from beneath him in the mayhem as Peanut bared his teeth and snarled.

The dog made contact a second time, this time sinking his yellow, razer-like fangs into Raymond's left thigh.

It was no use Raymond attempting to shake the furious creature off until Peanut himself decided to let go of his grip. Raymond scuffled backwards and into a startled Gracie, as he frantically kicked at the underside of the dog.

"Peanut, back," Mateo instructed, as he followed the sound of the racket into the hallway and rapidly assessed the struggle at the top of the staircase. Adamaria lay sideways on the cold, hardwood floor. She shot the boy a series of pleading looks from her vantage point at the top of the stairs. Peanut pulled back from his opponent at the sound of his master's voice.

Adamaria was aware of the sweet, metallic aroma of Raymond's sweat and blood in the rug beneath their heads.

Meanwhile, the heavily panting dog retreated, awaiting further instruction from Mateo, who, it appeared, had taken the stairs by flight. What happened next was so fast and furious, that Adamaria would struggle to remember the exact sequence of action.

The boy was smaller, weaker than Raymond. The older of the two was not much of a physical specimen, that was clear, yet it was the unfettered anger that lived inside of Raymond that gave him the strength to pose the most danger.

None of them had any reason to suspect the extent of experience that Mateo had under his belt. The abuse he'd endured in his young life trailed back way beyond the foster system. He had defended himself against other, more physically mature kids, having moved around a lot since he was small. It had come as second nature to him by the time he'd entered care, knowingly avoiding eye contact, making his moves in as swift and unexpected maneuver as possible in order to prevent himself from being close enough for his opponent to make striking contact.

Raymond's power control over the situation waned as one hand hung protectively over the ripped and bloody section of the rain-soaked pants on his punctured thigh. The sight of his own blood, compounded by pain and the general panic and confusion of it all did not bode well with his coming down from the medley of drugs and alcohol he had pumped into his system over the previous twenty-four hours. Fury raged in his pumping heart.

Wind and rain rattled and shook the thin pane of glass in the small window at the end of the upstairs hallway. A bolt of lightning lit up a theatrical set of entangled bodies.

"Stop this," Adamaria demanded. "What the devil are you doing, Raymond?" She employed a last-ditch attempt to talk reason into him. "Think of your children."

Gracie had scooted and was huddled in protective guard by the door of the girls' bedroom. She'd yet to recognize the boy as the kid from outside of the church that afternoon as she curled into a ball-shaped doorstop as she gripped her knees within the space inside the restraints on her arms. The sour, acidic taste of shock and disorientation settled in her stomach and nausea waved through her core. She closed her eyes and lowered her head down onto her knees in an attempt to block out the sight of the moaning, marauding Raymond.

Next, Mateo, upon the direct impact of a rapid charge into his narrow shoulder bone, was knocked clear to the floor. Nobody would have believed such a small dog capable, yet Peanut, undeterred, despite his limited frame, leapt up into the fray, biting hard a third time, as he sank his molars into Raymond's right arm. His jaws set in firmly as he swung from Raymond's limb. No amount of fury would fling him off.

The wind wrenched a gutter from the exterior siding. It flapped, noisily, like a metal flag as it hit against the exterior and crashed down audibly into a heap on the concrete pathway at the side of the house.

The look of righteous anger on the boy's face belied his years. His lack of physical maturity and strength was bolstered by his raw emotions — an overriding urge of self-defense. It was as if this fresh, furious sense of injustice had lifted him clear from the ground. A year of pain and suffering, wrath and rage merged into one small, insignificant-looking frame and filled him with fury.

Peanut dropped to the floor, spent. Raymond missed as he attempted to drop-kick the animal with an unhinged furor that was unable to maintain its center of gravity.

Raymond did not anticipate his young mystery opponent's left hook, which came, after, abruptly out of nowhere, leaving him reeling — like his head had surely separated from his body. He was certainly fitter, lighter and better balanced than Raymond who was by then wobbling on his feet, aglow with sweat and blood, lashing out into thin air.

The next of Raymond's furious air-punches made contact, though it soon backfired in snapping an inch-long fracture around the baseline of his right thumb. Adamaria lay close enough to see the dark-blue veins on the inside of the boy's wrists that ran up his skinny forearms. The indignant little dog continued baring his teeth and growling as Raymond's mouth twisted into an ugly shape. He changed tactics and aimed another furious shot into the shadows. This time his fist making target beneath the kids' ribcage.

The boy bent double, though he reared back up again and in a most surprising move, he charged Raymond with his head and deployed, with the grace of a dancer, what was surely his thunderbolt-move. The younger of the two then pounded his fist on his opponent's chest with such sheer force that Raymond's jaw visibly slackened, his eyes widening in shock as he tumbled backwards, his head hitting the hard base of the wooden stair rail and knocking him out. Peanut, having caught his breath, leapt on top of the heaving chest of the downed man — spraying a stream of drool on his face.

"Good dog," Adamaria praised, her lips pursed as her shaking hands instinctively fumbled to release the knotted robe-belt from her waist: "Keep him down, Peanut."

Gracie scooted toward her mother as Adamaria deftly bound a soon-wakeful Raymond's hands at his bony wrists, raising them above his dazed head and securing them to the upper stairwell with a rapid loop of her belt around the newel.

Gracie groaned, scuffled and pointed her foot in the direction of the gleaming steel blade that lay within the reach of Raymond's foot. Adamaria slid over and snatched it up, sliding herself back to where her daughter was crouched to cut through the tape that bound her wrists. Gracie winced as she worked the duct tape from her mouth.

Adamaria, confident that her daughter was able to breathe without fear of hyperventilating, eased herself into a semi-standing position. Her curved back creaked in resistance as she reached down to reassure the still-growling dog.

Raymond roused. And in an instant, before Adamaria had time to catch her own labored breath and move herself out of his orbit, she felt him strike the back of her calf with the full force of the underside of his still-swollen foot. Gracie watched in silent, helpless horror as her mother buckled at the knees and proceeded to roll, face first, half-way down the staircase. Adamaria hit the wall twice as she tumbled. Her rotund little body settled motionless at the bottom of the stairs, curled up into a ball of robe and flesh and fluffy slippers, face down and muted in shock and pain.

Gracie slid forward on her hands and knees and grabbed the knife in clenched hands. Peanut leapt down the staircase, followed in hot pursuit by a knife-wielding Gracie. The panting dog settled by Adamaria's side, whimpering as he gently nudged her white cloud of hair.

"Oh God, no," Gracie repeated, as she felt for her mother's wrist, checking her pulse. Even though she wasn't sure she should, she slowly, carefully, rolled her to one side.

Adamaria was breathing steadily, though her face had turned a scary, ashen color. She lay unconscious a short while before she came around. Her own thoughts were that she was nowhere near ready to give it all up. There was no way she'd ever allow Raymond the satisfaction of being the one to put her out of commission. She had far too much left to do to secure her family's safety and security before she would even think of joining her beloved Aldo on the other side.

Later, sometime after she'd regained consciousness, she swore to herself she'd seen a path of Aldo's muddy footprints on the floor by the side of her resting head. Had he come to her? Had she been so close to crossing over? She figured it must have been the concussion that had put such silly notions into her head.

"Thank God, you're alive, Ma. What I want to know is who are these two? Why are they here for heaven's sake?" Gracie asked, breathlessly, as she tentatively reached for the dog's collar. If she hadn't seen it for herself, she never would have believed the creature capable of such a sustained attack. She was balanced on her heels beside her mother's crumpled frame.

"Do I know you?" she addressed the terrified-looking kid at the top of the stairs diligently making sure that Raymond was not able to worm his way free. "What's your part in all of this?"

The boy remained silent. He clutched his ribs and focused on Raymond, avoiding eye contact with Gracie. She remembered that she'd left her phone on its charger in her bedroom the night before.

She placed her hand gently on her mother's forehead. "Hold on, Mom, hold on. I'm calling for help."

Please God, let her be okay, she prayed, as she ran back up the stairs, knife in hand, panting for air. She had the sense in her panicked state to take a wide berth to avoid the reach of Raymond's curled-up legs and feet, though, without a further thought, she stopped in her tracks and crouched down to what she deemed a safe enough distance from his grimacing face.

"It's my turn now, Raymond. Look at me." She bent low and spoke slowly and deliberately. "Let's see how you like it. Are you ready?" She gritted her teeth and pressed the tip of the knife into the thin stretch of pallid skin beneath his trembling chin and his nervous, wobbling thyroid cartilage.

"Gracie, baby. I'm hurt, can't you see? I'm bit. I'm bleedin'. For the love of our kids, don't you get it? You swore an oath. We both did."

"Call this love?" she replied, bitterly as she pressed harder with the knife's steely tip. Her hands were sticky with adrenaline. Her heart beat fast. For the first time in her life, Gracie experienced the thrill of the instinct to break skin, to press a knife deep into his scrawny neck, to twist it, finish it.

"You're out of your mind, Raymond," she said, holding steady with the tip of the blade. "But you know what? You'll never break me. I'm stronger than you. Always have been. Always will be."

Raymond begged, he blubbered, he sobbed at his wife's knee. He never would have believed it of her, but in that moment, he feared for his life. Gracie finally released the knife from his throat. She stood to her full height and dug the heel of her bare foot into the side of his bruised ribcage.

"Just so you know, it would've been self-defense," she added. Would she have possessed the nerve to slash his throat, at least superficially? She wasn't sure, but she was empowered to have made him think so.

Her nerve-endings were on edge, her sizzling fingertips igniting a strange sensation that shot from the hand that held the knife, up through her arm, across her chest and up into her throat and mouth. It was the bitter, toxic taste of revenge, that of the newly uncaged — a true first for Gracie. Sweet, angelic Gracie. For a brief while she had been someone else entirely. She could smell an alien odor emanating from her pores, taste it. It was as if an altogether foreign being had briefly taken over her body. All the moisture had left her mouth. It tasted like she had taken a teaspoon of bitter baking soda onto her tongue and held it there, un-swallowed.

That fight-or-flight survival instinct, a powerful inner surge had taken hold when it had mattered most. And yet, as she drew breath, the old Gracie prevailed, rational, able to make decisions based on intelligent thinking rather than emotion.

Sweet Gracie, loving daughter, devoted mother, dedicated teacher, was, if she were to admit it, not nearly so much as newly transformed. It had been a long process of becoming true to herself and she had barely recognized it until now. It wasn't that she hated Raymond for all his sins. She'd admitted as much to Julian. What she hated was that she'd ever allowed herself to be aligned with him, a man who knew nothing other than the need to dominate to make himself feel powerful. The compliant, long-suffering wife she'd let herself become was gone. The Gracie who had emerged had given herself permission to finally, fully, let herself in, raise herself up and fight, for what she deserved, for how she wanted her life to be.

"Don't think for one more minute of your miserable life that you are worth my trouble, Raymond," she added as she paced into her room to retrieve her cell phone, and, with shaking fingers, dialed 911. Her eyes remained glued to him as he pulled his knees into the fetal position and moaned.

"Ambulance. Emergency. Yes . . . police. A fight . . . yes, I confirm, two in need of urgent medical care."

Gracie's next call was her most-recently dialed. It was Julian and his family she turned to instinctively, waking him from his sleep, without a second's pause.

# CHAPTER TWENTY-ONE

# NO PLACE TO RUN

Mateo fled. He sprinted, shoeless along the wet, tree-lined city block. To bolt was the instinct he'd acted on first, his deepest fear of being turned-in. He gradually slowed and loped along a ways and stopped for a second to draw breath, the morning air filling the lungs beneath his bruised chest with a sharp, cold, tang.

He'd made a run-for-it the second he'd heard the younger woman call the cops. Peanut, who had followed close to his heels initially, had taken a sudden and unexpected about turn, inexplicably abandoning him after the first half a block, darting back to the house.

It was darkish still, not yet dawn. The storm had passed and the purplish mist that engulfed the street smelled of freshly-washed evergreens doused by the plump raindrops that hung, visibly, like portly diamonds on bare, winter branches. Mateo's sopping-wet socks made a disconcerting sucking sound on the wet sidewalk. He lifted his left foot and bent down to retrieve a sharp rock from the cold, damp fabric between his toes.

He knew he should not have acted on impulse, but there was no getting around his fear of being picked up and taken back into care — or worse, Juvenile Hall for any infractions pertaining to the other man's injuries. He figured he and Peanut had given the dude a pretty good going over between them. And yet, there was no way he would possibly leave Peanut behind to face the consequences alone. His mind raced with fruitless options.

"Shit," he vented, as he reached down and rubbed his feet. Wet socks rendered him all the more vulnerable, offering him little chance of escape. Mateo calculated that he wouldn't get far without footwear and not even his hoodie for disguise before some cop or other was sure to pick him up. Briefly, he weighed up the narrow chances of his sneaking back into the house and grabbing hold of Peanut. The jarring blare of sweeping sirens turned onto the block. A fleet of emergency responder vehicles backed a cop car with its round of flashing lights blasting the sleepy street just as the last of the dark sky lifted over the neighborhood.

Officer Angela Rodriguez was bright-eyed for that hour, it being the start of her shift. She'd volunteered to work on Christmas Day in recent years since she had no kids of her own and considered it a basic kindness to those of her colleagues with little ones at home. It would prove fortunate for all concerned that it was Angela who spotted the boy as he swiveled and ducked for cover behind a heavily laden camellia bush. It was a healthy, mature specimen on the brink of breaking out with a heavy spray of winter blooms against a dense green foliage.

Helper to the priest, the Latin name for camellia the officer noted with regards to the boy's specific choice of hide-out. How appropriate, she figured. As good a Holy Season refuge as any. Only she'd seen him already so it was no use him hiding.

Emerging blooms revealed a white flowered varietal. Her favorite, as an avid back-yard gardener and not as common as the various shades of pink camellias more popularly planted around town.

Given that the officer was in a good mood after a relaxing Christmas Eve, she was in no immediate hurry to bust the kid. Her intuition told her she had this under control.

The movie *To Kill a Mockingbird* had put her to sleep in her recliner, early the previous night. She'd awoken after midnight and had slept soundly in her bed until her alarm went off a few hours later for work. It was even more curious, the kid picking this specific bush for cover, she thought, as she remembered the part in the movie where Jem had cut off all of the camellia flowers in grumpy old Mrs. Henry Lafayette Dubose's yard.

She'd lost count of how many times she'd watched this same old classic since she was in high school. One of these days, I'll sit myself down and read the book she promised herself and not for the first time.

Officer Rodriguez was one of only a handful of female cops in her department and at the tender age of thirty-eight, she was the oldest at that. The most important aspect of her job she believed was to listen up, pay attention, be fair. In what she considered her humble opinion, this basic philosophy was in short supply in way too many police departments around the country.

It was Angela's brand of tried and tested composure that she'd built on over the years, coupled with a finely-tuned character insight that enabled her to size-up the frightened boy in a calm and compassionate manner.

The kid definitely had something to do with the 911 call, she figured, given the timing and circumstances and yet she calculated that his culpability of instigating a premeditated crime was unlikely given that he'd taken to the street in such a state of undress. Poor creature looked scared to death as he'd ducked behind the budding camellia, squeezing himself into as tight a ball as possible on the cold, damp ground.

Officer Rodriguez made an on-the-spot decision. She'd move in with unflappable precision so as not to make matters any worse for the kid, whatever his part in what had gone down.

"You'd best pull over and let me out before you proceed on to the house," she advised, addressing her patrol partner, Officer Jimmy Flynn. It was Jimmy who was behind the wheel. He was even tempered and as tolerant as she was and yet the two of them were as different as apples and oranges in their enthusiasm for action. They'd been paired in the most recent buddy system the chief had doled out.

Angela unbuckled her seat belt in an instant, opened the passenger seat door and, with the grace of a well-toned cat, sprang onto the sidewalk. She had dreamed of becoming a dancer back when she was in junior high and still considered herself more than decently spry.

"Watch yourself with that move," Officer Flynn remarked, employing his trademark deadpan tone as he leaned across the passenger seat to reach for the door. "You ain't no spring chicken no more, Ang."

"I resent that, Jimmy," she replied, turning to give him the eye. She swiveled back on her boot heel and narrowed a set of toffee-colored, wide-set optics, flanked by a striking set of micro-bladed, semi-permanent eyebrows she feared had rendered her face in a somewhat regrettable constant state of surprise. As she launched herself toward the bulky evergreen bush, she ducked to avoid the glistening chandelier of an intricate spiderweb that hung from its upper branches.

"Stop right there. Don't move." She circled the camellia's perimeter, readying herself to frisk the frightened boy. There was no need to escalate the kid's elevated emotions any more than was absolutely necessary. She knew she was taking a chance on the child being unarmed, a knife potentially, though she seriously doubted he was carrying. She'd seen him slip to the ground like a salamander. He knew he was trapped though he'd made a valiant attempt to uncurl himself and slink out into a puddle of mud around the other side of the bush.

"There's no place to run," Angela announced, maintaining her practiced, authoritarian, yet motherly-tone. "Best you give it up, hon." She stepped toward him, hands on hips so that he was able to better size her up from where he was crouched on the ground. A distinctively downy, pre-pubescent face stared up at her. He was younger than she'd thought. After a brief jostling amongst the foliage, she grabbed the boy firmly beneath his arms and yanked him to his knees. In a second, equally smooth maneuver she secured his arms behind his back. This was one of her most tried and tested moves and it had yet to let her down.

"There's no need for handcuffs, as yet," she informed him, "as long as you settle down and answer a few of my questions."

The sky was heavily overcast, the thinnest strips of daylight cutting through the mist. A brief flash of sunlight beamed directly onto the dark green leaves and white camellia buds, turning them momentarily iridescent. Mateo knew not to fight back when it came to a cop. Besides, his knuckles throbbed and his ribs ached. Wet mud seeped through the knees of his loaner sweatpants.

"If you come along with me peacefully, young man, you'll be savin' yourself the serious charge of fleein' the scene of a crime, or worse still, assaultin' an officer," Angela warned.

Mateo groaned, motioning in the direction of Adamaria's house. "It's not me you should be goin' after, it's the dude that's tied to the staircase."

"Then you'll have no problem accompanyin' me, will you?" Officer Rodriquez replied, as she frog-marched the dejected, shivering youth a block along the sidewalk, up the porch steps and back in through the open door he'd run from less than ten minutes before.

As the boy was being led into the house a dazed and bloodied Raymond was escorted down the staircase by Officer Flynn. The two found themselves face-to-face, flanked by an officer-apiece. A wounded and defeated Raymond glared as Officer Flynn multi-tasked with his radio in his free hand as he instructed the driver of a back-up police car.

Mateo and Officer Rodriguez sidestepped a team of paramedics who were expertly strapping the injured and immobile Adamaria to a stretcher.

A forlorn-looking Peanut emerged sheepishly from the shadows beneath a console table, his head held low in his primal shame of having abandoned his master. He yelped with joy, however at the sight of his return. And as the boy broke away from the officer briefly and attempted to scoop the frightened animal into a constrained embrace, Peanut licked his face with such affection and relief, it fairly burst his heart. Angela was able to assess him better by the hallway light as she caught sight of the intriguing, blooded and letter tattooed knuckles on the boy's fingers.

"What's this?" she asked. "SONG BIRD?"

The last of anything close to love and loyalty in Mateo's life had been lost to him in the brief time that the boy and dog had been apart. This much was evident in the form of his four-legged companion's display of adoration and allegiance as Mateo's eyes fast-welled with relief. It was clear that this reunion with his best friend, this furry-family of his, rolled into one wriggling, wiry package of unconditional devotion, was worth whatever trouble he was in.

Officer Rodriguez couldn't help but be moved by the boy's brave attempt to brush away his silent, salty tears with his slight shoulder. She recognized something in the dark, deep pools of his eyes — the measure of grief that was anchored there.

He would risk it all for Peanut. When it had come to the old woman, he justified, he'd at least waited until he'd been sure she'd survived her fall before he'd taken off.

Now, he feared, he was sure to pay the price of him and Peanut being picked up by social services and sent back to the foster home, the place where they'd made him feel like he was a total weirdo, a loser, barely human. Worse still, it would surely be one of the rank group homes he'd been warned of, even in the beat-up condition he was in.

Mateo's needs had been minimal: a taste of Adamaria's home cooked food, the fleeting sense of a home that belonged to a real family. It had seemed to him how he imagined heaven, if there was such a place, one with a fireplace and a real Christmas tree with twinkling lights that stayed on through the night. He should've known such a taste of good fortune was too sweet to last.

Gracie, who had held it together long enough to slip back into the jeans and top she'd worn the previous evening, clothing that smelled of the bar, kept her cool as she methodically gave the officer an abbreviated version of the general picture. Numbness gripped her as she recounted the events of the early hours of Christmas morning. It was as if another person entirely was speaking through her, while anger and outrage festered below the surface. She explained, in as controlled a manner and in as few words as possible, how it was that this total-stranger had mysteriously come to their defense.

"My mom, she had to have let him in. They banded together to protect me, the three of them."

Mateo watched, transfixed as Officer Rodriguez looked from face to face, as yet, she appeared unconvinced.

"Alright then, though I'm not sure what exactly it is that you two are workin' so hard to convince me of." She scratched her head. She was confused. If he was so innocent, then why had the boy run? And what was he doing there in the first place? It would take some deconstruction.

Adamaria struggled to speak clearly in an urgent attempt to back up her daughter's assessment. Her words jumbled on her lips in sounds that were hard for her to form as she lay full-length on the stretcher waiting to be moved. After a while, she gave up, reached out and squeezed Mateo's arm — a signal he gladly accepted as an unspoken alliance as a team of paramedics transported the stretcher carrying Adamaria's motionless body through the front door.

Mateo shook at his core. Try as he might, he could not curtail his display of nerves, a heady combination of half-fear, half-relief. He had no real idea as to why this Adamaria woman was insistent on looking out for him, especially after he had left her like that — laying there on the floor in a crumpled heap. Officer Rodriguez released her hold on his arms and he immediately wrapped them across his narrow chest in a move to contain any more of the raw emotions that revealed how utterly exposed he'd found himself.

Gracie and Mateo were required to give separate, formal, brief statements before she'd be permitted to follow her mother to the hospital. After Gracie made it known she was anxious to make a move, she informed the officer that a friend was on his way to sit with the boy and keep watch while her daughters slept.

"I've asked him to bring his mother," she said. "To take care of the girls."

"Alright, then please first do the kid the decency of a pair of dry socks," Angela replied. "Meanwhile, I'll clean and wrap his hand."

"He may need to see a doctor," Gracie suggested, taken aback at how seemingly rational and in control she saw herself in the other woman's eyes given the immediate aftermath of all that had gone down. "His ribs took a beating and all."

Mateo shook his head in an effusive no. A heavy-set sadness had settled in his eyes. His sorrow was palpable. Angela, who had been unable to carry a pregnancy to term, would have loved a son of her own. After her husband took off, he and his girlfriend wasted no time in producing a couple of kids in the handful of years that had followed. She'd had little choice but to accept and move on, though the loss of what might have been still hurt. Whenever she was around kids of Mateo's age, she was reminded of all that she'd sacrificed.

An auntie to her sibling's kids however many times over, she tended toward a soft, nurturing spot for her nephews and she felt her big heart reach out to this needy looking boy in much the same way. He appeared sad, undernourished, wily and beguiling in a way she was unable to resist. It was something in her DNA. Angela couldn't put her finger on why she was so drawn to rectifying the empathy deficit in the world. It was, as she saw it, harder for her to not act on easing a troubled child's suffering than to put herself out there each time and actually do something about it.

"One in a million," her boss called her. "We need a million more of you in the force."

Mateo could've been any one of her five nephews, not one of them a stranger to her as they sprawled out on the lawn in the back yard of her condo like a pack of long-legged, gangly puppies. The boys frequently scootered or cycled to join her for hot cocoa in the evenings or an ice cream cone on the hot summer days when she was off-duty. Angela liked to think of herself as the go-to aunt in the family, good for confessions and confidences, occasional mediation and treats and, due to her work, she was not easily shocked. What's more, she was able to send them home to their parents after spending auntie quality time, which was a bonus.

This intriguing young fella was being given a cover for some good reason, she reasoned. And that was in his favor. In her experience, if he had been a white kid, his skin not as brown, assumptions on his being guilty of any kind of wrong doing would have been significantly reduced. The system was completely unfair.

"Any specific kind of bird?" she asked, gesturing back to his knuckles. He'd not answered her the first time.

"I'm saying' nothin' I don't have to," Mateo muttered, avoiding the officer's studious gaze as she gently but adeptly rinsed his injured hand under warm water from the kitchen faucet. "'Cept to say that's what my mom c-c-called me. She used to tell me stories about the pajareros, the wild bird grabbers and traders in Mexico — how they take them from the wild in the early morning and sell them as p-p-pets."

"Yeah, and you know what? Songbirds are actually prized in religious ceremonies all over Latin America," the officer's interest was piqued by her memories of stories surrounding the yellow caged-canaries that her dear, late mother had taken such diligent care of under her small, covered deck, in her mobile home plot in neighboring Sonoma.

"It's the fledglin's and the males I heard that are swiped from their natural habitat. The male birds are especially valued for their song."

Gracie returned, her face pale and hollow from holding back tears. She presented the officer with a bandage and antibiotic cream and the wide-eyed boy, in turn, with a pair of thick, brown, slipper socks, a tag still attached.

"An unused gift of my dad's," Gracie explained, her hand shaking as her eyes began to slowly glass over. "Don't worry, he won't miss them. He's no longer with us. We still have a bunch of his stuff."

The continued presence and close proximity of the police officer fostered an uneasy atmosphere in the room, despite Angela's taking considerable pains to maintain a civil, friendly, even chatty tone. It was easy to see that because of her, the two of them, the young woman and the boy were holding their emotions under extra tight control.

Mateo was unable to relax. He visibly twitched and avoided eye contact. He knew too well what it was to be degraded, humiliated, to be put in a position where there was no way out even if it was none of his fault.

"Let's try again with a few more basic questions," Officer Rodriguez continued, softening her voice as Gracie stepped forward to help her with the bandage. "Are you in any way related to any of these people?" she asked the boy, although she was quite sure from what he'd already said that this was not the case.

Gracie stepped between them as an unexpected surge of protection cut through her numbing exhaustion. "No. He's not. But I think it would be fair to ask that he have the opportunity to talk to a lawyer before he's asked to say anything more, pertaining to his personal situation, that is."

"Well, that's okay, but if it should transpire that you're a runaway, Mateo — and homeless," Officer Rodriguez responded, gently. "I want you to know, I've seen plenty of kids get help around here, those who've been out on the streets a short time or months. In the dead of winter, no less. And that being said, homelessness is not a disease."

"The friend I'm waiting on — I should tell you, he's a lawyer," Gracie added, acting on high alert, instinctively repositioning her body to stand directly in front of the boy. "I'd like for them to have a chance to speak in private before we take things further."

"I have no problem with that," said Officer Rodriguez. "Mateo is not under arrest."

The three of them made stilted and awkward small talk until Julian arrived within a quarter of an hour. His mother, Lena, bundled up in a hat and scarf and a heavy, red coat, stood by her son's side.

It came as some relief for Gracie to find out that Lena was well accustomed to dealing with emergencies. She worked as a medical office administrator in town and, conveniently, it transpired that she was known to Officer Rodriguez. The news of this helped ease some of the tension in the room.

"Are you in need of medical care, sugar?" Lena asked Mateo.

"No ma'am," he replied. "I was plannin' on helpin' out a little is all — you know, clearin' the overgrowth in the b-b-back yard for starters," he blurted, downplaying his injuries as he desperately mulled over any plausible excuse for his being there. Julian gave him a subtle once-over, impressed with the kids' youthful ingenuity.

"You all can see this ol' place is in need of a m-m-makeover," Mateo added, for good measure, acting on an intuitive desire to stick close to this rambling safe haven he'd so randomly stumbled upon. He'd never so much as had a sniff of security, not even for one previous second of that past lousy year.

Julian stepped into the light of the hallway. He stopped, inches from Gracie, their eyes searching, interlocking. He had yet to find out exactly what had transpired since he'd seen her home the previous evening other than that it had been unexpected and violent. It didn't take a law degree to connect it to Gracie's ex.

She was holding herself remarkably still. Her overall demeanor was forced, a contrived calm when inside, he knew she was surely roiling. He felt a strong desire to make things right, to help restore a sense of safety after whatever physical and emotional shock it was that she'd suffered. She might appear to be holding herself together, but he guessed the shifting degrees of her inner coping mechanism would show themselves soon enough. Although he was emboldened that she had turned immediately to him, Julian's first priority was to figure out just how comfortable she was in the level of his jumping in to help.

Gracie needed him in the moment, that was clear — but if he'd learned anything the previous evening, it was paramount in his mind to remain respectful of her need to maintain control of her situation. He wasn't about to barge in and take over. Whatever was to happen next was her decision, not his.

They held each other's gaze. There was no need for words. He would simply follow her lead. The bond that had tied them together as teenagers had survived, that much was evident in her desperate call to him that morning. It was more than intact, he realized, despite her extremely precarious situation, the decade apart and all that had happened since. And somehow, she confirmed all of this and more in the way she looked at him that morning.

It was Gracie who broke their silence. His presence brought with it an unspeakably intense relief. She stepped forward and embraced him, tightly.

Her whole being was reassured. It simply seemed to say: "He's here. Julian. At last."

His solid, stable demeanor, his genuine, grounded presence carried a palpable warmth into the cold, narrow hallway. She'd never in her whole life been happier and more grateful to see another person. So, this is what it feels like, she consoled herself, relieved to experience anything at all, let alone such a rush of positive emotion.

Her gravitational pull had called him back into her orbit, she believed. She had let go of the pain, the fear, the inertia (at least prior to the past night's injustices) — and Julian had materialized. He'd come back into her life as if by some cosmic beckoning. Even if it was in nothing more than friendship alone, she reveled in his return, his presence.

"Jeez," she said as she released him from her clutch. She clumsily attempted to lighten the obvious intensity of her need. "Some start to Christmas."

Her knees buckled. She reached out for his arm as beads of sweat formed on her brow. "It's like it comes over me in waves — the shock, small at first, then along comes a rogue, one of those brutal tidal sleepers, knocking me off my feet and sucking me under . . ."

"Hey, you've made it to the other side, Gracie. Whatever happened, it's over —I'm here, we're here," Julian gestured to his mother's presence. "You're unhurt, physically, right? The kids? Where are they?"

"They're sleeping. Thank God for small mercies they sleep through anything."

"They're safe now, with us, you go see your mom."

He turned his attention to the cowering, terrified boy who had retreated and was lurking in the shadows by the stairs.

"I'm Julian," he addressed, holding out a solid hand in greeting. "So, if you're planning on sticking around, then how about you and me go sit ourselves down in the kitchen? Maybe you'll see to it to fill me in on what else it is that you're doing here?"

"He's a little on the young side for a landscapin' position," said Officer Rodriguez as she moved in close enough to make a grab for Mateo's arm if she felt it warranted. She'd been as impressed as Julian by the boy's fast-thinking. But she couldn't risk him doing a second runner.

"But hey, diggin' your hands in the dirt says a good deal about a person," she added. "If you ask me, plants are way easier to handle than people, any day of the week."

Since gardening was how she preferred to purge and re-energize, Angela wondered just how much trauma and loss had led this boy to seek refuge in the brush of an overgrown yard. He may well prove to be a con-man in training for all she knew, buttering them up with his talk of making himself useful around the place. And yet she couldn't help but follow Gracie's lead and soften her stance with him.

"Why don't you tell our friend Julian here what's goin' on? And after that, I have to agree, if it works out in your favor, if it does appear you might make yourself useful around here in the short term at least, then maybe you don't have to take off so soon."

Gracie was grateful and relieved that Julian's mother had been willing and able to rise to the occasion so swiftly in her hour of need. Her own reasoning was intact, if not impaired, given how distressed and frightened she'd felt. As far as her girls were concerned, they had no idea Julian even existed, let alone his mom. But she'd instinctively known that a motherly figure in the house was the best she could have asked for at this moment. Leaving them in the care of a police officer, nice as she appeared, would not have been an option. Order was not entirely lost amidst the chaos.

At least, she figured, her girls would awake to discover the calm and kindly Lena along with Julian in the kitchen, aside from the boy and Officer Rodriguez — though strangers all. But first, Lena took Gracie aside and insisted on driving her to the hospital.

"You're in shock, sugar," Lena said. No arguing, no nonsense. "There's absolutely no way you're driving yourself across town."

"Okay. Then I'll leave it to you to explain who you are to the girls when you get back," Gracie conceded, as she reached out and took Lena's firm hand in hers. It was a comforting gesture, the simplest of pacts between two mothers. Gracie's face tightened. Don't cry, don't cry, she warned herself as she fought to hold in her elevated emotion.

She was unable to stop herself as she let out a loud, convulsive sob, tears welling and tumbling and running free down her flushed, pink cheeks. Julian moved toward her as her eyes settled on a faded square on the wall behind Lena's head. It was where her wedding photo had hung.

"I'm so sorry for all of this, for dragging you both into this. But you being here for me, for my mom and my girls and on Christmas especially, I can't thank you enough."

She wiped her eyes with the back of her sleeve and tried not to choke too uncontrollably as she sobbed. "Please don't think of us as a disaster. It's done. I just need to be sure that my mom's gonna make it through."

Lena held on to Gracie's hand. Julian stood beside Gracie, his arm around her shoulder. In one fluid move, Lena wrapped Gracie and Julian in an enormous bear hug, which was so unexpected, it brought a fresh stream of tears to the younger woman's eyes. Gracie was by now completely spent. Though she remained on high alert, internally, furious, disgusted and saddened by Raymond's behavior. The sense of humility she felt toward the small group in her midst that had turned out in the early hours to support her helped.

And yet it was hard for her to move, the blunted effect of trauma on her mind and body had slowed time to a crawl, though she'd not had a second in which to begin to process any of it. She felt her stomach muscles constrict and her heart skip a beat.

"Hush now," Lena urged, soothingly, as she released Gracie and Julian from her embrace and removed her cream-colored cashmere hat and scarf. She shook out a peal of loose, shoulder length, soft, grey curls and duly set about fluffing them into shape in the hallway mirror. She grinned at a largely speechless Gracie, in such a reassuring and spontaneous manner that everyone, not just Gracie, felt at least a little better than they had about the situation before the capable, solid and unflustered Lena showed up.

# CHAPTER TWENTY-TWO

# JAILBIRD

Raymond slumped awkwardly in the back seat of Officer Flynn's patrol vehicle. He had been read his rights and arrested on suspicion of attempted kidnapping and aggravated assault. His head hung low on his chest. He winced at each throbbing beat from his injured foot to his pulsating thumb, the puncture wounds on his thigh and arms. The early morning street scene was deserted, aside from several nosey neighbors as they peered out into the dawn from their bedroom windows.

Officer Flynn had instructed him immediately after his arrest that he was to undergo a brief psychiatric evaluation and an initial assessment of his wounds. All Raymond was able to focus on was his urgent desperation to be numbed, to not feel anything, the physical pain, the despair, the anguish inside of his head. He cared nothing more in that moment but to have it all obliterated. This was not at all how he'd planned his holiday reunion with his wife and children. His plan had gone diabolically wrong from the start.

Now he wished as much as anything that he'd given up his calamitous campaign after the women had failed to show for the children's service. Raymond shut his eyes and pictured the unopened gifts on the floor of his truck. It was the kid with the crazy mutt, that furious, scrawny-ass dog that was locked in a jaw clamp that came to mind. Who the hell was he?

What had he been doin' there? His addled imagination raced with a million unanswered questions, not least that his wife was now entirely free to return to cheating on him. Raymond was bleeding still from the dog bites and worse, he was humiliated, taken down, defeated as all hell — first by himself, then by Gracie, her bitch of a mother, a stupid kid

159

and his dog, the screwed-up legal system, the goddamn cop who was taking him in. He didn't know which of it hurt most.

Damp air hung heavily over the valley after the overnight storm. It had settled in his lungs after his initial furious inhale out on the street. His last image of the house where his kids would soon awaken would stay with him for the remains of the day, that and the sight of festive paper and food contents, the tell-tale garbage of the pre-dawn foraging of the racoons, trash strewn across the sidewalk. He'd been escorted through the chaos of it all, a loser's parade, his head held low in the new dawn light.

"Oh well, at least those fuckers got what they came for," he muttered.

He glared out of the cop car window as it transported him over the heavy, steel draw bridge across the Petaluma River. Mist rose from the water in circular coils like ghosts greeting the dawn. A flock of Canada Geese flew alongside in a striking, low formation, heading into the emerging daylight. What he would have given to have broken free of his restraints, taken flight with them, up and away from all of it.

Jealously, Raymond guessed the birds were headed to the nearby wetlands, the same natural habitat where he'd hit the trails for a hit of weed and a liquid lunch break back when he'd worked for the big poultry processor across town. After the rains, when the marshland was filled with water, every kind of bird and wildlife flocked to the swollen riverbank and into the flooded pools.

Raymond had taken uncharacteristic pleasure in looking out for the red-wing blackbirds that were everywhere in the wild marshlands, the males, especially, with their bright-red shoulder pads. He'd learned how to recognize the grebes, gulls and terns, kingfishers, pelicans and cormorants, raptors, the occasional turtle wandering the path. It had been the only good part of working the poultry plant — its proximity to this wide, open space with its big skies — a total escape from all his troubles for a frequent half hour or so. It was as if the creatures of the wild had been placed there just for him as he remembered the big, fat king snake he had almost stepped on in the heat of the summer the week before he was fired.

He'd not once considered the prospect of sharing the place with his wife and kids – not even on a weekend or holiday when the park was filled with families with little ones, out taking a stroll outdoors together in the clean, fresh air. No, he had held on to it as a secret place of his own, away from the pressure and every demand of his dreary life. It was one of the few times in his adult life he'd ever done anything close to taking care of his mental head space, aside from the self-medicating smoking and drinking part, which is what had gotten him fired in the end. Now, he was afraid the only place he was headed for was jail, at least until he'd talk his old man into making bail. Raymond was many things but he wasn't delusional when it came to his calculating all that they might attempt to pin on him.

Nature continued its witness to his state of distress in the watchful form of a flock of ravens perched on a powerline at the entrance to the emergency room. In his mind, they mocked him with a loud and throaty, collective clamor as the officer escorted him beneath.

Nothing would have been of less appeal than a visit to the ER in handcuffs on the early hours of Christmas Day had he not been hurting so. Raymond was in no mood to make eye contact with the motley assortment of injured and sick, many of them late night holiday revelers by their attire, most of them still sobering up while they waited in line to be seen.

He resented being seen handcuffed and limping as he was escorted and duly paraded by the pan-faced Officer Flynn, conscious of the blood-stiffened fabric sticking to his skin around the incision marks.

"These goddamn bites are fuckin' killin' me, man," he yelped in protest, after the miserable news was delivered of a two-hour or more wait from his place at the bottom of a list of the random assorted medical emergencies that had taken place between the night of Christmas Eve and the early hours of Christmas morning.

"Come on now. How much harm can a five-pound dog cause?" Officer Flynn, Jimmy, loosened his belt a notch to relieve his bloated stomach from the lingering effects of the prime rib supper that he and his wife, Marla had cooked up for the two of them and his folks the night before.

"Screw you, dude," Raymond replied, giving him the middle finger.

Finally, a doctor appeared, a spray of runaway salt and pepper tangles escaping from her braid. It had been a long night. Raymond was mesmerized by the lines on her tired but attentive face as she deftly administered a tetanus shot and tended his wounds by first flushing the shallow punctures on his arm and thigh. He tried to read her take on his condition, his being there in handcuffs, though she remained neutral, giving little away with regards to judgement except to recommend an X-Ray for a suspected fracture to his thumb and a series of antibiotics.

"Given that we don't have access to the dog's immunization records as yet, until animal control is able to make a full assessment, that is, I'm making notes for a full re-check for any signs of potential redness, swelling, warmth, foul odor, or any whitish, yellow discharge that may indicate infection or possibly even Rabies," the doctor advised.

Jimmy jotted down her instructions. Raymond, compliant throughout his care, grew increasingly jittery.

His lacerations failed to present any initial overt cause for concern. A temporary cast was set on his hand. However, the pressure of Peanut's tiny jaws and razor-sharp teeth had, as Raymond was about to discover, already inflicted serious damage to the tissue under the skin on his thigh. Unbeknown to all, it was an underlying injury that would, and in shocking speed, severely impair the healthy function of his body.

Completely oblivious to this, a bitching, moaning and by-then thoroughly depleted Raymond was informed that he would be booked in at the police station, county jail being full to overflowing. He overheard Officer Flynn recount on the radio that a seasonal spree of offenders was awaiting trial for felonies and misdemeanors ranging from a particularly grisly first-degree intentional homicide to multiple Driving Under the Influences, trespassing and a rash of holiday shoplifting.

The officer, who was feeling the effects of a self-induced punishment of a microwaved breakfast of his left-over holiday dinner escorted Raymond through the secure and controlled entryway to the police station. He felt a twinge of indigestion as he ordered Raymond to stop at a yellow line for a routine weapon and illegal contraband check.

Jimmy, having determined there were no additional weapons, promptly set about inputting Raymond's personal details into the computer. Afterwards, he duly instructed the injured arrestee that he would, as a matter of routine, be entitled to a full follow-up physical within fourteen days.

"So, keep on whinin', Raymond, by all means – though you'll get all the care you'll need in due course. Including a permanent cast."

Raymond's rapid breathing picked up pace, his mental distress all the more impacted by the symptoms of sepsis that had begun to spread a series of tentacles throughout his body.

By the time ten digital fingerprints, mug shots, saliva, hair samples and a second, more comprehensive and demoralizing strip search were complete, Raymond's minor criminal background records, electronic court orders and child support arrears having been made evident to the officer were the least of his worries.

Raymond's knife, which had been confiscated by Officer Flynn at the scene of the alleged crime, was neatly wrapped in a plastic bag and put away as evidence. His keys and wallet, removed from his bloodied clothing during the strip search, were impounded along with the knife. Raymond struggled to keep his mouth shut as he was issued a folded, orange jail uniform and a receipt for his personal belongings.

"All yours," Officer Flynn said in an attempt to make light, given the Christmas booking date.

"I wanna talk to a lawyer," Raymond rebuffed the offer of a subsequent round of antibiotics along with a plastic water bottle.

"Oh, you'll have access to court services in due course," Jimmy replied, ushering a jittery Raymond to an uncomfortable-looking chair. "What I suggest you do right now, bud, is down the meds like the doctor said. Drink the water and place your free phone call to a family member or friend, someone who'll advocate for you from the outside in the short term."

"And how long do you expect all this bullshit to take?" Raymond asked, looking around with disgust at his grim surrounds. There were no beds in the holding cell which otherwise housed a stark urinal and an old model television set which was airing the Bay Area holiday morning's breaking news.

"Oh, well, typically, arrestees generally expect to be here anywhere from twelve to twenty-four hours before bein' transferred to County," the consistently non-plussed officer replied. "But come to think of it, unfortunately for you this bein' Christmas and a Friday to boot makes for some real bad timin'."

Typically, as Jimmy explained, in order to hold Raymond for the full seventy-two-hour review rule period, a prosecuting attorney's office would have to file criminal charges. The officer winced.

"See — the thing is, the seventy-two-hour review rule period does not include Saturdays, Sundays or holidays."

"What the fuck?"

Officer Flynn calculated Raymond's specific roll of the dice on the calendar of crime. He felt bad for him, given the circumstances and his injuries as he matter-of-factly laid out, in detail, how it was that the precise day of the week that Christmas had fallen that year made it an especially unlucky day for Raymond to have gotten himself arrested.

"Pretty much gives the authorities an extra three days on top of the seventy-two-hour rule to decide if they have a case against you — or not."

Raymond wasn't sure which was worse: the stark holding cell in the police station or the prospect of waiting out all they'd attempt to charge him for in the medium/maximum security facility of County Jail. Pre-trial and sentenced inmates were hardly the company he'd had in mind for himself in the period between Christmas and New Year.

It was a miracle and he knew it that he had evaded jail time thus far, considering his sketchy past. And so, it was Raymond's vivid imagination and the grim scenes from the prison shows he watched on tv that conjured the unwelcome images in his mind of a bunch of violent, depressed criminals mooching around in a mass incarcerated, post-Christmas funk. And then there'd be the stench, he reminded himself. One of the things he could deal with least was the notion of being trapped amongst a legion of stale, male body odor — heavy traces of ammonia and laundry detergent he imagined mixed up with a bunch of old fried food and fear.

He wasn't left alone for long within the lesser-offending walls of the holding cell in the early hours of Christmas morning. Raymond stared, silently, as an older man, his skin, turkey-like, gaunt and creased, faded ink on every visible inch of his salmon-colored gizzard-like neck, was ushered in a half-hour after he himself had landed there. The old man shuffled past him, wordlessly, as if Raymond were invisible, his bloodshot, watery blue eyes swimming listlessly around the ceiling of the room searching for cracks in the corners for what was left of his conscience to slide through and a chair in which to slump his bag of bones.

Raymond demanded to make his phone call. He woke his own old man from a whiskey-soaked slumber to break the news. Least of Raymond's worries, he announced, was that he'd not be making it over to the casino restaurant in Rohnert Park for their pre-booked dinner for two. To think, Raymond had fantasized calling his father that day to cancel, to announce that he was back with Gracie. All he'd wanted was to get his own damn wife back.

"The woman's hell bent on my sufferin'," Raymond muttered into the phone after he'd impatiently repeated his current predicament at least two times. His insistence on it having been Gracie at fault was met with deaf ears. Even his own father declared he'd had enough of hearing it.

"You fucked-up pressin' on with it, son," was the extent that Raymond-Senior was able to muster in the way of sympathy after mulling the situation over for a minute or two. "Royally, I'd wager, though the drill is that you're gonna be classified accordin' to the level of danger they consider you pose. You're askin' me to make your bail? My answer, Ray-Ray, is that you made your darn bed one time too many."

While father and son were hashing it out, lethal bacteria further infiltrated itself within the deep tissue beneath the laceration on Raymond's thigh.

By the time he ended his call, the area around the bite to Raymond's thigh warmed to the touch and it had since begun to swell. He was preoccupied with his wasted life, wondering too late where he had gone wrong, demanding of himself what might have been. Though he was unaware, there was too little time for him to rectify the past, his mistakes, his lost opportunities, his bad behavior.

Officer Flynn had witnessed the tetanus shot and Raymond's wounds having been thoroughly flushed not hours before. He had no reason to suspect the litany of disaster about to further unleash within the offending thigh hidden beneath a layer of Raymond's orange jump suit.

Raymond experienced a strange, new, dizzy sensation.

"Sucks for you," he said, rather than voice his concern. "Spendin' Christmas with me."

"It's my job," Officer Flynn retorted, with a shrug. "And if I were you, I'd focus on gettin' myself outta here by New Year."

# CHAPTER TWENTY-THREE

# DOCTOR'S ORDERS

Gracie stepped out of a rideshare vehicle onto Liberty Street under the bright canopy of an orange-blue, watercolor sky. The heavens had taken on the familiar, washed-out effect that followed a big storm and the palette of blanched colors that saturated the street was surreal, a film-like exposure over the sidewalk in front of the house.

All around, proud and steeply-pitched rooftops, stately Sycamore trees and even the two tall church spires were brushed by the faintest of winter sunlight that hovered celestially above the earth's atmosphere.

So much rain. It had been calming and restorative coming in after wildfire season, but its relentless downpour had grown steadily depressing by the time Christmas rolled around. As she climbed the steps to the front porch, Gracie glanced back at the tree-lined sidewalk, the natural world appeared to her now satiated and everything man-made had been refreshingly, stonewashed clean.

Gracie had remained by her mother's side at the hospital that morning as they'd awaited the attending emergency room doctor and, afterwards, to see Adamaria settled into a room where she was to remain for at least a couple of nights for further tests and observation.

"Well, you know what? We're still here, Ma," she'd encouraged, her voice trembling as she'd held tightly on to her mother's hand. She'd almost watched her die. The two of them had suffered a brutal attack. Though Gracie was reeling in the added after-shock of Raymond's assault in her room, she was clear-headed in her realization of how close they'd been to something unspeakable.

Adamaria had suffered a minor stroke. Gracie had composed herself once again, attempting to control the shakes. It helped to learn that her mother had escaped a fractured wrist, or worse still, a broken a hip from the fall.

The attending physician explained to her how the movement of a clot from Adamaria's heart to her brain had caused an embolism. Though Adamaria was weakened by it she persisted on in her usual, determined manner.

"The boy," she'd insisted, gesticulating with her hands in an animated fashion. "My little Mousebird. Don't let them take him away."

"But Ma," Gracie had placed her hand on her mother's arm. "Who the heck is he? Really, it's time to spill the beans. What business did he have in our house last night?"

Adamaria squeezed her daughter's hand. Her eyes drooped and welled with tears. "A little kindness is all…"

"Yes, yes, I know . . ." Gracie had replied, squeezing back. "Isn't that what you're always telling us?" she asked. "Be kind, for everyone you meet is fighting a harder battle? Or something along those lines."

"Plato," Adamaria replied, attempting a nod, her mouth working hard to form the words.

"Ah, well if you say so. You're the boss, Ma. Though I never expected you as a softie — you of all people, exposing the security of our house to a total stranger. On Christmas Eve. Aren't you the dark horse?"

Gracie had figured if it had been one or both of her girls who'd been put into the precarious position that she'd found herself plunged into during Raymond's marauding, early morning invasion, she wouldn't have thought twice as to throwing herself into the ring, either. Adamaria had unselfishly put her own life at risk for her daughter.

Gracie couldn't fathom all that had taken place in the hours between her returning home, the boy making his appearance and Raymond's crazed intrusion. Whatever had prompted Adamaria's seeing fit to take in the mystery kid along with his feisty little dog in the first place, her mother, unable to articulate with ease, had refused to throw any light on the subject. Gracie hoped at least that Julian was getting to the bottom of it all back at the house.

If their cloistered existence, the home she'd considered her one safe space, would remain untarnished by the events of the past night, Gracie prepared for whatever strange new forces were at play.

"Okay, I sort of get it, Mom," she'd assured. "Whatever's going on with this boy, if it was those angels of yours that brought him to us, then the very least he deserves is our cutting him some slack, offering a little support — the few things we are able to offer as it happens."

Adamaria had beamed, a reassuring flush of color returning temporarily to her cheeks.

Gracie had added: "Julian will help us figure out what's up, I'm sure. And we'll make room, temporarily if that's what will make you happy. That's only if the kid and his dog is open to cooperating, to playing by our rules."

The doctor had encouraged Gracie that the right thing to do was for her to return home, to leave her mother to some hours of rest.

"Assuming you have support, yourself. You've had a harrowing night by the sounds of it," he'd added.

He'd detailed to Gracie that it was vital for Adamaria to keep an eye on her blood pressure and cholesterol going forward. Gracie quieted the many unanswered questions in her mind as the doctor recommended her mother ease up on the more rigorous of domestic tasks. "What she needs most is a significant reduction in stress coupled with the gradual introduction of daily gentle exercise," he'd said.

Before she'd left, Gracie spoke candidly to her mother. "You hear that, Ma? Things at home are gonna change," she said, "You've no choice now but to loosen your grip." Gracie understood how Raymond's desperate move had, in effect, brought the crisis of their household's loaded tension to an unavoidable head.

She'd sat back long enough and allowed her single-minded and tenacious mother to orchestrate the myriad duties of full-time caretaker for their house and family.

The new year promised a shake-up in the order of things, starting with Adamaria being given no alternative but to accept a period of bed rest, followed by rehabilitation and drug-therapy to prevent any more clots from developing.

As it turned out, Gracie had another two weeks of winter vacation ahead of her, which, she assessed, would gift her time to fast-track changes in their domestic regime.

She promised herself she'd resolve a workable schedule in which Adamaria was no longer responsible for the brunt of the cooking and house work. If Gracie and the girls were to remain in the house with her mom (with the addition of the boy for the time being), then she would just have to get on with stepping up her impromptu role as next-generation matriarch without making her mother feel stripped of the title that meant most to her. Given her mother's incapacitation, it would be a challenge that neither of them had any option but to embrace.

Officer Rodriguez was standing in the open doorway making a call as Gracie climbed the steps, two-at-a-time, still thinking it all over and relieved to be back at the house. She was by then eager to reassure her girls that all would be well with their Nonna. The numbness she'd felt earlier and her subsequent wobbles she'd felt in the hospital subsided sufficiently for her to stride up the steps. The friendly-faced officer pulled the front door to a partial close so that they were able to talk in private.

"So, the dog was chipped," Angela explained. "Peanut is registered to a family in Stockton. The boy, Mateo, is reported a runaway, as I'd suspected. Foster home. Well known to protective services."

"And?" Gracie asked. "Why did he run away? That's what we need to know." Gracie suspected that if he had been a white kid, there would have been more of a concerted effort to find him by now.

"I'm hopin' that your very capable boyfriend has managed to get him to open up a little," the officer replied. "They've had a chat, but from what I was able to decipher, Mateo was reluctant to go into detail as distressed as he is at the prospect of bein' sent back."

"What happens now? And, by the way, Julian and me, we're not . . ."

"Right. Whatever you say," Angela dealt her a loaded look, the kind that one woman gives another when discussing matters of the heart. "Well, it bein' Christmas and all, if you and Julian . . ." she emphasized his name, making Gracie blush, "especially with him being a lawyer and all, should agree to look after Mateo in the short term and the boy is not considered too much of a flight risk, I figure he may be allowed to remain in your care until we work out what's goin' on with him. Whatever he's facin' today will be the same tomorrow, right? Christmas calls for somethin' of a special circumstance in my opinion. He seems to want to stick around. The dog will remain in animal services until all tests are in."

"I see," Gracie replied. This officer was certainly out of the ordinary in her experience. As a teacher, Gracie had met several police officers with skills in dealing with minors, but Officer Rodriguez was special when it came to the compassion and humility she'd shown. "Thanks. Whatever the situation, the kid sure made a big impression on my mom. This kind of connection doesn't happen very often, let me tell you. And it's a fact — he and his dog saved our skin."

"And I should tell you, it's your daughters who made my day this far. Don't often meet such sweet and well-mannered kiddos," Officer Rodriguez added, smiling ear to ear. "They've been the perfect little hosts while you've been gone, despite them wakin' up and findin' me in their kitchen in my scary ol' uniform."

"Too young to be intimidated," Gracie replied. "I guess they shared the Panettone?"

"Yes, a small slice and it sure was delicious. And that kitchen — all those vintage fixtures, like steppin' back in time. And on Christmas." She paused as she met Gracie's tired eyes with her own. "Are you okay, hon? I mean, we have services to help at times like this."

Gracie looked away. "If you wouldn't mind letting Julian, Lena and the girls know that I'm home, I just need a few minutes to myself, to freshen up," Gracie replied, changing track as she forced a self-conscious smile. Her eyes had given her away. It had been a harrowing morning. All she really wanted to do was to curl up in a ball and collapse.

She summoned the energy to take the stairs slowly and softly in her socks, careful not to slip on the smooth wooden surface and pausing at the top of the staircase. Did it all truly happen, she asked herself, as she replayed the hideous events of the early hours? Someone had left a sponge and a spray bottle of stain remover on the rug where the remnants of a fresh blood stain had seeped into the fibers. Gracie shuddered. She shook off a sudden onset of goosebumps, a repeat round of delayed shock. It manifested itself in an overwhelming urge to dissolve into a puddle, a bottomless pool of liquid relief. Somehow her sheer mental strength lasted long enough to carry her through the events of the morning and back up those stairs, though she knew not how or even that she'd fully had it in her.

Gracie flopped on the edge of her bed. Someone, most likely Lena, had thoughtfully put it back together for her in neat, nurses' corners. She felt like a hollowed-out rag doll that had lost its stuffing. Her hands brushed her soft, flannel bedsheets with their cheery, faded snowflake design as she fought off the urge to collapse, to burrow under her duvet. But it was still morning and the noisy crows were back, calling to her absent mother from their usual perch. It was not yet noon and she remembered that her girls were downstairs patiently awaiting her return, confused at the very least by the presence of their unexpected guests, despite their reportedly chatty demeanor.

Off came her jeans, next the shirt that smelled of the bar and now the hospital. Again, Gracie pushed aside her desire to dive deep beneath the covers and submit to the sleep of the bone-weary. Though a part of her brain was still on high patrol, scanning for threats, the concept of freedom, at long last, was intoxicating. Raymond was under lock and key. He'd gone too far this time and she knew she was freer of him than she'd ever been.

Rather than encase herself between the warm, flannel casings and risk the pull of sleep, she flopped back against her pillow for several minutes, her eyes propped open, soaking in the kaleidoscope of colors and patterns, textures and daylight that played out on the ceiling. Raymond had intended on wreaking havoc in that same spot only hours earlier and yet, here she was, back home, her strained senses still alert and agog with the sheer adrenaline of having resisted his force.

You're more than this, she consoled herself. Don't you ever forget it.

What to tell the children with regards to her reckoning on their father's inevitable jail time? This was what concerned her most. Gracie was accustomed to dealing with more than the occasional family drama at work. She prided herself on her thinking on the spot when it came to never coming close to overloading a child with too much information — or not enough.

She would be honest with them, she decided, as always. An edited version, but honest. Best the girls understood, going forward, that their daddy was not about to show up at any time soon, upsetting them all, unannounced. She fixed her gaze on a strip of peeling, rose-pink, trellis-patterned wallpaper that she'd disliked intensely as a teenager, but, now, considered oddly comforting given its own original legacy of stalwart endurance.

Gracie readied herself to face the little group gathered around the kitchen table, but not before a quick change into a fresh pair of jeans and a comfortable, long-sleeved, t-shirt emblazoned with the head of a reindeer motif on the front. She'd laid it out on a chair before bed the night before. It felt like an eternity ago. It would be the extent of her cheerful holiday attire for the children's sake.

Gracie lingered a short while longer as she stood and slowly brushed her hair before the open-drawers of her dresser, beside which a gentle, smiling Jesus gazed directly back at her, his twinkling blue eyes set into all-familiar creamy white face. His cascading sandy-hair fell to his shoulders in gentle waves and there was a fluffy white lamb tucked tenderly beneath his blue-cloaked arm. A ray of sunbeams arched above his beautiful head. This saintly, benevolent being met her directly at eye level. As a child, her mother had insisted nightly that Gracie make the sign of the cross in reverence to what she now considered a culturally misleading interpretation of the Almighty as she'd readied for bed.

Gracie considered her mother's over-zealous taste of Catholic symbolism was over-doing it for modern times but she hadn't the heart to offend her by removing this softly-focused, over-romanticized and thoroughly white-washed version of Jesus from her bedroom wall.

And yet, that morning, for the first time in more years than she cared to recall, Gracie stood before him. She traced the outline of an upright cross on her chest, thanking any and all of the many and unnamed additional powers that had delivered her safely to that moment. The fact that she and her family had survived the shock and horror of Raymond's failed abduction was testament enough in her mind that higher forces were in play.

Also, as I'm not done yet, she added, looking him in the eye, for whatever reason it is that you've seen fit to send us this stranger and his dog, I promise I'll do my best to pay it forward.

Downstairs, Lena looked up and her warm smile lit up the room as Gracie walked through the kitchen door. Lena sat directly across from Julian and Mateo, the girls flanking her on either side at the kitchen table. The youngest, Rosa, was enthralled by this new friend's every word. They so rarely had guests, if ever. Lena, peppermint scented and perfectly manicured, was an instant hit. Gracie noticed how Mateo's bandaged hand rested on the table. An enticing aroma of hot chocolate, vanilla and cinnamon filled the room.

"How good it's been getting to know these two young ladies," Lena exclaimed, as she extended a polished hand to each of the children while holding Gracie's eye. "Bless them." Izzie and Rosa, peachy-cheeked and cozy in their warm, holiday pajamas, were mesmerized by the crimson varnish of her perfect nails. They barely batted an eyelid at their mother's late appearance. Though Gracie had anticipated their concern as to her whereabouts, she was nothing but relieved by the sight of two sets of saucer-shaped blue eyes lighting up, as yet unaware as to the specifics of why their grandmother had been taken into hospital. Gracie had decided to postpone a more detailed explanation until the next day. Let them have their Christmas first.

"Isn't Nonna comin' home?" Izzie implored, her cheerful young face suddenly crestfallen as she scanned the room and the space past the kitchen door into the hallway for signs of her grandmother. Julian and Lena had deliberately outlined only the basics of their presence in the house along with Officer Rodriguez and the boy. As far as the children were concerned, their grandmother had fallen on the stairs. Gracie had taken her to see a doctor to make sure she hadn't broken any bones. They'd unquestioningly assumed that the boy had arrived with Julian and Lena.

"Now, listen-up. There's nothing for you two to worry about," Gracie answered, self-regulating any urge to overshare the drama that had ensued. "Nonna will be home before we know it, a day or two at most. The doctor says what she really needs is a good rest and some peace and quiet after such a nasty fall."

"Is she goin' to be all wibbly wobbly?" Rosa asked. A thought struck her that maybe it was something she and her sister had done to wear their Nonna out.

"A little," Gracie smiled at her youngest daughter, selecting her words sparingly. "But she'll be fine in no time. And I'm so happy that you've been nice to my friends — Julian and his momma and Mateo. Wasn't it good of them to come take care of you? I can see you've not wasted any time making everyone at home."

"We ate breakfast already," Izzie explained. "All of us. Mateo too. He's Nonna's friend, you see. We saved you some food, Mommy. Your favorite. It's yummy."

"Thank you!" Gracie replied, sweeping the smallest of the girls off her chair and placing her on her lap as she avoided the subject of what their guests were really doing there. "Breakfast sounds so good right now."

Lena stood, refilled the tea kettle and placed it on the stovetop to heat. "How about some tea?" she asked, tapping her nails on the side of the kettle. "You must be famished."

"I think I'm about ready for something a little stronger — a double espresso will do," Gracie rubbed her sleepy eyes.

"I'll make it, Mom," Julian offered, as he joined his mother in sorting through the various containers on the countertop. "I make a mean espresso, you'll see."

"It looks to me like you two have things handled," Lena announced, sensing the need to give them some room. "If it's alright with you, I'll leave you all to your day."

"But Mom, what about Dad? Will he be okay with me bowing out on the honey baked ham? On Christmas?" Julian was torn. He'd been looking forward to the cornbread and scalloped potatoes.

Lena reached up to pinch his cheek.

"Oh, you'll figure out how to make it up to him," she replied. "That ham of his makes for great left-overs in any case," she added.

Izzie reached over to run her finger along a star-shaped sparkly paste brooch that Lena wore pinned onto the lapel of the coat that matched her festive nails. The child had been demonstrably enchanted by her new friend's easy warmth, her rhythmic speech and lingering south eastern charm.

"Pretty huh?" Lena remarked, as she ran a finger across the brooch that had belonged to her own mother. Though it had been little more than one of her mom's old 1950s drug-store, holiday-bargains, Lena cherished it, digging it out of her jewelry box each December for its sentimental value. "You like sparkly things, too, I see."

"Tell us about the brownies again before you go," Izzie begged. "The ones you made for Julian when he was a little boy." Lena had succeeded in holding the girls' more probing questions at bay while their mother was gone, regaling them with tidbits of the Christmases of her childhood. The lighting of the great tree on Rich's Department Store Bridge in Atlanta, a ride on the Pink Pig, real reindeer. Iced brownies in the basement.

Adamaria's house had appeared to her as something of a curious time-warp. It brought back memories of the drafty old Victorian in which she was raised in-so-far as its layout of small, square rooms, its high ceilings, the natural wood floors – its built-ins of narrow pantry shelves, a pie cooler even. Cold, drafty hallways were imprinted in her mind along with the winter snow. In contrast, she and her husband Reggie who was also raised in Georgia, had jumped at the chance to purchase and renovate an open-plan 1960's single-story, ranch-style house not far from Adamaria's Victorian neighborhood shortly after he'd retired from his last post in the coast guard at neighboring Two Rock.

Over the decade since they'd settled, they'd been encouraged to see their adopted community gradually evolve and become more welcoming as more families of color and non-traditional households were drawn into the country hometown feel of the area.

"Oh, those iced brownies," Lena tickled the back of Izzie's head. "Best treat in the world, aside from the bakery's rum balls and coconut cake. Made them myself when I moved to California."

"Ooh," Rosa said, "are they soft and chewy?"

"Disgustingly so," Lena replied.

"Best brownies at any pot-luck," Julian added. "Come to think of it, Mom, when's the last time you made a batch?"

"I dare say, not since you were last home for Christmas." Lena patted her stomach. She glanced over at the boy who had unglued himself from the hallway wall an hour earlier, having given up the fight of looking like he might make a run for it at any moment. He'd slowly warmed to them, though he'd contributed little to their conversation.

"Then, I think it's time to resurrect the recipe, don't you?" Julian asked.

"Do you like brownies?" Lena addressed a question to Mateo amidst a chorus of resounding approval from the girls. The boy responded by simply raising his eyebrows and giving her a weak thumbs-up.

"Come to think of it, I do remember stealing a brownie or two from Julian's lunch pack —in high school," Gracie piped in. It felt surprisingly good to be talking about something as innocuous as baked goods. "I'm not sure my two care much for chocolate."

"Yes, Mommy yes . . ." Rosa implored. "Course we do."

"Well, how about I make up a batch this week?" Lena suggested.

"Ooh, yes please," Izzie beamed, licking her lips in anticipation.

All eyes were fixed on Lena as Julian walked his mother to the kitchen door. "By the looks of your Nonna's kitchen, I'd say there's already plenty for the five of you to feast on today," she remarked, looking around one last time as she buttoned her coat.

"Be sure that you sit down together and savor your mother's hard work," she said as she reached out to gently brush Gracie's arm. "She wouldn't want you to miss out on such a delicious meal. And don't fret, Adamaria's in good hands with the staff at the hospital."

"Yes, you're right on all counts. It's not exactly how we pictured our Christmas," Gracie replied, glancing from face to face at the small, intent group that was gathered in her mother's kitchen. Lena's graciousness was not lost on her.

Lena had been nothing but kindness itself as she'd driven Gracie across town in her neat, hybrid vehicle earlier and she had gone so far as to have accompanied her as they'd checked in on Adamaria's admittance.

It was a testament to Lena's superior character in Gracie's eyes that she would stand by her son in his support of a family who had been considerably less than gracious toward him and in turn, Lena and her husband, all those years ago. To forgive and move on was different than to forgive and completely forget, she feared, but at least it was a start.

"What your mother needs is absolute rest," Lena added, picking up on Gracie's misgivings as she leaned in to land a light kiss on the younger woman's cheek. "And I dare say that knowing you are safe and sound and enjoying the holiday at home will be just the tonic for her."

"And Mateo." Rosa added, not missing a word. "He's stayin' too."

"Yes, Mateo and Julian will be sharing our Christmas with us it seems," Gracie replied, as she watched him guide his mother through the door. It hadn't crossed her mind until then that her patient young daughters had yet to open their gifts.

"How is it that you always know the right thing to do and say, Mom?" Julian asked, out of earshot.

"I like to think I rely on my instinct," Lena replied, a twinkle in her eye. "And just so you know, I've always thought you make a fine pair. Life's all about timing. Be patient. Don't rush it. Things have a habit of shifting. You'll see."

## CHAPTER TWENTY-FOUR

# THE BEST THINGS HAPPEN WHEN YOU'RE DANCING

Adamaria struggled to settle into the confines of her stiff and narrow hospital bed. It was a double room and there was a hushed conversation taking place on the other side of the curtain.

A male nurse with a pleasing smile, a compact and bustling young man in his mid-thirties, she estimated, emerged from behind the curtain to greet her alongside a taller female doctor, younger, not much older than her Gracie, who towered over him as she took her position at the foot of her bed. The nurse, she noticed, was in possession of a set of impressively smooth and sculpted arm muscles that bulged like tennis balls beneath his silky, tan skin, a startling contrast to her recollection of Aldo's wiry, white-haired arms, which had been all skin and bone at the end.

He leaned over and attached a heart-monitor into the opening of her hospital gown. Adamaria was startled by his touch, though he was suitably gentle and professional. This was the closest she'd been to a member of the male species since her husband had passed. Being cared for by a man made her blush although she was fully aware of how silly this was. She knew full well he was doing his job and could likely care less about her ridiculous, old-fashioned modesty. The distracting sight of a television set mounted above the doctor's head on a retractable metal hinge came as a relief.

"How about a Christmas movie?" the nurse, "Daniel", as printed on his name badge suggested in more of statement than a question. He'd sensed her discomfort and her general impression of him shifted to gratitude. What a kind soul and so well suited to his vocation. She'd never heard such a thing as a male nurse back when she was young. Path of progress, she figured. Not that I'm complaining, she assured herself. She was going to make it after all. I'm clearly not dead yet, she reminded herself and she chuckled.

Adamaria turned her head and rested it on a pillow in order to take in the view from the window next to her bed. She didn't want the nice nurse to think she was staring at him or that she found him a novelty in any unsuitable way.

Outside, beyond the trees and suburban sprawl of multiple decades of housing developments, Adamaria's eyes scrolled the rolling hills of velvet green that flanked the foot of the Sonoma Mountain range, its upper peaks reaching up into the mist-veiled, purple colored sky. It was a breathtaking scene after the rains, the only time in her life she had viewed the mountain from a second-floor vantage point on this side of town. Adamaria imagined the mountain teeming with native plants, birds and other wildlife, especially so after the long, green, seasonal grasses had come in.

Her head raced. She was still so disorientated. For some reason she was reminded of the pesky gopher that had made such a hot mess of her garden during the dry summer months. It upset her to think of disorder. That darn gopher, she assumed, was likely the same destructive creature that had decimated her geranium beds and gobbled the fallen figs from the tree that Aldo had planted shortly after they'd married. She and Gracie had spent an entire weekend hacking down overgrowth behind the unruly flower bed that had, over time, formed a small jungle by the shed, making it hard to access tools and other useful items.

As she watched the nurse move in and out of the curtained-off area surrounding her mystery roommate, she recalled how Gracie's girls had been disappointed at the jungle being cut back since they had made a fort in the bushes. And yet, she'd almost worn out her patience in her constant warnings of the black widow spiders that lay in wait.

She feared her late husband and her long-deceased parents would have disapproved of her letting things go so to seed in the backyard they had tended so devotedly in their time. Adamaria fretted anew. And whatever, she wondered, would they have made of her winding up in this hospital bed on this day of all days? Decades of dedication to the garden had ground to a slow stop after Aldo was no longer around to tend it. She'd been a fool for thinking herself invincible in the yard and on the stairs. Her mind raced. What else could she have done in the circumstances? Aldo would certainly never have allowed Raymond to force his way into their home and get away it, hurting their daughter any more than he already had.

Adamaria's guilt was her cross-to-bear, her letting her guard down during the night and the otherwise inconsequential thought of her overgrown yard gnawed away at her obsessive tendencies despite her precarious state. What she wouldn't have given at that moment to have mustered the energy to head home and set-to in her worn-in gardening gloves and boots, Aldo's rusty shears in hand. She'd have something to say to that soon-to-be-ex-son-in-law just as soon as he was behind bars, she vowed. And yet, she had to face the fact that she'd been given a warning. Her days of single-handedly boss-managing her family, her house and yard were over.

"Workaholic, that's my trouble, my whole life," Adamaria declared. She was ever the compulsive talker, though her mouth didn't seem to want to move the right way. Defeated, she turned her head back to the tv set.

"Then it's time to slow things down a tad." Daniel had overheard her ramblings and had no trouble deciphering her slurred speech. He picked up on her thread.

"Trouble is," Adamaria admitted. "I feel like if I give it up now, it's the end. It would be like having been shoved into a dark room —in a pair of lead boots no less. Slowin' down terrifies me half to death if I'm honest."

Daniel paused in his sorting of a tray of medical supplies and caught her eye with a knowing nod. "Hey, life is for livin'. And you know what? We only get one go around. Good time to bust out with somethin' new and improved — surprise 'em all, why don't you?"

"Easier said than done," Adamaria replied, a weak smile forming on her misfunctioning lips. Their candid conversation eased her heavy mood. "Though I've always hankered after tryin' my hand at paintin'. Pictures. Not walls."

"That's a good one."

Adamaria closed her eyes and envisioned Gracie's taking her turn at the helm. It was a daunting amount of work to ask of a young person, she feared. So much responsibility. And yet, hadn't it taken the events of the previous night to open her mind to recognize the fragility of her own mortality? And Gracie had surely shown her own considerable mettle. Adamaria was beginning to come around to the idea that Gracie did in fact possess the wherewithal to take on a good deal more than she'd been given credit for.

Her mind continued to run circles. What was it the Mousebird had shared about his being drawn to the garden? Yes, she remembered it all, now. A yard, she figured, was as good a safe-haven as any for a soul such as his. Her family's neglected property was crying out for attention. It dawned on her, as the nice nurse Daniel fiddled around with the remote control that if she and Gracie were able to persuade the authorities to let the poor mite stay a while, at least until things were sorted out properly that is, then why not reassemble all the pieces together as a kind of team?

Would their making room for another only add to their troubles, she asked herself? And yet, despite her concerns, Adamaria refused to imagine launching him back out there into the hands of the cold, hard world, poor kid. She felt a rush of something like hope. It was good to be making such new and unexpected plans after all.

And in the meantime, there were soft pillows beneath her head and crisp sheets to envelope her into the cocoon of the pale green walls, the sound track of rolling carts laden with gloves, sterilized wipes and syringes, the distant intercoms and squeaking wheelchairs that lulled her into a sense of submission.

She'd been unceremoniously plucked from her hectic domestic holiday routine. And yet laying there, giving in to it all, Adamaria was secretly enjoying certain aspects of it. She actually dared to look forward to a time when she might take a moment to relax, to sit in her own back yard — surrounded by the reassuring tones of the street beyond and the general buzz of nature, her family safe around her. She even dared to imagine what life would look like with a watercolor pad and brushes in hand.

The woman in the bed behind the curtain snored heavily, her vocal tissues vibrating in a loud yet steady rhythm. Adamaria envied her faceless roommate's ability to sleep. Her own mind, however, continued to buzz, primed by the combined stimulus of the air exchanger blowing indoor air outside and sucking outdoor air in, the feel of cold metal bedrails beneath her hands, the sound of doors sliding open and shut.

It was still fairly early on in the afternoon, though time appeared suspended under the fluorescent lights. Adamaria's thoughts inevitably wandered back to the familiar comfort zone of her kitchen. At that hour, she'd be heating up their Christmas meal she'd so lovingly and painstakingly prepared the day before. She pictured the salad greens that were in need of a good rinsing. They were tucked away in the vegetable draw of the refrigerator.

She wondered, had Gracie even thought to leave her with her phone, let alone remember to wash the salad?

"Here you go," Daniel returned to her side. He interrupted his patient's endlessly troublesome thoughts by fluffing her pillow at the back of her head. He elevated the bed to a suitable resting point and set down fresh water. Cheerful sounds and colorful pictures played out before her eyes.

"*White Christmas.* The best. Nothin' wrong with a little Bing and Danny," he remarked.

Gracie had offered to stay with her throughout the day but Adamaria had insisted she'd be all right. And it was true, it felt good to be taken care of and fussed over by someone else for once. Gracie had support back at the house. That was a comfort. Besides, there was nothing much her daughter could do for her besides anxiously fretting over her all afternoon. They would have plenty of time later to deal with their shared after-shock. She was sure that they'd only feed into one another's adrenaline if Gracie had stayed on with her.

And Adamaria was adamant that the children's Christmas not be any further spoiled by Raymond's antics. If their mommy had been gone all day, it would have been left to Julian and his mother to tell the girls what had happened and Adamaria, like Gracie, was in no rush for them to learn of all that had transpired during the night.

"I'd like to send a message to my daughter," Adamaria informed the nurse nonetheless. She was unable to resist issuing orders, despite the distraction of the movie. Daniel opened the drawer beside her bed and rummaged around.

"I don't see a phone," he replied. "Would you like to make a call from the landline?"

Adamaria fought her urge to interfere, opting to leave her daughter in peace for a few more hours. "No. I'll wait," she replied, her eyes drawn back to the television screen.

She had been a child when *White Christmas* was released, back in '54. It was a classic and it would become one of her family' favorite movies, a group of entertainers attempting to save a failing Vermont inn during the Second World War. Memories flooded back to sinking into a velvet covered chair in the old movie theater in town, her folks either side of her like a pair of human bookends.

She hadn't thought of it in decades as she recalled how her mother and father had been bowled over by the entire, glitzy, big screen extravaganza —its romantic, uplifting story, the vivid pictorial quality, the sound and songs by Irving Berlin. Danny Kaye was considered a decent dancer in his day and Adamaria remembered how her mother, a big fan of his, had honed in with her eagle eyes that first time on the part where he accidentally tripped Vera-Ellen near the end, ironically in *The Best Things Happen When You're Dancing.*

Now here she was, all those years later, all of their lives later, an older woman herself, enthralled by the cast of *White Christmas* on the small screen suspended above the foot of a hospital bed. Vera-Ellen once again, for the millionth time, twirling around with a whirling Danny, catching her foot on his and, as ever for time-immemorial, promptly making her graceful recovery without so much as a stumble.

Silly goose, Adamaria chided herself. Did you think she'd somehow miss his big ol' foot this time? The cast of *White Christmas*, she assumed, like her dear, departed parents as well as her beloved Aldo, was long since dead and buried. Yet there on the screen, as if by magic, they lived on, all of them, forever.

By the time the final scene rolled around with its snowfall and dancing ballerinas, a boy choir and magnificent tree, a cabaret cast and revelers resplendent in their festive red and white, all velvet, satin and fur — Adamaria had slipped into a deep, overdue and surprisingly contented sleep.

# Chapter Twenty-Five

# A House Without a Woman

Julian set about clearing the dining room table after the five of them had made a substantial dent in a large tray of zesty baked ziti with its creamy ricotta layer and multiple slices of a succulent leg of roast lamb. He'd taken charge of its slow roasting, elevating the meat out of the pan juices, as per Gracie's specific instruction, after he'd emptied several quarter pails of rain water that had leaked in patches through the house.

It was a first for Julian, in so far as a holiday meal, the leg of lamb-roasting part, at least and though he'd been nervous, concerned he might have easily destroyed Adamaria's meticulously prepared Christmas spread — all of it, starting with the pasta, tasted wonderful, a gooey, tomato sauce melded with the soft cheese that whet their appetites for the second course, which turned out a blushing pink and carved alongside a crisp green salad that Gracie had thrown together at the last minute.

After they'd eaten, Gracie and the girls had set about dusting off an old wicker hamper they'd retrieved from the closet under the stairs. He watched as he washed dishes and passed them over to Mateo to dry as she neatly lined the hamper's interior with one of her mother's hand-embroidered dishtowels before packaging up a selection of cookies into a cardboard container which she tied with a sparkly gold ribbon from a pile of recycled wrappings she pulled from a drawer.

She'd sent the girls upstairs with orders to retrieve a pink poinsettia from under her bed and, after flipping one side of the lid open on the hamper, she gently set it inside. A couple of handfuls of satsumas and grapes from the fruit bowl tucked in snugly between the plant and small tubs of leftover pasta, bread and meat.

Gracie voiced her concern that the hospital staff might not allow outside food into her mother's room, but added if she was sure of

183

anything, it was that a questionable meal from a partitioned tray would not do much to lift Adamaria's bruised spirits.

"It'll make her happy to have some element of a homemade Christmas on her tray table, even if she has little appetite," Gracie shared, remarking how surprised she'd been that she'd been able to eat such a feast herself, considering the day's roller coaster of emotions.

As she prepared to make a move, leaving Julian in charge of Mateo at the house for an hour or so, she bundled the girls into warm fleece jackets for her second trip across town that day. This time she insisted she was perfectly all right to drive. They passed the big CVS store and a couple of tire shops as the lights ran green through several sets by the city fairgrounds and the drive-throughs on East Washington. It took no time, there being barely any holiday traffic on the flat ribbon of shiny road that was washed clean from the rain. Though the sky was clear at that hour, the girls looked out at a small river that ran through the roadside gutters.

Meanwhile, Adamaria dreamed once more of Aldo being back by her side. It was as if he were flesh and blood, real as life, right beside her. How she yearned to reach out, draw him in, but Aldo simply shook his head and laughingly reprimanded her in his native Italian. With one of his favorite proverbs, the warmth of his familiar voice caused her heart to leap: "Una casa sensa donna e come una lanterna senza luma," he proclaimed. A house without a woman is like a lantern without the light.

"Andare a casa, bella," Aldo urged. Get better, go home. Back to Gracie and the girls. It wasn't her time to join him, she'd been told twice that day, no matter how tired and tempted she'd been to reunite with her husband.

Adamaria awoke with a start as Gracie and the girls piled noisily into the narrow space beside her bed.

Gracie fussed around, arranging the hamper on a chair. She held a finger to her lips to make the girls aware that whoever the woman was in the bed on the other side of the curtain was sleeping. The three of them giggled at the sound of a series of impressive snores. Daniel, the ever-attentive nurse, jumped in to help Gracie find a spot for the pink poinsettia. Adamaria presided over it all, drowsy initially, though uplifted by the presence of her family.

"She's Italian, she told me — I get it," Daniel smiled, obligingly, when Gracie broached the subject of her mother requiring her basic home comforts.

"It being Christmas," she nodded.

Izzie and Rosa clambered onto the chair by the side of the bed, arms and legs entwined. Their curious eyes probed their grandmother's face.

"When are you comin' home, Nonna?" asked the youngest of the two. "We miss you. And why are you speaking weal funny?"

"As soon as the doctors say so, Bella," Adamaria replied, slowly sounding out her words as she reached out to touch each of her beloved granddaughters. She needed to be sure they were there in the flesh. She wasn't fully convinced how much of what was happening around her was real and what of it might still be a dream.

"Your voice is wonky," Rosa blurted.

"Shush," her sister rebuked, digging her in the ribs with her elbow.

"It's okay. It is a little strange. And it will be for a while. Thank you for the beautiful plant — my favorite. Aren't you the cat's pajamas?" Adamaria reassured herself through touch that she was firmly back in the here and now. "Come stand by my side and tell me if Santa came through."

"Yep," Izzie exclaimed, matter-of-factly. "Santa doesn't let little kids down, don't you know?"

"That's as may be," Adamaria replied, ruffling Izzie's tangled hair. "Though he's gettin' on in years. We're all forgetful sometimes."

Izzie looked her Nonna directly in the eye. She sighed and took a deep breath as she thought through what it was that she wanted to say" "Actually. I wrote him a note. I asked him if he'd come up with somethin' to make Mommy happy again."

Gracie sat upright. "Oh really? That's news to me. And what did you do with it, this secret letter, Izzie?" she asked her daughter.

"I folded it and propped it up against his treats," the earnest child replied. She turned her face to avoid her mother's searching eyes.

"And — did you hear . . . Santa, last night?" Gracie asked, fearing for the first time that the children may not have slept through the events of the early hours after all.

"No," Izzie replied, rather too quickly in Gracie's mind. The girl shot the briefest of glances in her sister's direction.

"Me neither," Rosa added. She wasn't known for keeping secrets, though Gracie wasn't sure if she was fully convinced that they were telling the truth. "But we found it there this mornin'. The note was still where we stood it and he never even ate any of the nice food we left for him."

Grace looked from one child to the other.

"But Mommy's friend, Julian, well, then he came to the house this mornin' and he made her laugh when she came home and her cheeks turned pink when she smiled at him," Izzie was quick to add. "Santa must've read it, see, I'm sure. Do you think he sent them, Nonna? Julian? And Mateo as well, I mean?"

"Girls," Gracie announced, firmly, taking control of the conversation before it veered any more off track. She drew her children toward her as she perched on the end of her mother's bed.

"If there's one thing that I'd like us all to learn this Christmas, it's that we're not hanging around for someone else to come along and fix things or make us happy. It's not Santa, or anyone else for that matter who is responsible for whatever we wish for most. We're each of us perfectly capable of making whatever it is we dream of come true. It's nice to ask for material things — toys and books and art supplies and whatnot, but for real, it's how we feel about ourselves and the people around us that really matters. For me, it's you two and Nonna. It's all about being our best selves and taking care of each other."

"Yes, Mommy," Izzie persisted. "But do you love him? Julian?"

"I love him like you love your very best buddy, the friend you've known the longest."

"Do people marry their best buddy?" Rosa pressed the point.

Gracie chuckled and ruffled her daughter's hair. "Someone is getting way ahead of herself," she answered. "All kinds of people love one-another, you don't have to be married to show it."

"Anyways, Mommy is married to Daddy, silly," Izzie announced. "Aren't you?"

"Technically, yes," Gracie replied. Honesty always her best policy, especially when her children asked such pointed questions. It had proved a prudent strategy throughout the long court battle. She had so often gritted her teeth in a determined effort to endure the girls' need and right to know what was happening in their world without her laying on any excessive details of blame onto Raymond's shoulders. One day she would share more, but they were far too young to process the detailed complexities of why they were estranged from their father.

"But one day soon your Daddy and me, well, we won't be married anymore. And that doesn't mean we're not still your parents. Or that we don't both love you two. It's totally fine for you to ask me whatever you'd like to know."

"But not today," Adamaria interjected, meeting Gracie's eyes as she wagged her finger and reached out her hand to her oldest granddaughter. "Today is Christmas and what I would like most is for you three to make your way home. Enjoy what's left of the afternoon and evening. Those boys are waitin' for you to get back." She squeezed their small, warm hands in turn. "That young 'un sure could do with a friend or two."

"How long is Mateo gonna stay with us?" Rosa asked. "Why doesn't he go home to his own family?"

"Maybe Santa did send him after all," Adamaria replied. "Not everyone has a family of their own like ours to spend the holidays with. Santa must have figured that we had room in our house to welcome Mateo — at least for a while."

"Did Santa think you needed a boy, a gwandson kinda thing?" Rosa asked — and, as she turned from her grandmother to her mother: "Does that make him our bwother?"

"Well. Not quite, but then we're all brothers and sisters in God's eyes," Adamaria replied. And for the first time in her life, she really, truly considered the notion. She thought about what she'd said as she smoothed a crease in the soft thermal blanket that topped her bedsheets.

"What Nonna means," Gracie explained, as she tightened her arms around her huddle of girls, "is that we don't all have to be born into the same family to help others to feel that they belong. We don't have to look like one another, either."

Rosa considered her mother's statement for a moment. "Okay," she said. Izzie nodded in agreement.

Gracie figured she'd done something right in the accepting and unquestioning nature of her daughters. And it was Adamaria who had set the example for kindness this time. She had not rushed, as Gracie would have expected, into making her usual rash judgements — instead, her mother had showed her compassion in offering a young stranger the emergency shelter he so badly needed.

"And you know," Gracie said, as she kissed her mother's forehead. "When we see the good in someone, well — we shine."

# Chapter Twenty-Six

# Calling All Angels

Officer Rodriguez braced herself as she took the porch stairs in her energetic manner of two at a time. The afternoon was dwindling and her energy was fast diminishing, along with the hour. A cup of coffee would be nice, she thought, something to reenergize her spirits after she'd spent considerable time tracking down animal control to check in on Peanut's whereabouts and status. If she was honest with herself, she'd feared for the dog's chances as slim. And having seen how attached they were to one other, the boy and his dog, it pulled heavily at her heartstrings to consider Mateo's most probable loss.

Soft, multicolored lights of Adamaria and Gracie's Christmas tree reflected through the window, bathing the porch in a twinkling carpet of muted rainbow hues.

So much for the most wonderful time of the year, she thought. Christmas was an especially hard time — her parents had passed and though she had a big extended family, she was a divorcee with no kids of her own. The tree lights conjured images of her childhood, her bittersweet coping strategy to banish her grown-up holiday blues was to reminisce on the happier memories of the brash and shiny dollar store décor she'd been so enthralled in outfitting her folks' house with as a kid. All the good things, her big, boisterous family, the homemade tamales and platters of cookies, a few simple gifts, these were the remembrances that helped elevate her mood.

A large part of Officer Rodriguez' method in the carrying out of her law enforcement duty was steeped in a firm and unshakeable belief that angels come in all shapes and sizes. Although she certainly did not consider herself to have yet earned a place amongst even the lesser of the winged-ranks of heavenly hosts, Angela was well aware of the power vested within her to take a benevolent stand when she felt it was especially warranted. Over the years, there'd been many ways for her to implement this personal standpoint of hers while keeping within the parameters of the law.

Softening the blow of potential worse-case news about Peanut was top of her mind at that moment and though she would assure young Mateo that she was doing all she could to reunite him with his beloved companion she knew she had to be honest with him and not raise his hopes too soon.

The more the boy had attempted to stifle his sobs as Peanut had been pried away from him, the greater she'd resolved to do everything in her power to save the pair from being permanently parted.

Julian greeted her at the door, his sweater sleeves rolled up to his elbows. Gracie and the girls were on their way home from their afternoon visit to the hospital.

"Come on in from the cold," he said. "Care for coffee?"

Angela replied that he'd most certainly read her mind. She nodded. "It's been a long day for all of us, for sure."

Julian appeared to have had something of a steadying influence on the boy in the time they'd been left alone. Before they reached the kitchen, he had managed to explain to her how he was a firm believer in the simple act of building on a kid's strengths as opposed to his weaknesses. "Makes a huge difference in a troubled life."

If anyone had been able to encourage the boy to open up and talk a little, it was him, she figured. It wasn't as if they'd faced the same issues, but Julian had overcome his own hurdles.

Angela looked Mateo over as he sat quietly at the kitchen table.

"You know — I couldn't wait to leave home, ditch this place," Julian confided, as he made a pot of strong coffee and poured it into holly-patterned mugs.

"This town drove me crazy as a teenager," Julian continued, as he stood at the kitchen counter, stirring cream into the hot, aromatic liquid. "Especially so for all the grief I was dealt as one of the only Black kids in the whole darn school. It wasn't easy back then, not for me or my family." He acknowledged Mateo's background and circumstances being altogether different than his own but he was able to relate.

And Officer Rodriguez could see how it was that Julian had been able to make a start in building Mateo's trust by letting him know how far from ideal his own youth had been.

"Wanna talk about Peanut, honey?" Angela's approach was to set to it and tackle the elephant in the room head on.

Mateo looked down at his hands — he closely inspected each of his stubby fingernails. "Things are gonna get shitty enough — without them t-t-t-takin' my dog."

Julian sat the mugs on the kitchen table. "They don't have to be," he said. "I can help you sort through whatever mess it is that you've gotten yourself into."

Gracie had texted Julian before she'd left the hospital. She and her mother had agreed to take the kid in, at least temporarily.

"You're a good guy, Mateo. Adamaria and Gracie believe this. I believe it," Julian added, his eyes steady and reassuring. "In time, I may be able to work it out for you to see your little sisters. Who knows, maybe your aunt will agree to your moving up there, after all. In the meantime, you're to stay here for a while. This is what we're all willing and prepared to do for you if you want it, that is."

"Why would any of you do this for me?" Mateo asked. He looked up earnestly as he wiped a tear from his eye. "I'm messed up, ya know."

Julian held his hand out in front of him, palm forward. "Hey, we all have our flaws, bud. Learning how to trust is a good place to start. Figure out how to make yourself a good house guest. Earn yourself some respect in turn."

Officer Rodriguez listened intently as she added a second teaspoon of sugar to her coffee. It hit her empty stomach and bounced around her insides. On cue, Julian passed around a plate of biscotti and the last of the Wandi wings.

"There appears to be no shortage of offerings in Adamaria's ample kitchen," he remarked, as he crunched into a biscotti.

Angela was grateful for the boost of the light refreshment. She refocused her attention on Mateo. "You know what? On the rare occasions in life when someone actually steps up and offers care and comfort, however broken you might believe yourself to be," she suggested, "I'd take it as an opportunity to learn how to be a little kinder to yourself, and not just you, but to others. What you're being offered here is a win-win, Mijo, but only if everyone pitches in. And besides, the alternative's not so pretty."

"Goin' back into care, you mean?" asked Mateo.

"That or juvenile detention, dependin' on whatever else there is you may not be tellin' us."

"I've not done nothin' to be l-l-locked up for," Mateo insisted, frowning. "Why'd you try to pin somethin' on me I never did? I never done nothin' to no one without being pushed to it. I don't get why I'm always the one being punished."

"Look, all the classes you take in school," Julian explained, deflecting the tension that was building — "every time you pass one, it's kinda like winning a round in a boxing ring, right? — your own way of beating the system. All you've gotta do man, is figure out how to take care of yourself for starters. I've seen plenty of kids in trouble turn it around, get on with school, make a path for themselves. Do this and one day, if you stick with it, you're gonna look around and find that you've gotten yourself into a way better place."

# CHAPTER TWENTY-SEVEN

# STAY THE NIGHT

Julian placed the palm of his hand lightly in the hollow of Gracie's back. They were face to face at last in the kitchen in the dim light of late afternoon, not quite a foot apart. His eyes followed her hand as she reached up to secure the same loose strand of hair that had captivated him so the previous evening. She took his free hand in hers and raised it to rest on the side of her warm face. A spark of energy passed between them —a wild zap of body chemistry, impossible to ignore. They laughed. Their connection was undeniable. Julian's cool palm absorbed the flush of her cheek as his hand lingered in place. It was effortless, their physical draw to one another, easy and comfortable, a natural, magnetic pull.

In his mind, the kitchen was not ideal as romantic settings go considering this was their first, real, private reconnection. And yet, much as he knew he should try to conjure far more reserve, there was no holding back their mutual desire as she leaned in gently and brushed his lips with hers. He moved closer toward her, lowered his face to hers. She raised a finger to his lips and shushed him from whatever it was he was about to say.

"There's no need to get into anything too heavy duty," she said, caressing his face with her hand. "I think we both have more than enough to process right now."

Officer Rodriguez had bid them goodbye a few minutes earlier. She'd made them an assurance that she would do her best to see to it that Peanut would be released into their care.

Mateo and the girls had subsequently settled in the parlor to watch *A Charlie Brown Christmas* on Gracie's tablet which was propped on the coffee table so that the boy, who'd been easily drawn in by the mellow, jazzy soundtrack of the 60s special was able to watch it with the younger two.

"It's Peanuts, see," Izzie had declared as he rested in the glow of the fireplace, his arms wrapped around his knees as he leaned somewhat awkwardly against a pile of cushions the girls had propped against the couch.

"But I want you to know," Julian said as he released his hold on her, stepped back and looked her in the eyes: "I'm here for you, Gracie, however much you feel you need to share, it's up to you. And the minute you need your space, you let me know."

He had no intention of pressuring her into anything she wasn't entirely comfortable with. "I know you don't need anyone to take care of you. I can see that," he added. "And the last thing I want is to come across as forward or pushy, but I think it's best I stay here at the house initially, keep an eye on the boy from the sidelines, at least for tonight."

Gracie smiled. "Aside from all that's swirling around in my head right now, not to mention in here," she motioned to her heart. "I'd say we best have a drink."

She feared if she held on too tight, she'd suffocate him. It was all happening so fast. The last thing she wanted was to dump any more of her already excessive baggage on him. She stood on tip-toes and reached into an upper cabinet where Adamaria stored the few bottles of liquor they kept in the house. He watched as she poured generously from a half-full bottle of a rich, amber-colored brandy, the house favorite, a vintage Italian Vecchia Romagna. As she set the two drinks in cloudy crystal tumblers before them on the kitchen table, Julian pulled out a chair with a gesture of gentlemanly flourish that made her laugh.

"Take a seat, ma'am," he said. He would not over-step the mark, he'd decided, even if she asked him to.

Brandy dribbled down the side of her glass.

"I feel like my brain is encased in molasses, if I'm honest," she said. "This probably doesn't help, but all I know right now is that I've gotta get through the evening first. Get the kids off to sleep."

Neither of them knew exactly what to make of their fast-forward reunion except that there would be time for talking later. The initial fireworks they'd experienced at each another's touch settled down to something of a steadier fuse with the help of the smooth, spicily-warm liquid that slid too easily down their throats.

It had been a tumultuous twenty-four-hours.

"Things will look a little clearer tomorrow," Julian promised, as he swirled the last of his liquor around in his glass. "Life has its own way of connecting the dots if we can manage to stay out of the way."

"I want you to know you're free to walk away and without a second's fear of hurting my feelings," Gracie replied, the loosening effects of the alcohol had created a sense of urgency in her desire to be totally upfront with him. She leaned in closer and locked eyes with him. "I've thrown you in at the deep end."

"Hey, no judgement," Julian replied. Gracie relaxed. She had willingly let her guard down with him. She laughed again. The very sound of it was an oddity, a strange, out-of-body-experience. She felt herself lightened, wrapped in his familiarity, the comfort of him, like a moth that had been deprived of light.

"You can count on me to keep a respectful distance," Julian added, aware of her foot touching his beneath the table.

Despite all they'd been through, there was a peaceful normalcy in their togetherness. That he had thought of her so many times over the years, most often last thing at night, or in the still, early hours whenever he'd had trouble sleeping was not lost on him now, for here she was. Here he was. The same Gracie. The same Julian, only older, wiser, both. She took his hands in hers, rested her head on his shoulder.

"Stay," she said. "And hold me."

# CHAPTER TWENTY-EIGHT

# CHRISTMAS WHERE WE ARE

Adamaria eased herself into a semi-upright position as she took one last look through the hospital window before darkness set in. Though her body ached for sleep, it was a comforting sight to watch the distant dining room chandeliers and holiday lights illuminate the many homes that were nestled amidst the green-rolling ranch land set into the oak-studded peaks of Sonoma Mountain.

The winter evening lightshow created a sparkling scene, a million small, twinkly pin-pricks in the misty hue that was the onset of early evening. As she propped herself up onto her pile of plump, white pillows, Adamaria pondered what had led to her having landed there all alone as Christmas Day drew to a close, except for a sleeping roommate she had yet to set eyes on, as they rested their bodies in their respective hospital beds.

Nurse Daniel was back, puttering around, this time intent on closing the blinds — inadvertently eliminating her unexpected vantage point on the sparkling, hillside light show that so enthralled. Daniel turned to Adamaria with a half-smile. She took it for an apology of his for the sudden muting of the outside world. In her opinion, it was too early to ask her to tune out and call it a day, even though she was meant to be resting. She supposed there was likely some hospital rule and regulation involved and so she stifled an urge to object.

Daniel tucked Adamaria's ruffled bedding into place with a pair of smooth, deft hands. "I'll be heading home myself, soon," he said.

Adamaria had been greatly reassured by his having attended to her, for she'd found him a calming, most caring presence at the end of what had been a terrifying night and long, difficult day. The universe was telling her something, she had to admit. There had been no one other than her and Gracie and the girls for the longest time and now there were all these people who'd come along in so short a time to help her rethink her position. She felt giddy almost, strangely not guilty at all as she lay there, propped on her pillows and pampered by her charming nurse.

Daniel asked if she had any other children, other than her daughter. "And those two cutie-pie kiddos. Any other grandkids?"

"No, I had Gracie in my forties," Adamaria explained. "She's my only one. My Birdie, my one and only. Until the little ones came along. I always wanted a full house. And, now, well, as of last night, it's beginnin' to look that way. There's a teenager at home — a new boy. He showed up in need of some place to stay."

"That's sure nice of you to take him in. Is he family?"

"No, as a matter of fact, I never even met him until the early hours of this mornin'."

"It's none of my business," Daniel raised a neatly sculpted eyebrow as he glanced at her sideways. "But I sure hope this surprise visitor didn't have anythin' to do with you landin' up in here?"

"It's a long story," Adamaria replied. "But, no, suffice to say it was the boy who rather saved the day — or night, I should say."

She was exhausted after all. She settled herself back into her nest of pillows and closed her eyes, recognizing how her little family was not alone in their having experienced an especially troubled period in their lives. The boy, Mateo, hadn't he suffered even greater sorrows in such a young life? It fairly broke her heart. And yet, somehow, the darker it had grown that Christmas, the brighter the light now appeared at the end of it.

The old ways Adamaria understood, all that she had held onto over the years and with such an unbendable zeal, the way she'd tended to jump in her judgement of others, her stubborn, unjust bias, her denials — it had all come dangerously close to choking her. It struck her as fortunate indeed that her beloved and patient family had not been torn apart by her many stubborn insistences.

It pained her that she'd been so self-centered and rigid for so long, reluctant to embrace any kind of change. Adamaria had pressed her daughter and grandchildren to follow her rules, abide by her wishes. She'd been blind to the times and, as a direct result, to Gracie's and the girls' own needs.

Well, she informed herself, her shoulders bristling, there's nothin' more to do than to step back up, dust it all off and darn well start over afresh.

As if he'd read her mind: "Don't you worry. We'll see that you're rested and ready for that household of yours before we let you go," Daniel said, as he dimmed the lights and left the room.

Outside, although Adamaria was by-then oblivious to the scene, only a handful of cars remained in the hospital lot as Christmas evening drew in. Leaves twirled and flew in the wind and three or four big ones settled briefly on the glass before floating off into the dark.

*"You can't go back and change the beginning, but you can start where you are and change the end,"*

Unknown

# Epilogue Christmas, 2020

# One Year Later
# — The Kids Are Alright

It was Christmas morning during the second lockdown of COVID and the girls were intrigued to discover a large mystery envelope addressed to them and tucked under the modest pile of gifts they'd torn into beneath the Christmas tree. Izzie turned the envelope around in her hands several times as she inspected a series of gold, shiny star stickers that decorated the back of the envelope. She scrutinized the handwriting. It wasn't her mother's or Nonna's familiar penmanship. Even though she was less convinced than ever that he was real, a part of her wanted to believe, to hope that Santa had returned her letter this year or at least read it.

"Go on, open it," Gracie encouraged.

"I will if you won't, slowpoke," Rosa said, itching to wrestle the envelope from her sister.

"Dear Izzie and Rosa," Izzie read out loud, slowly and deliberately sounding out a large, cursive script that swirled across the snow-white page in a heavy flourish of thick, blue ink. "Santa here with some special news. By the time the middle of summer rolls around, a baby brother will arrive to keep you company. I hope that you'll be as excited about this news as the grown-ups are."

All eyes immediately turned to Gracie. Three sets of jaws dropped open and hung in suspense. Though the girls were clearly surprised and not unhappy, thin sheets of steel had dropped instantly behind Mateo's eyes. Peanut sat, attentively, at his feet, licking his hand. It had taken the boy a full two years to shake the edge off the trauma of his own mother's devastating labor. A chill ran through him. There had been one brief, outdoor, safe-distance-mask-mandated visit with his sisters, awkward and emotional for the two older siblings that summer. His by-then toddler sister had no idea who he was and his aunt, who for her own reasons remained reluctant to warm to him, made little attempt to explain.

Julian had been prepared for the boy's reaction to the news. "It's alright, bud, I'll be right here for everyone, especially for Gracie and the baby. We all will." For Gracie and Julian, the pregnancy was a joint decision that they'd not taken lightly but felt was right, timing-wise, what with their desire to have a child together and the girls growing fast. With everyone at home for an unknown stretch of months ahead, Gracie had said there was no time like the present. And they'd been lucky to conceive a good deal faster than they'd reckoned on.

"There's plenty of room in the house for all of us," Gracie added, as she patted her belly, it's subtle bulge hidden in plain sight beneath the beautiful, brand-new emerald-green silk blouse Julian had gifted her after venturing out on a downtown holiday shopping expedition on Small Business Sunday.

Adamaria was over the moon when they'd broken the news to her in confidence a few days earlier. She had been sulking somewhat beforehand, after a subtle reminder that she was, under no circumstances, allowed to take on too many of the holiday duties. Still, the consensus was that Christmas Eve was hers and always would be, as long as she wished to chop and sautée and simmer a deep pan of sauce that would scent the house the whole day long. The idea of a grandson more than made up for the unscripted holiday pot-lucks that she'd learned to grin and bear.

What a difference a year had made. And what a year with the initial shock and fear, the fog of seemingly endless stay-at-home orders, school closures, months of unrest during the peak of protests and countless, unimagined restrictions. Yet, Adamaria was extraordinarily grateful that there they all were, they'd made it that far, all together, into an unknown future as one big, unexpected, blended family, under not one, but now technically, two roofs.

Officer Rodriguez, Angela, had moved into a three-quarter-time position — supervising community relations. It suited her and she was a good deal more self-fulfilled and pleased to be making a difference in a new way. She'd taken up COVID mask-making in her extended off-hours and had stopped by with a small pile of freshly-stitched masks in a range of holiday fabrics for a safe-distance porch visit Christmas morning. She'd kept in touch closely by video messenger throughout the early lockdown and with frequent backyard visits during the intervening warmer months. Angela proved a constant in Mateo's life and the two had bonded almost as if he was another of her beloved nephews.

"Look at what you've accomplished in a year," she reminded him that morning, before she headed to her brother's house for her first off-duty Christmas in years. "It would have been a rough road — a life out there on your own, Mijo, the fact you and Peanut are still welcome here with these good folks means that you've earned it."

Peanut had, as it had transpired a couple of days after Raymond's arrest, exceptionally poor teeth. They were prone to tartar and a build-up of plaque, the result of which was a nasty influx of Capnocytophaga — the germs that live in the mouths of cats and dogs (without so much as making their hosts even the slightest bit sick). Any amount of which had unfortunately posed a particularly dire threat to Raymond given the state of his weakened immune system.

Raymond's last hours in the holding cell were spent without the slightest idea how deadly the pestilent blisters would be that had emerged around the bite area on his thigh. He'd been all-consumed by his powerful emotions, the bitter taste of regret, while a fast-inducing, death-dealing redness, swelling and the draining of a foul-smelling pus set in, rapidly escalating into an excruciating litany of feverous stomach and muscle pain, diarrhea, vomiting, headache and confusion.

In fact, such was the violent, toxic nature of his infection, it was a worse-case-scenario for Raymond in that his stark fate was to become little more than a statistic. The one in every three sepsis victims to succumb to subsequent kidney failure followed by a fatal heart attack.

Ultimately, it was Raymond's double-dose of extraordinary bad luck in having been stuck in limbo in the holding cell that sealed his fate, for the bacteria's stealth attack on his body had remained wholly and devastatingly undetected.

Until — it was too late.

Officer Flynn and Officer Rodriguez had informed Gracie of her estranged husband's death in custody in person. It had been almost an entire year since the terrible events and though Raymond no longer posed any threat to her, their daughters, himself or her family, Gracie took no solace in the tragedy of the circumstance of his passing. It had happened so fast that no one was ever held responsible for any lack of procedure. Fate had continued to play the ultimate hand in that Gracie had continued direct payments from her salary on a modest annual life insurance sum for herself and Raymond even after they had separated. Although she'd feared the insurance company would refuse to pay out due to Raymond's arrest, the fact he did not die while in the act of committing a crime was ultimately to his favor.

Gracie and the girls had attended Raymond's funeral service two weeks prior to her first visit to southern California to visit Julian. Raymond Senior, the girls' grandfather, had reached out to her several times in the days and weeks after the shocking news of his son's sudden passing. It was agreed that his wish to reunite with his granddaughters was acceptable to Gracie and, after careful thought, she chose to take them with her to a low-key, pre-pandemic afternoon gathering at Raymond Senior's house following the crematorium service. She hoped it would help bring some closure for the children after she'd explained that their father had passed.

Meanwhile, unbeknown to Mateo until sometime after social services had given the go ahead for him to remain in the care of Adamaria and Gracie, Julian had succeeded in connecting the dots between the state and the boy's aunt and uncle in the handling of his father's unlawful-death suit.

The California Occupational Safety and Health Administration had indeed closed in on finalizing an official investigation into the incident that claimed the life of Mateo's father. This meant that with Julian's legal input and subsequent agreement, Mateo was eligible to become Julian's ward of court until the boy came of age when he would receive a third of the payoff from the winery's insurance carrier.

Peanut, who had been given a fortunate and wholly unexpected reprieve by animal services, largely thanks to the constant input, influence and dental care fundraising efforts of Officer Angela Rodriguez, continued to keep Mateo constant company, watching his every move. Mateo found the act of sliding a putty knife between the old wallpaper and the drywall of a room-of-his-own to be especially satisfying as he deftly and patiently eased-off the sheets of old paper and glue in long, thick curling strips. Everyone admired the final layer before the lath and plaster that revealed an intriguing original pattern of Victorian stripes and tulips in rose red and gold.

Julian and he had shopped together, Peanut in tow, at the hardware store downtown. They'd brought home plastic tarps and wallpaper-removing-sheets for the more stubborn areas, along with a large sponge and a bucket. Together, they'd carried in the same old ladder that Raymond had employed a year before this subsequent, pandemic holiday season, so that Mateo was able to reach the top parts of the high walls. Because the room was so spacious, a consensus had been made to divide it in the middle, creating two smaller, single bedrooms from the original one.

It had been shortly after Thanksgiving when Adamaria made a monumental-to-her move out into her newly completed granny unit, her tiny home, or Liberty Street Nest Number Two as she named it. Thanks to Gracie's having generously allocated a large chunk of Raymond's life insurance they welcomed the addition of a small, cheery, pre-manufactured one-story structure with a modest bedroom, living room, kitchenette and shower room.

It fit snugly, as if it had always been there, nestled in the clearance that Mateo made good on his word on, having labored in the early part of the stay-at-home orders, out in the yard where the overgrown bushes had been. And it was Mateo who Adamaria had charged with designing and building a narrow, gravel pathway from the main house to the studio. Blooming garden beds surrounded her compact new space after they had planted them together in the early summer months with Adamaria's choice of heirloom roses and lavender and several colorful pollinator plants.

Everyone had noticed Mateo's stuttering had lessened significantly. He smiled readily and had grown taller, gained several, much needed pounds. Peanut had filled out along with his master. Adamaria quit calling the boy Birdmouse, referring to him by his proper name, though she would always think of him that way, privately and affectionately.

While Adamaria was busy fussing happily and organizing her new space, content in the knowledge for the first time in years that the house and property would stay in the family after all, Gracie and Julian moved into her former, freshly painted, large and airy bedroom. It had taken the better part of a year for the pair of them to take the plunge to live together full time — not because either of them had any reservations. Lock-down logistics had prevented them from moving any faster.

It was not long after Gracie's second weekend visit to southern California (with the blessing of Julian's mother who had taken the girls and Mateo in at her house so as to ensure a few days peace and quiet for Adamaria) — that news of COVID-19's imminent spread had hit the airwaves.

The Black Lives Matter movement had followed hot on the heels of the pandemic, reaching a peak in early June when half a million people turned out in close to 550 different towns and cities across the country. Julian was up in Sonoma County on June 6th and he and Gracie gathered his parents, Mateo and the girls to join a peaceful rally through the streets of downtown Petaluma. Nobody was more surprised than he when Adamaria in her floppy sunhat and cat-eye shades announced that she was coming with them in what would become the largest ever single day protest in the country's history.

Initial lockdown separation had made for hearts that grew stronger-by-the-day. Long-distance video calls and late-night chats provided the space for Gracie and Julian to talk for an hour or two each night. It had provided them ample time and opportunity to broach any subject that might have raised any red flags, including the acknowledgment and better understanding of the added layers and complexity of their relationship.

Gracie's confidence in her own decision-making grew to unexpected heights as she'd overseen plans for the tiny house, plus a new roof and replacement windows on the main house. Her new role as capable and competent decision-maker empowered her sense of self and confidence as she took on the reins of running the house and the start of its myriad much-needed improvements.

All that Adamaria asked of the restorations was that they'd remain especially sensitive to the preservation of the home's historic architectural details. And anyway, Gracie, being of the mindset that less is more and mindful of her budget, preferred not to bring in too many new elements all at once.

Despite the presence of Peanut, the family of racoons that had wintered in the crawl space beneath the house hung on until workmen discovered them mid-Spring. Their months of feasting on mice, rats and gophers generated the natural pest control that saved the spring and summer garden they planted as a family in the old raised beds out back.

Lena had decided to reduce her week and work part time from home and in her newfound hours volunteered to help out the extended family bubble in its challenging and often chaotic online schooling at the kitchen table. Adamaria proved a natural leader with arts and crafts. Gracie set up her own Zoom teaching station which she somehow managed alongside the commotion of the extensive work being done on the house. The rooms and furnishings of the house on Liberty Street were called into play like a game of musical chairs.

Lunch hours found Adamaria staunchly in charge of soups and sandwiches with a mutually agreed-upon, full-run of the kitchen in the middle of the day. She was often to be found lingering afterwards soaking a bowl of beans or chopping vegetables for dinner prep — though the evening meal was a daily task that Gracie, and later, Julian, had been most insistent on taking over.

By November Julian, who discovered like so many during lockdown, a passion and talent for making bread, had secured himself a relocation package with a new position in neighboring Napa County District Attorney's department.

Adamaria had not been nearly as peeved as Gracie had expected when she'd revealed her tiger tattoo on the first warm day of summer. "Your body, your choice," she'd said and left it at that, though Gracie frequently caught her studying the image with interest as they'd sat together in the sunshine in the backyard.

It made complete sense to Adamaria to live this way, as if she'd planned it so, her own little melting-pot, though she was aware that Gracie didn't approve of her using such an old-fashioned term. Never-the-less, stay-at-home orders had brought them all closer together in ways she never would have dreamed of. And as Gracie frequently reminded her, this sensibly-shared space of theirs reduced their family footprint significantly. Though it was tight quarters at times, they were all of them so very thankful for their home, this sanctuary, for one another, for all of the many shared resources and various ways of looking at life and especially, for the plentiful food on their table.

By the time the eight of their Liberty Street bubble, including Julian's parents, had finished clearing dishes in a noisy, enthusiastic group-effort following Adamaria's first-ever giving of the green light on a Christmas Day pot-luck, it had begun to rain.

She stoked the fire in the parlor and thanked her blessings for all of it, praying for her growing family's safe passage thus far into the wild unknown of another strange new year. Her eyes rested on the modest, living tree that Gracie, Julian, Mateo and the girls had picked out at a nursery mid-December. After Christmas, they would plant the tree in a special spot in the backyard.

"It's for the children to remember their dad," Gracie had explained. "They'll have many more questions as they grow and it'll give them somewhere to sit beneath and process."

Adamaria wasn't sure she'd have been anywhere as near as benevolent toward Raymond's memory if she were her daughter, but she supposed he had loved his children and they should know that. She herself was far from perfect, she had to admit, and if Gracie had forgiven him, then she would try to also in time.

A home on Liberty Street with such an unconventional tribe wasn't nearly all clear sailing and Adamaria was sensible enough to figure it wouldn't be at all easy going forward, either. Family life wasn't designed that way. She knew that. It would be messy and confusing, maybe even painful at times. But for Adamaria, love was all she needed. All any of them needed. And acceptance. A roof and windows that didn't leak. And a deep pan of homemade lasagna on a regular basis.

There were moments when the past and the present did still converge, though more and more she was inspired by the constant revelations of this new, modern family that they had created together. She understood it as a place where memory, intimacy and growth were somehow able to co-exist, side-by-side. Adamaria had adapted. Against her natural instincts, she had opened herself to new people, a dog, to new ideas and at a perilous time in which she didn't know how she would have survived alone if she hadn't.

Adamaria had fought hard to save what was important — The House on Liberty Street, her family, all that was dear to her.

# ACKNOWLEDGEMENTS

It's not easy to write a novel, especially, I discovered, during a pandemic. For me, the most positive aspect of the past few years was already having work-from-home as a way of life during a return to full-house mode after only a brief dalliance with empty nesting. Since raising a family was the best thing I ever did, I missed my three sons and their youthful energy after they all left for university and their own lives beyond that. Thankfully, my second and third born twenty-something sons, Luc and Dom joined us back at home and we all hunkered down in remote-work mode with my husband, Timo and me, our dog Rosie and COVID kitten Moxie.

My cousin also came to stay for a couple of months after being stranded in Boston soon after relocating from the UK. Timo, being first generation Italian double immigrant, embraced the spirit of the European lunch hour with gusto. Our motley crew gathered around the kitchen table as we took our collective breaks from all the remote work (and sporadic writing) that was taking place in various parts of our home. It proved as ideal a pandemic retreat as we could have hoped for given that we have plenty of shared and open space. Although my writing has been slow going, the nourishment of a British Italian American family, along with the boys' girlfriends and various friends in our little pod certainly revived my motherly skills, as well as my culinary and housekeeping repertoire.

I'd started writing The House on Liberty Street just before the world turned itself upside down. Though I had the evolution of Adamaria's family in mind from the outset, I had no idea how much the concept of coming together under one roof and the strength of community would be given cause to develop in my storytelling.

My concept editor Elaine Silver, whom I've worked with on all four of my books, declared the multi-generational cohabitation concept the way that we all should live. As ever, I am so grateful to Elaine for her encouragement, her wise counseling and thoughtful redirections at the outset and into the first few drafts of my stories.

The characters in this story came not fully formed. They grew more outspoken, bold and opinionated as the months passed. As in any good work of fiction, their lives evolved with the unfolding of their actions. All of this was born from my imagination, a desire for a more just world in troubled times and a deep appreciation of the culture and heritage of Petaluma, Sonoma County, the city in which the story is set and I've chosen to live since 1992.

Rocco Rivetti, super smart oldest son, multi-media editor, director and Los Angeles stalwart throughout these most challenging of recent years began mailing me his astute, insightful, sage and enlightening pen and ink insights, cartoons and suggestions for sensitivities and quickening the pace of chapter by chapter of The House on Liberty Street once I was several drafts in. This is the second novel we've worked on together and I can't imagine anyone more in tune with my thoughts, direction and process than he. Thank you, Rocco for being so clever and kind, constructive and sincere and for never making me feel like I can't fix something I've written so that it's better all around.

Adamaria's Italian American heritage is uniquely Northern Californian. It differs from the East Coast Italian American perspective, influenced as it is by the West Coast, Mediterranean-like topography and climate. It's even more removed from the culture I know so well of my mother-in-law, Giuseppina, to whom this book is dedicated, who immigrated from Southern Italy to England as a young woman in the 1950s. Still, at 85, Giuseppina's devotion to family, hearth and home is remarkable and it's her much-admired culinary skills that I've attempted to conjure in Adamaria's kitchen. Nonna Pina, as we fondly call her welcomes all at her table. She likes to say that she doesn't have a big house, but she has an open house. And it's true. Thank you, Pina for being the most loving and generous mother-in-law and for the many thousands of delicious homemade meals (and platters of Wandis) that have emerged from your humble kitchen.

Thank you, restoration historian Christopher and Elaine Stevick for the tour of your cherished Liberty Street Victorian home. We had to postpone our visit until after we all were all vaccinated but it was worth the wait for an in-depth walk-through the quirky characteristics of a Gold-Rush era house. I'm frequently asked about the specific location of the ranch and house in Big Green Country and though I explain that it is a fictional property based on several that fit the bill in coastal Sonoma/Marin Counties, I expect that I'll be equally pressed for the precise location of The House on Liberty Street after readers find themselves immersed within its gently sagging lath and plaster walls. Again, please know that this is a make-believe house, a blend of several Victorians in West Petaluma's heritage home neighborhood and not any one house in particular.

Early readers, Amery, Carol, Dana, Dom, John, Luc, Lindsey, Kerry, Gail and Timo, I'm so grateful for all of your focused input and enthusiasm and I'm glad that you all felt like you were right here on the ground with me and my characters in Petaluma as you read. Carol went the extra round with a copy edit and I think she caught most of my typos.

My son, Luc invented a mousebird as his secret pal during pre-school years. It was always mousebird who ate the last cookie. It was a revelation, over two decades later, when my research revealed to me that mousebirds actually do exist.

The Italian gnome stories and folklore in this story are based on traditional beliefs and stories passed on through generations by word of mouth.

Book cover illustrator Gail Foulkes is a fellow transplanted Brit to the Petaluma area and dear friend. I am so delighted to have worked with Gail on the collaboration of original and micro-regional cover art for The House on Liberty Street. Gail's fantastic brown paper bag series that you can see on her website Gailfoulkes.com came to life during COVID when she found herself with a mound of paper grocery bags due to reuse restrictions. The scenes from around Petaluma that Gail painted are so refreshing, original and alive and I just knew that Gail was the one to capture the essence of the house in my story. Thank you, dear Gail for your original mind, sharp eye, humor, love, can-do attitude and collaborative spirit.

My husband, Timo, remains my number one cheerleader and receives a high five for being so patient with my seemingly never-ending drafts, every of one of which he diligently read through in his favorite chair by the fireplace.

The outreach and efforts within my community to be ever more inclusive and aware of its shortcomings in the diversity arena is encouraging. I look forward to a future without prejudice and bias and one where we learn to live together in new and smart ways.

# About the Author

Frances Rivetti is an Independent Publisher Book Awards Gold Medal winner for her 2019 debut novel, Big Green County. She trained as a newspaper reporter in her native UK and has made her home in the Northern California city of Petaluma, Sonoma County with her British Italian husband, Timo and their three sons since the early 1990s. This is her fourth book and second novel. Northern California natural history, pioneer ranch culture and European settler heritage inform her work as she explores the rambling backroads of coastal Sonoma and Marin counties.

Join her Reader's Club at www.francesrivetti.com. Look for her on Instagram, Twitter and her author Facebook page.

CPSIA information can be obtained
at www.ICGtesting.com
Printed in the USA
LVHW032017260323
742647LV00002B/277